GETTING LOST

Visit us at www.boldstrokesbooks.com

GETTING LOST

by

Michelle Grubb

2015

GETTING LOST

© 2015 BY MICHELLE GRUBB. ALL RIGHTS RESERVED.

ISBN 13: 978-1-62639-328-8

THIS TRADE PAPERBACK ORIGINAL IS PUBLISHED BY
BOLD STROKES BOOKS, INC.
P.O. BOX 249
VALLEY FALLS, NY 12185

FIRST EDITION: MARCH 2015

CREDITS
EDITOR: CINDY CRESAP
PRODUCTION DESIGN: SUSAN RAMUNDO
COVER DESIGN BY SHERI (GRAPHICARTIST2020@HOTMAIL.COM)

Acknowledgments

Rarely is a book written without the valuable input of special people. Here are my thanks, etched on paper for now and evermore.

Thank you, Alanna Cannon, for all your encouragement, your handy red pen, and for believing in me.

Thanks also to Jenny Cashin, Jane Johnson, and Jill Stone for your support and valuable feedback. I couldn't ask for a better bunch of friends. Malcolm Honey, your kind message back when I was getting started is treasured.

To Monique Gorham, I have a lot to thank you for, but for now I'll just say thanks for the medical advice.

A big thank you to Bold Strokes Books; Radclyffe, Sandy, Cindy, and Sheri. I'm thrilled to have this amazing opportunity.

Lastly, I'd like to thank Kerry Grubb-Moore. Thank you for your amazing mind, your fantastic ideas, endless support, and for the exciting world you offer me every day.

Dedication

For Kerry.
My inspiration, my big fish.

CHAPTER ONE

I'm not your mother." She smiled sweetly, but her tone meant business. "And Russo here, he's not your father."

Russo, a pale, tattooed, skinhead Australian with stunningly handsome features and eyelashes that were the envy of girls, momentarily took his eyes off the road to glance back, giving a cheeky wink.

"We're all adults here, so unless the problem you have requires the help of a tour manager or a coach driver, I suggest you buy a phone card to call home."

The first day spiel was second nature to Stella. Commanding the attention of everyone on board, she stood at the front of the coach, sporting her much despised corporate-issue lilac polo shirt and beige cargo shorts. Her wardrobe usually consisted of designer European branded jeans and shirts, but on day one, she conceded to wearing the common corporate crap.

"I love the new hair." Russo was referring to her short blond haircut. Stella always sported the latest look.

"Don't even ask, wise guy."

"Go on, how much?"

Russo shaved his head and was constantly astounded to hear how much she would pay London designers to cut her hair. "Your weekly salary."

Russo whistled. "It suits you. Pity you're about two feet too short for the catwalk."

Stella had no comeback. She was short, but she mouthed the words "Fuck off" just to have the last say.

Her boss, Janet, had told Stella there were three extremely important rules to being a successful tour manager, and she wouldn't find them written in any handbook. Rule number one: be single. Never have a partner, boyfriend, girlfriend, husband, wife, or obvious relations of any description. Even if you never intended to sleep with anyone on your tours, the trick was to make them think you could if you wanted to. Anyone with the slightest attraction toward you should be led to believe they're in with a chance. Sex, Janet would say, is what makes the world go round. If you're not single, learn to lie.

That, incidentally, was rule number two: lie convincingly, pretend, and fake it. Janet had emphasised that these tours were full of idiots. And make no mistake, she had said, "You'll scarcely like any of the bleeding fuck wits," so the best thing was to learn how to pretend and lie convincingly. The third rule was never, *ever* get caught sleeping with the driver. If it wasn't bad enough the group thought you weren't available, sleeping with the driver—whom everyone also wanted to bed—could lead to mutiny. European tours were for sex-crazed or sex-starved idiots with too much money, Janet had said. Minutes after being hired, as Stella swaggered triumphantly from Janet's office, she heard Janet whistle and mutter under her breath, "That little arse will see some action."

Stella had lost count of the times she'd stood in front of an excited coach load of tourists, mostly Australians, and repeated the exact same lines as the coach weaved out of London, fifty pairs of beady little eyes watching her every move and hanging on her every word. It was becoming a little monotonous now, however, and she and Russo, who always looked so handsome in lilac, had been together doing this route all year long—London, down to Greece, and back again—in all, a journey of twenty-eight days. Between them, they had nine years of touring Europe under their belts, which afforded them the prestige of hotel tours. No more campsites or cabins; they were assigned to the newbies.

Stella had a reputation as one of the slickest tour managers on the European circuit. Her organisational skills were impeccable, the clients adored her, she consistently achieved higher bonuses than her colleagues, and absolutely every other tour company had attempted to headhunt her at one time or another. It was reaching the ridiculous stage where prospective clients were e-mailing the company to ask for her summer roster, hoping to book her tours after being referred by a friend. Of course this was impossible to facilitate, but it was a compliment nevertheless.

It was rumoured that Janet was eventually intending to move into a higher role in another company specialising in older age groups. Older and richer. If Janet had contempt for the sex-crazed young traveller, she had equally as much contempt for the lazy, rich, old ones. Ironically, while Janet despised the clients, she was exceptional at delivering results.

At twenty-seven, and after living out of a suitcase for four years—at least during the warmer months—Stella was ready to leave the transient life of a tour manager. Between tours, she occupied a room the size of a broom cupboard in her cousin's flat south of London, but it wasn't home. For the first time in her life, Stella craved a place to finally lay down roots. She had Janet's job in her sights—it was time to take the reins in a managerial position.

With a sense of familiarity, Stella settled down in the single chair opposite Russo, resting her head back; her next speech wasn't due until the approach to Dover. She was a little hungover—an unexpected drinking session with a colleague saw her stumble in at three that morning—but she forced herself to pull the client list from her satchel to confirm the hotel room booking for their first night in Paris. She ignored the nagging, dull ache that pulsed in her temples. It was overcast leaving London, but she wore her sunglasses regardless. Six couples requiring double rooms, thirteen twin rooms, three triple rooms, and three single rooms.

A hard line was required on the first day of any tour. It was necessary for Stella to establish, from the outset, that she was in charge. She was keen to avoid some of her bolder clients from developing any bright ideas about questioning her authority. Her reputation usually preceded her, but her clients expected the best, and she nearly always delivered. The drug-like high that sent her ego soaring from constant adoration was simply a valued added extra.

It was a huge talking point among tour companies just how much people would play up on holiday. Of course, there was nothing wrong with a bit of fun, but the number of people who would leave their real personalities at home, assuming a completely reckless persona, was remarkable. Ten thousand miles away from their real lives, these folks were wound up and ready to go off. They would flirt like never before, have sex like it was going out of fashion, and the risks they were prepared to take were astounding.

This group were well mixed, not too young—younger meant more work—and not too old, although a tour of predominantly over thirties meant it was more like a holiday for Stella herself. Her new crew were diverse, slightly fewer males than females, ranging in age from eighteen—an American from New Jersey travelling with his cousin—to thirty-eight.

She scanned the names to see if any rang a bell. On too many occasions, she'd been on tour with people she went to school with and hadn't recognised. It had been embarrassing. Now, as a matter of interest, she always checked the list for any potential long lost classmates. No names stood out from school, but there was one name that seemed familiar. Phoebe Lancaster—single room. Unable to place the name, she dismissed the hint of recognition, scrolled through the numbers in the memory of her phone, and dialled the hotel on the outskirts of Paris. With a mixture of English and poor French, Stella confirmed her reservation for the required rooms and, as usual, secured two of the quietest single rooms for herself and Russo.

The name *Phoebe Lancaster* bounced around the fogginess of Stella's lethargic brain. She was sure no one of that name had been at school with her, but it nagged at her regardless.

Russo glanced her way. "Everything okay?"

"Yeah, hotel's confirmed."

"And have you anyone in your sights for some company this evening?"

Stella rolled her eyes. In the early days, she held the record as the only female tour manager to bed a conquest on the first night. But that was history now. As it stood, she could hardly be bothered bedding a conquest at all. The shine had certainly worn off. Russo, on the other hand, was a self-professed sex machine.

"I can't imagine why that's any of your business."

He grinned and took the next corner a little late, waking up any dozers on the coach.

Stella leaned closer to him and softly asked, "Hey, does the name Phoebe Lancaster ring any bells with you?"

Russo's eyes sprung wide. "Why? Do you know her?"

"No. Well, I don't think so. Her name's on the room list."

His voice grew louder and higher in pitch. "*What?*"

"Shh!" Stella hadn't quite expected that reaction. "Keep your voice down!"

"You mean she's on the coach?"

"Yes."

"*This* coach?"

"Yes, you bloody idiot. This coach. Who is she?"

Subtly twitching his head, Russo indicated Stella needed to be closer still for this revelation. "She's the bird who killed Rebecca Dean!"

"Who's Rebecca Dean?"

Russo sighed dramatically. "What are you, fucking twelve years old or something? Oscar Dean's daughter, you twat!"

Stella's face indicated she was drawing a blank.

Russo rolled his eyes. "Oscar Dean practically owns every media outlet in Australia. His daughter was murdered five years ago. Remember I was telling you about it?" Vague memories were seeping back to Stella. "Lesbian love triangle stuff?"

Suddenly, it all came back. She remembered Russo reading something to her from a newspaper in Australia. The story hadn't really made the news internationally. "Oh *that* Rebecca Dean."

"Yes, *that* Rebecca Dean." Russo slowed down, as if unable to maintain speed while discussing this issue. "Phoebe Lancaster was her lover. She killed her."

Stella frowned and cocked her head. "So, how come she's on our coach?"

"Well, obviously she wasn't convicted. No one really knows who did it, but she was charged. They released her eventually. Seemed a bit suss at the time."

"So, which one is she?" Stella jerked her head back toward the passengers.

"Beats me." Russo's brow developed a moist surface shine.

"But what does she look like?"

He thought for a moment. "Dark. No, blond, I think. Shit. I really can't remember."

Stella shook her head and returned to her seat to digest this revelation. With the knowledge a murderer could be on the coach, she desperately needed to find out which passenger was Phoebe Lancaster.

Russo sped up again and glanced nervously in the rearview mirror.

Stella wondered if anyone in the office knew about Phoebe being on this tour considering half the office staff was either from Australia or New Zealand. A heads-up would have been helpful, but for the time being, she would give them the benefit of the doubt. In the privacy of her room that evening, she would call Janet.

Stella formulated a plan to establish the identity of Phoebe Lancaster. She unbuckled her belt, grabbed the list of passengers, and switched on the microphone.

"Hi, folks, sorry to interrupt, but can the three people with single rooms please raise your hands?"

Three people indicated with a wave. Stella discounted the male from Perth; she wasn't interested in him. She analysed the remaining two quickly. Neither sparked any twinge of recognition, and rather inconveniently, neither had *Murderer* tattooed on her forehead. Her eyes lingered longer on the stunning blonde, and she recalled the pleasant and unexpected spark that had ignited between her legs earlier that morning as she completed the mandatory passport checks. She had been so mesmerised by the aloof woman, she failed to actually register what name was on the passport. *Idiot.*

Perhaps now it was her fascination of this lean, tall beauty with amazing glowing skin that convinced her to discount the possibility she could be a murderer. Subsequently, she settled her gaze for an extended moment on the other woman.

Stella intended to speak while her courage remained intact and resolutely marched toward a dark-haired, freckled, pleasant looking woman. As if she had no idea who she was, Stella pretended to read the name from the list. "Phoebe, is it?"

The girl frowned.

"No." Stella heard a smooth, deep voice from behind. "I'm Phoebe."

Stella swung around as the dashing Phoebe Lancaster stood up. She hesitated awkwardly and felt exposed because she'd singled Phoebe out. Stella backtracked and spoke to the dark-haired girl first, but with no idea of her name, she clumsily consulted her list.

"Hi, Melanie?" The girl nodded. "Look, there may be a problem with the hotel tonight. I'm awaiting confirmation, but a suite may be the only available room. It will have two quite separate bedrooms." The girl nodded again. "For Paris only, would it be okay for you to share with the other lady who has asked for a single room?" The lie was easy to retract; she would simply say the hotel had received a cancellation.

Melanie spoke with a strong South African accent. "Sure, no problem."

Stella treasured how willing clients were to accommodate her, somehow hoping this would enhance their European experience. "Great, Mel. Thanks for being so understanding and flexible. It may not come to that, but I thought I'd prepare you. Just in case. I'll let the other lady know."

Stella drew a deep breath on the approach to Phoebe Lancaster. "Phoebe, hi. Look, I don't know if you heard me chatting to Mel, but there may be a problem with the room allocations in Paris."

Phoebe's expression remained indifferent, and Stella wondered how she could feel a pang of attraction and fear all at once. Surely the fact that this woman was once suspected of murder would be enough to quell her unpredictable urges. Apparently not.

Phoebe was remarkably attractive, and her shoulder-length blond hair appeared natural. Her most appealing feature was her amazing, flawless complexion. Stella couldn't detect even a hint of makeup, and she was pleased she'd left her sunglasses on so she could stare a little longer. There were no blemishes, merely a light dusting of freckles and only faint laugh lines. Her lips were glossed, her blue eyes sparkled, and her high cheekbones accentuated features Stella was sure never to forget.

"Yes, I heard. It's certainly okay with me." Phoebe paused, frowning. "Plus, it may not eventuate yet."

Stella wasn't sure, but she thought a smug grin fleetingly flickered across her face. "Thanks, Phoebe. These things happen.

Fingers crossed the hotel receives a cancellation and we don't have to worry about it."

"Yes." Phoebe sighed, disinterested. "Fingers crossed."

Without further interaction, Phoebe turned toward the window. Stella was dismissed.

❖

With Dover soon approaching, it was essential Stella prepare the group for passport control.

She wedged herself between the partition behind Russo and the first row of seats to inform her troops of the process—she was exceptionally comfortable with a microphone in hand. Her unquestionable ability to control fifty strangers gave her a thrill second only to that of an orgasm. She loved their willingness to please her.

Power and control aside, Stella had a job to do. More often than not, a French immigration officer would simply question Stella and Russo—Stella was obligated to site every passenger's passport before departure that morning—but sometimes the impulsive officials kept them on their toes, boarding the coach and checking documentation.

As instructed, the passengers were on their best behaviour as the coach joined the end of a long queue on the slow crawl toward the ferry. Cars, caravans, coaches, motorcycles, and trucks all lined up.

The low-lying clouds of London had long disappeared, and Dover was aglow with bright sunshine reflecting off the cliffs and the crisp blue water. Russo had slid open his window, and a fresh warm breeze wafted toward Stella. She loved summer in Europe and would miss it. The people, the places, the amazing weather, and there was always something exciting happening in every country. Once upon a time, Stella had felt more at home on the road in Europe than anywhere else in the world. Now, the road felt long and the desire to unpack her suitcase and leave it unpacked was more appealing.

On the approach to the immigration checkpoint, an officer boarded and spoke to Stella, requesting a copy of their client list. He was almost out the door after scanning the list when he stopped abruptly, a serious expression creasing his weathered face.

"I think today, mademoiselle, we will check."

"Is everything okay?"

"Oui, I'm sure it is fine. Instruct your group to have their passports on hand, s'il vous plaît."

Eyeing Russo, Stella gripped the microphone and addressed the quiet, apprehensive group calmly. "This is simply routine, folks. Can everyone please have their passport ready for inspection, and by ready, I mean in your hot little hands."

Stella, hiding behind her sunglasses, intently watched Phoebe Lancaster for any sign of distress. Nothing. In fact, she appeared calmer than every other passenger. Phoebe gazed out the window, ignoring the girl fidgeting in the seat beside her.

In no time at all, a murmur swelled and gathered momentum. Annoyed expressions and enquiring glances brought the group to life. The only words Stella could distinguish from the utterings were, "Phoebe Lancaster." Exasperated, Stella sighed—there was nothing listed under "Accused Murderer" in the handbook.

Stella spoke firmly to regain control. "People! I said this was routine, and I meant it. Passport checks happen all the time. Get used to it. Now, can we have a bit of quiet while the officer does his job, please?"

Silence. Stella had bought some time. A coach half full of Australians had been bound to realise, sooner rather than later, that a high profile accused murderer was on board. With their backs to the group, Stella and Russo anxiously discussed options.

"I love it when you speak to them like that." Russo forced an anxious grin.

"This is not the time, Russo." She gripped the back of her neck. "How the hell did she get on my tour?"

"Paris is only hours away. Let's just bide our time until then, assess the damage, and salvage what we can."

Stella knew that was all they could do. Dissidence so early was often irreparable. She also knew it was going to be hard work. Between now and Paris, she would identify some strong personalities amongst the group and focus on keeping them onside. Twenty-eight days together was a long time. "I agree."

"Hey." Russo smiled. "You'll work some magic later. It'll be fine."

A kerfuffle toward the rear of the coach broke out, distracting Stella, who swung around to watch the officer escort Phoebe Lancaster down the aisle. Phoebe held an expression Stella couldn't interpret and eyed her all the way. Stella couldn't help but be in awe of her composure. The moisture in her pants suggested she was in awe of something else altogether. *Christ, Stella, hold it together.*

Once again, the Australians in the group erupted in discontent. Stella thrust the microphone at Russo and calmly followed Phoebe and the officer off the coach. As they briskly crossed the tarmac to the immigration office, Stella heard Russo demand silence on the coach yet again.

"What's going on?" Stella stood protectively close to Phoebe in the small, cream-coloured office. Although, nearly a foot shorter than Phoebe, she was hardly an imposing figure. Forty-nine paying customers sat waiting on the coach. It was in everyone's best interests to have this resolved promptly.

"Do you know who this lady is?"

"Yes, she's a client who's paid nearly seven thousand dollars to be on my coach."

"Oui, the money is important to you. I know. But Mademoiselle Lancaster on a coach, travelling to Europe." He shrugged. "This requires some attention from me."

"Okay." Stella wanted to do this the easy way. "What do you need from her?"

"Right now? Only her passport." Phoebe tossed her passport on the bare desk, ignoring the outstretched hand. "I have to make some calls. I will return soon." He disappeared through a glass one-way mirrored door.

Phoebe stepped away from Stella, and after a minute of awkward silence, she spoke, her voice deep and velvet, almost foreign to her porcelain doll appearance. "I suppose you're wondering why I didn't change my name."

The thought had crossed Stella's mind, along with hundreds of other disturbing notions. Something was horribly wrong. Phoebe Lancaster was as cold as ice, and Stella wondered how to survive a month with this woman on her coach. Of greater concern was the raw physical attraction gripping her. She trusted her body to eventually ignore the growing lust and finally work out that she did not have, nor ever would have, a connection with this woman. It was essential when constantly dealing with fifty new clients, that Stella rely on instincts and intuition. At that moment, with Phoebe leering at her, her gut feeling was stripped down to basic fear. Phoebe Lancaster scared her. She was, however, unwilling to reveal how intimidated she felt. "Might have been easier?"

"I'm not a criminal," Phoebe said. "I have never been convicted of a crime. I refuse to change my name, or my face, purely for your comfort, or anyone else's."

You asked! It occurred to Stella that an opportunity had presented itself. Had Phoebe been anyone else under the microscope of French immigration, Stella would continue to take control of the situation and conduct as much of the negotiation as possible. Given that a refusal of entry from French authorities could efficiently solve this serious problem, Stella elected to let Phoebe fend for herself. If Phoebe was refused entry, she would deal with her soaring desire later or suffer until a suitable alternative distraction presented itself. Stella kept her responses to a minimum, not convinced her voice would remain even. "I'm not judging you. You asked and I answered. Forgive me if this sounds rude, but why are you even on a coach tour of Europe?"

"It sounds rude, because it is rude." Phoebe glared intensely, but offered nothing further. They waited in silence, Phoebe appearing calm, while Stella's head throbbed with the pounding of her racing heart.

The officer re-entered the room, faxed documents in hand and a serious scowl upon his brow. "Mademoiselle, I am going to stamp your passport with a visa requiring you to report to immigration upon leaving France in precisely four weeks' time."

You're kidding. Stella's heart sank.

He continued. "If you remain in France or the European Union beyond the date on this visa, your stay will be unlawful, and upon arrest you will be deported, jeopardising any future travel to Europe. Is that clear, Mademoiselle Lancaster?" He turned to Stella. "If she is not on the coach when you return, you will have some explaining to do."

Stella knew perfectly well the movements of a client were out of her control and beyond her responsibility, but she nodded regardless.

In a tone Stella had not heard, nor thought Phoebe capable of, she smiled sweetly and assured the officer she would abide by the generous conditions imposed upon her.

What a piece of work. Opportunity missed, although a small part of Stella enjoyed the idea that Phoebe's continued presence was out of her hands for the time being. Phoebe Lancaster was not going away that easily.

"Thanks for your support in there." Phoebe oozed sarcasm as they strode toward the waiting coach.

"Excuse me? You appeared to handle it well enough."

"Yes, I did. That's what I do. I handle things—in all kinds of ways. You'd do well to remember that."

"And what precisely does that mean?" Stella pulled up and Phoebe followed suit, stopping only centimetres away. "Are you threatening me?"

Phoebe smiled. And although Stella admired her ability to change demeanour on a whim, it unnerved her. Phoebe's shoulders visibly relaxed. "You'll never have to ask me that. Trust me; you'll know if I threaten you."

"Look." Stella's composure wouldn't hold for long, and the words rushed from her. "I have fifty people to worry about, not one, not just you. The real problem we have is sitting on that coach. If it weren't for the bloody Australians, you'd have gone unnoticed, but that cocky lot can make your holiday hell. They'll happily be judge, jury, and fucking executioner, so we need to think about how we're going to deal with this."

"We do, do we?" It was impossible to tell if this episode raised Phoebe's stress levels at all. "I don't have a problem. I don't care what you, or those idiots on that wretched bus, think of me." She strode defiantly toward the coach, but called over her shoulder, "Perhaps it would be better if I were to share with *you* in Paris tonight?"

"I don't get paid enough for that shit." Stella looked down as something in her stomach performed a back flip. "And damn it, you can just quit it, too."

With any other client, Stella would have read them the riot act. Under normal circumstances, nothing aggravated her more than self-centred, spoilt, rich kids. Not that Phoebe Lancaster was a child. Her date of birth indicated she was thirty-one. But something put Stella on edge—her instincts told her not to mess with this woman. And it wasn't like she wanted to mess with her anyway. Racking her brain, she couldn't fathom one valid reason why Phoebe Lancaster should be on a coach tour of Europe. The entire scenario was bizarre, and until she could find out more, she remained hesitant and wary of rocking the boat.

Stella boarded the coach, and Russo raised his eyebrows questioningly. There was no time to confer with him as she observed the group eyeing Phoebe with contempt. With Phoebe back in her seat, forty-nine pairs of questioning eyes fell upon Stella for answers.

"Right, folks." Her voice bellowed loudly through the sound system, demanding attention. "I'm under the impression you're all unhappy about something, so let's get it out in the open. Some of you have obviously recognised Phoebe." The group nodded and groaned in agreement. "Now, unless someone here knows her personally, or has some inside information about her that the rest of the world isn't privy to, I suggest we all pull our heads in and quit being so selfishly judgmental. Not one of you has probably spoken a word to her, yet you're all terribly keen to pass judgment. You'll get nothing from a month in Europe if you all play judge and jury with everyone you meet." The softening of faces reassured Stella her rant was working. "So, can we all please focus on having a good time and keeping ourselves open to new and exciting experiences?"

Utterings of confirmation murmured throughout the coach. It was unfair that she had to berate this group for their actions when her own feelings toward Phoebe were questionable and possibly tainted with an unwanted attraction. If Stella hadn't known better, a fleeting expression of victory, almost pleasure, flashed across Phoebe's beautiful face as she switched off the microphone.

To Stella's amazement, her speech appeared to work. The deathly stares directed toward Phoebe somehow dissipated, not that Phoebe gave the slightest hint of acknowledgement. A distinct look of petulance, followed by indifference settled on Phoebe's face as she disengaged, leaning back casually and placing headphones in her ears. Stella shook her head. *Thanks, Stella. Thanks for helping out.* She settled back into her seat stewing over Phoebe's attitude and wondering why the hell it even mattered. *Damn those blue eyes and lean legs that go on forever.*

The mood on the coach lightened considerably, and a glance toward Russo, who gave her an affectionate wink, eased her stress. It was a struggle pushing all thoughts of Phoebe from her mind—the fear *and* the attraction—so instead Stella focused on the shipping workers skillfully organising the impatient traffic onto the waiting ferry.

Stella's thoughts inevitably returned to Phoebe, and it occurred to her, after watching the negative reactions of a busload of predominantly Australians, how frustrating it must be being constantly recognised as the accused murderer of Rebecca Dean. *Accused murderer.* The words lingered in Stella's mind, and she shivered, recalling the steely gaze that almost tore right through her in the French immigration office. Gauging by Phoebe's reaction, she took sadistic delight in observing how nervous and fidgety people became by her sheer presence.

What bugged Stella was that she couldn't think of one valid reason for Phoebe being on her tour. Phoebe clearly thought she belonged in a higher class, and by the countless immigration stamps she caught a glimpse of in her passport, she was well travelled and obviously not lacking in funds. With the clear intention of not enjoying herself *and* making everyone else's life a terrifying misery, Stella was at a loss to even begin to explain why Phoebe Lancaster sat annoyingly smug on her coach.

She couldn't help but wonder if that smug grin belonged to a murderer.

CHAPTER TWO

Stella worked the coach as they sped toward Paris. It wasn't the safest thing to do, and certainly against regulations—standing in the aisle chatting—but considering the events of the morning, a little extra effort was required to keep this group on track.

Negativity spread like a rampant disease when left to fester. On rare occasions, Stella and Russo had been oblivious to niggling problems, and before they could intervene, the morale and attitude had slipped to irretrievable depths. It was understood not everyone on the coach would get along, but when things went awry, divisions would surface, and the outcome was unpleasant, not to mention extremely hard work.

Stella's most precious talent was flirting—simple, but effective. Her small stature worked to her advantage. The difference between an accomplished, flirtatious tour manager and one who lacked the skill, was between one and two thousand pounds per trip in tips. The men were an easy target—half of them were attracted to her immediately. The other half fed off her authority and then, soon after, developed an attraction. The women were a different story. Some wanted to be her—they were usually easy to get along with—some fancied her, and that was no problem, but others felt threatened. This minority of insecure girls required subtle attention, but eventually they fell under her spell. Then, of course, there were those who no matter what she did, they disliked her regardless. In the early days, she would waste precious time seeking to win over this faction, but it was often to the detriment of the rest of the group. Experience taught Stella to concentrate and focus on the ninety percent of people she'd already charmed, forget the rest. Her first year on the job, Stella flirted to land a bed partner; the extra cash was incidental. Now, she flirted for the cash—scoring a conquest was often more trouble than it was worth.

A laid-back couple from Brisbane, Matt and Belinda, appeared to be the leaders, or at least the most outspoken, of a group of eight travelling together from Queensland. Stella and Matt hit it off immediately, but to remain on side, she focused her attention on Belinda, and during the course of their discussion, promised to take her—and anyone else who cared to join them—to the best crepe stall on the Champs-Élysées. Hook, line, and sinker, Stella reeled them in. Personal, almost one-on-one interest from the tour manager was guaranteed to keep clients on side. Winning over this group of eight was a good place to start.

Throughout the course of the tour, she would interact on a personal level with everyone—special chats, time alone, thoughtful comments, jovial banter—but the first few days were imperative. Considerable time and effort was spent including everyone in the early stages.

Matt and Belinda were like the opposite sex version of each other. Not like siblings. Stella had toured with many brother and sister travelling teams; their closeness could be defined as comfortable, almost intuitive. But couples like Matt and Belinda had a certain physical sexuality about them. Without knowing, Stella guessed these two had been together for at least ten years.

"So, Stella, what's the plan for tonight?" Matt, slightly chubby with narrow eyes and mousy brown wavy hair, appeared eager to begin the trip with a hangover.

"Dinner and bed for you, I should imagine. You'd be too old for nightclubs, surely?" Stella winked toward Belinda and some others in their group. The simple wink was a powerful tool, and while a happy group meant a greater tip for her and Russo in the end, it remained an effective and genuine way to put a smile on someone's face.

"Pig's arse I'm too old. How old are you?"

"A well-mannered gentleman like yourself should know better than to ask a lady her age."

"A lady, yes, but you?"

Touché! Yes, Stella was going to have fun with this lot; down-to-earth, insulting, and intent on enjoying themselves. For a moment, lost in the good-natured banter, Phoebe Lancaster slipped her mind. "Twenty-seven, but I'm sure I don't look a day over twenty-one."

"No, not one day. Millions maybe. Will you be joining us tonight?"

"Some nights I come along, so does Russo—with and without the coach—but tonight we drop you off at a club. I'll tell you where the hotel is, how much a cab should cost, and you find your own way back."

Stella hated nightclubs. The music drove her mad. For the most part, it was her job to go out with the group, but on some nights her job was to travel back to the hotel with Russo and any members of the group who wanted an early night. "Don't worry. There'll be plenty of other nights when I can watch you all get rolling drunk and make complete arses of yourselves." They all laughed. Stella sealed the deal with another wink toward Belinda, asking for incriminating photos the following morning.

Her dash back to the front of the coach was interrupted when she was accosted by an opinionated Texan, Piper Dixon. Pippy was anxious. Her fluffy brown hair appeared to perch atop her head like an ill-fitting wig and her blotched face was strained. She appeared genuinely frightened.

"E-ex-excuse me, St-St-Stella, can you please explain…I demand to know w-w-what you intend to do about that w-w-woman."

Please God! And she stutters as well. Give me strength.

Stella remained calm and professional as always. "What woman are you referring to exactly?"

"Th-th-that woman!" Her head jerked toward Phoebe. "Th-th-the m-m-murderer."

From the list, Stella recalled Pippy was roughly twenty-four or twenty-five. She was travelling with two other girls, cousins if her memory served her correctly, both listening intently to this exchange, but neither focusing directly on Stella. She guessed Pippy's questions weren't thought up all by herself.

"Honey," Stella said gently—she found insecure young girls especially liked to be singled out with pet names. "I can assure you, if

Phoebe was a murderer, she wouldn't be on this coach. Many people are wrongly charged with crimes they didn't commit. I presume Phoebe is a victim of this. Give her a chance. I'm sure she's a lovely girl."

Smiling awkwardly as if she wanted to say more, Pippy must have thought better of it because she remained silent, allowing Stella to return to her seat.

❖

Cruising along the motorway through the World War I battlefields in the Valley of Somme, Stella briefly provided some history concerning the area and its coloured past. She noted with interest a change in the atmosphere as most passengers relaxed, chatting amongst themselves. That is, everyone except Phoebe. Amanda, the girl beside her, had swung her legs into the aisle and was chatting with a couple opposite. Phoebe had plugged in her iPod, insolently oblivious to the people around her.

Stella found time to Google Phoebe Lancaster on her iPhone. The recurring facts she discovered were disturbing. Rebecca Dean (the daughter of media magnate, Oscar Dean), had been murdered. Stabbed. According to police, Phoebe and a man called Simon Threadbody were the last people to see her alive. During the days following the murder, Phoebe was interviewed, charged, but later released. Newspaper coverage in Australia was enormous. Every major paper had her photo splashed on the front page.

"We're an hour away, chief." Russo reminded her she had work to do, and she welcomed the distraction from the unsettling information.

Stella stood, microphone at the ready. "Okay, Russo, pick a song for this lot to wake up to." Stella pumped herself up to put on her best tour manager guise, engage the group, and equip them for their two nights in Paris.

"Yes, ma'am." Russo clicked through the iPod, pleased to replace the mellow tunes with something more upbeat. "How about this one?"

"Parlez vous Francais" by the Australian band Art Vs Science throbbed through the sound system and was a great choice. Stella watched, grinning, as everyone jumped to attention, suddenly wide-awake.

"Right, you lot, that's your wake-up song, for now." The group collectively cheered and then whined playfully at its abrupt beginning and the harsh volume. "Don't blame me. It was Russo's selection, and I don't know about you, but I'm not keen to argue with him." It was so easy. Stella commanded their undivided attention, and she loved every second of it.

"So let's get down to business," she continued. "The first sheet I'm handing out is extremely important. It's your *Get Lost* sheet. On it are the names of every hotel we will be staying in and the dates on which we will be staying there. I can't urge you strongly enough to go and get lost. You don't have to go where we take you. This is your holiday, remember. I am your guide, not your—"

"Mother!" everyone cried collectively.

"Precisely. We are all different in the things we enjoy. If you think a place I'm scheduled to take you doesn't interest you, don't come. I'm not here to make you do anything you don't want to do. Holidays are all about choices. You all have the choice to do whatever you want, whenever you want. So, view your *Get Lost* sheet as your freedom guide. If you do go off exploring, or miss the coach, I will presume you have made other arrangements and will meet us at the hotel. If, however, you intend to disappear for longer than a day, please call me so I don't alert the authorities unnecessarily. My number is on the bottom of the page, and I'm reachable all over Europe."

"I'll bet you are!" Matt yelled out from the back.

Stella grinned, but continued. "This brings me to departure times. It is unfair and inconsiderate to expect Russo and me to hold up the holiday of nearly fifty people because you can't make it to the coach on time. So, if we say the coach is leaving at two thirty, what time do you suppose the coach will leave?"

Again in unison, the entire group yelled with enthusiasm, "Two thirty!"

"That's correct. You catch on quickly. If you aren't at the departure point, I'll presume you've found something more exciting to do. Please—and I can't stress this enough—please do *not* call me if you're running late and ask me to hold up the coach. Bribes also won't work, Matt!" Stella threw this one to him for a laugh.

"But we have your direct number, right?" Matt yelled.

Stella sighed. There was always one in the group. "Yes, Matt. You have my direct number."

"Wow, we can call you anytime we like. Awesome."

"No, Matt. Not anytime. Besides, you will be having so much fun, speaking to me should be the last thing on your mind. Honestly, folks, there is so much to do in these places, actually getting lost is a great way to discover things that will never make it into the guidebooks. Which brings me to my second sheet of paper. This contains information on a map of Paris. You can see from the headings, it covers the major sights found in every tourist book. They're *in* every tourist guide for a reason. They're simply spectacular. Now, tonight we'll have dinner at the hotel, drive into the city centre, see a little known tower, I'll bore you with some history and information, and then, if you're in the mood, we'll drop you off at a nightclub and you can all dance the night away."

Whistles and yahoos filled the coach. "Righto, Russo, take us in!"

Stella was satisfied her group was back on track. The coach was abuzz with anticipation, Paris was only minutes away, but she was a bundle of nerves. The source of her apprehension sat calmly and attentively—a little too attentively—in the sixth row. Stella detected an arrogant, almost knowing expression upon Phoebe's face, until it turned into a smile. The knot in Stella's stomach tightened with attraction. Phoebe Lancaster smiled at her, a genuine smile even, and disappointingly, her body reacted. Phoebe held her gaze. The brilliant smile was addictive. Stella stumbled into her seat. She couldn't remember the last time she consistently felt the pang and excitement of attraction. But Phoebe Lancaster? *Please, God, don't let me feel this for her.*

CHAPTER THREE

The expression of wonder upon the faces of a group catching their first glimpse of the impressive Eiffel Tower was a sight Stella never tired of. Bursting with excitement, the awestruck travellers would rush off the coach, almost always running to stand under the tower and pose for countless photos. A group ticket in hand, Stella would round them up and watch, from possibly the most spectacular structure in the world, as Paris turned from dusk into a sparkling, radiant city.

This group were no exception, other than the notable omission of the mysterious Phoebe Lancaster. Phoebe had surely visited Paris before, probably staying in the most expensive hotels, but earlier in the evening, as they approached the rather modest Hotel de Concorde, she displayed no emotion whatsoever. Upon arrival, others rushed around, in and out of rooms, up and down to the bar, but Phoebe remained sombre in the background.

The single rooms were last on the hotel's allocation list. Only when a handful of people remained in the foyer awaiting room keys, did Stella notice Phoebe was dead last. It was too late to worry about altering the order of allocation now.

"So that just leaves you, Phoebe, and room number 4051." Stella attempted a light, casual tone as she extended her hand holding the electronic room card.

"And you." Phoebe smiled.

"Pardon?"

Phoebe slowly extended her hand. "It leaves you *and* me alone again."

A nervous shiver tingled beneath Stella's scalp, travelling the entire length of her body before dissolving in her toes. Alarmingly, a different sensation altogether settled like a stone in the pit of her stomach. Stella came to the undeniably dangerous realisation that she truly was attracted to Phoebe. And Phoebe's attributes were certainly easy on the eye. Stella hadn't been attracted to anyone, not like this, in such a long time, and the feeling was disturbing. Sure, she'd had women, decreasing in frequency of late, but this attraction was something new and dangerously distracting. Upon reflection, though, in various shapes and forms, Phoebe wasn't anything Stella hadn't had the chance to bed in the past. But the poise and the power were what had Stella's head spinning and groin throbbing. It was so alluring, Stella felt a little out of control. She had seen no real evidence to even suggest Phoebe possessed anything other than well-honed intimidation techniques, but there it sat, almost tangible, in her gut. Power and class. Phoebe excited her. *Fuck, typical, a bloody murderer makes me wet. Jesus!*

Stella glanced around. "Yes. We seem to be very much alone."

"I presume Melanie and I aren't sharing a room like you previously warned?"

Stella hadn't mentioned the room allocations since they left the UK, but it didn't surprise her to learn Phoebe remembered. "No. Everything has been sorted."

Phoebe leaned in close. "That's good then, isn't it?" She smiled. "Don't you want to run along?"

Stella's gaze lingered for a treacherously long moment on Phoebe's cleavage, her simple white linen shirt gaping. Then their eyes met. "I'm not in any hurry. Why are you still here?"

Phoebe straightened and her expression softened. "Drink?"

"What?"

"You're the tour manager. I imagine your room comes equipped with the minibar that I'm also imagining has been removed from our lowly rooms."

"Well, yes, it does." Stella was stumbling over her words. "You want to come to my room for a drink? Alone?" *Smooth, Cruz. Real smooth.*

Phoebe smiled, warmly this time. "Yes. Your room. Alcohol. You and I drinking it."

"I can't." Stella watched as Phoebe's eyes turned grey. "Don't misunderstand me; I want to, but Russo and I only have a small window of time alone before dinner to discuss work stuff." Phoebe's eyes softened imperceptibly, but Stella noticed it because she was looking for it. "Rain check?" *Rain check? Are you mad? Do you really want to be alone with this woman?* Unfortunately, the answer was yes. She was apprehensive, but the thought of them alone in her room was nothing short of appealing.

"Maybe." Phoebe turned and walked away. Over her shoulder she said, "You should be careful what you wish for, Stella."

Stella's knees nearly buckled at the low, husky voice.

❖

It was fortunate Stella had experienced the view from the Eiffel Tower on more occasions than she could remember. When accompanying groups to the breathtaking top level, she spent more time taking photos and posing for others to even spare a look over the beautiful city. And Paris was beautiful. Some argued it was dirty, predictable, or a tourist façade for the forgotten, lower class locals, but Stella didn't share that opinion. She loved its people, the food, the cafés, museums, galleries, shops, everything. It was, in Stella's eyes, terribly romantic. The French made wonderful lovers, and as she posed atop the Tower, Matt's hand only centimetres away from inappropriate on her rear end, Stella thought of Phoebe.

It was a fifty-fifty split—no surprises there—as Stella and Russo returned to the hotel with half the group. The revellers had been safely delivered to Club Pulse, a friendly night spot whose bouncers always ensured Stella's groups left in one piece. It was a convenient business arrangement. Stella took all her groups there, and Louis, the manager, ensured they had a good time and was guaranteed regular patronage. Stella received her little kickback when she met up with Louis for a drink the following morning.

Unfortunately, Pippy had chosen an early night. She was, much to Stella's dismay, sitting directly behind her. It became impossible for Stella and Russo to hold a conversation without Pippy interrupting every five seconds, so, begrudgingly, Stella turned to give Pippy her undivided attention. *Twenty minutes of my life I'll never get back.*

"I just love the Eiffel Tower, d-d-don't you?" Pippy leant over the barrier separating her from Stella's single seat. It was a good half metre higher than Stella, and to her disgust, her gaze focussed on the mass of nasal hair darting from Pippy's nose.

"Yes, it certainly is quite spectacular."

Pippy smiled, as if she must be the first person in the entire world to appreciate the marvellous structure. "I s-s-suppose you check on us all before b-b-bed? M-m-make sure we're all safe and sound?"

With practiced control, Stella reined in her amusement and refrained from rolling hysterically on the floor, asking, "Are you fucking insane?" but unfortunately, Piper Dixon wasn't the first idiot to think they were in school camp. "Sweetheart, we're all adults here. As I said before, you can all do what you like."

"So you won't be ch-ch-checking on Miss Lancaster, just to m-m-make sure she's okay?"

Phoebe's absence from the city tour and the Eiffel Tower had not gone unnoticed. Stella refused to acknowledge she was a little disappointed when Phoebe failed to board the coach, but she had sat in on many conversations throughout the evening, all speculating on the mystery that surrounded their absent companion. "Is something worrying you, Pippy?"

"N-n-no. I thought about w-w-what you said earlier, and I'm going to t-t-talk to her at breakfast. She c-c-could use a friend right now. I want to get to know her."

The advice Stella really wanted to give, not solely to Pippy, but to everyone on the tour, was to leave Phoebe alone and stay out of her unpredictable way. Unfortunately, this was not possible. Nor was it what she personally felt compelled to do. Stella opted to remain neutral in all matters regarding the elusive Phoebe. "I think you should do whatever you feel is right, honey."

"I'm just the person to br-br-bring her out of her shell and introduce her t-t-to the rest of the group. I'm already g-g-getting on fabulously with everyone!"

"From my experience, the more friends you make, the better time you are likely to have." Although not exactly a lie, Stella switched the focus to safer ground. "Actually, I'm keen to check out a section of the catacombs that's been restricted for the past decade or so. Perhaps you and your cousins would like to come along in the morning. It's only a short distance on the Metro."

"Really? I'd l-l-love to come."

Russo swung violently into the driveway of the hotel, jolting all the sleepyheads to attention.

"So," said Pippy. "We'll make arrangements in the m-m-morning for our little j-j-jaunt?"

"Sure. I'll let you know at breakfast what's happening for the day."

One by one, the exhausted snack-sized group trudged off the coach as Stella and Russo bid them all good night. Finally free of clients, she packed her satchel of work documents to ensure she was prepared for the following day, leaving Russo to clean the coach.

"Hey," Russo called from the backseat. "You want me to check in on you, seeing as though you appear to have lost your touch? Sleeping alone is no fun."

"Yes, please," Stella sarcastically replied.

"One night, Stella. That's all you'll need with me."

"It's almost tempting, Russo, just to see if you could satisfy me."

Russo sighed. "On second thought, you scare the hell out of me. I reckon I'd fail to perform."

"And don't I know it." Stella grinned. "Night, Russo. Sweet dreams."

"Night, Stella Bella."

❖

Although it was late, Stella stretched out on her bed, a gin and tonic in one hand, and confirmed via text to meet Manuel, the Notre Dame guide, at ten the following morning as usual. She then e-mailed the *Ou Est Le Can Can* to confirm numbers for the cabaret the following evening. Finally, with her work completed, she logged on to the Internet. This time she searched specifically for Rebecca Dean.

Stella read with interest: Rebecca was the only child of Oscar Dean. Unknown sources suggested that Oscar Dean was livid when he discovered his daughter was a lesbian. Publicly, he denied this, of course, remaining neutral in all things regarding Rebecca's sexuality. Oscar's plan had been for Rebecca to marry Simon Threadbody, his right-hand man.

Stella wondered how strongly Oscar had pressed Rebecca to marry Simon. Was Oscar Dean a difficult man to disappoint?

CHAPTER FOUR

The prearranged wake-up calls resounded in every room at precisely seven a.m. Never having been a big breakfast eater, Stella took her time; she would buy a real coffee near Notre Dame. Nagging her was the information she'd read regarding Rebecca Dean the previous night. She called her boss.

"Phoebe who?" Janet, bossy by nature as well as in job title, was a massive woman from New Zealand. Everything concerning her was big—her voice, her jet-black hair, and especially her salary.

Stella rolled her eyes and counted to five. "Phoebe Lancaster. She was arrested for the murder of Rebecca Dean five years ago in Australia. You know? The daughter of Oscar Dean?"

"Well, did she do it?" Janet bellowed down the line.

"I have no idea. She was let off. Look, does any of this ring a bell with you? I've got a bloody coach load of Australians who know exactly who she is. Surely someone there recognised the name."

"So what? Without a criminal record, she's free to travel wherever the fuck she likes."

Stella and Janet rarely saw eye to eye, but they shared a mutual respect for each other's abilities, although both would deny this publicly. "I know that, but a heads-up might have been helpful. I could have at least avoided the Calais fiasco. I looked like an incompetent idiot. Listen, I haven't got time to read up on all this, but can you please see what you can find out about her and e-mail it through?"

"You are an incompetent idiot, Stella." Janet laughed then coughed and nearly choked.

"Can you just e-mail the info, please?"

"Sure, whatever. I'll get that idiot PA I hired from Latvia or Libya, or wherever the fuck she's from, to look it up and send it through. She can't fuck that up, surely."

"Thanks." Stella sighed.

"Harden the fuck up, Stella. You'll be fine." The line went dead.

Stella sighed. Coming from Janet, that was actually a term of endearment.

Sparked by a renewed sense of adventure, and with the notion that things could only improve, Stella met the buzzing group at breakfast and found herself seeking out Phoebe.

The picture before her was jaw-dropping. Lounging comfortably in the middle of a growing crowd were Pippy and Phoebe, laughing and joking like old buddies. *Oh, please.* Stella was at a loss. Things should have been getting better, not weirder. And to top off her distaste, she was annoyed with the fleeting cramp of jealousy flaring in her chest. *God, Stella, she could be a murderer. Pull yourself together.* Her sense of unease surrounding Phoebe had not abated overnight; fear and attraction were a distracting combination. Stella busied herself with juice and half a slice of cold toast, preparing to address the group regarding the schedule for the day.

"Morning, everyone," she said, raising her voice above the chatter. "I trust you all slept well." Matt lifted his head from his arms to reveal a pale, clammy complexion. "All except Matt. I told you you're past it, old man." He raised his middle finger before gently replacing his head. "So here's the deal for today. Firstly, we're going to visit Napoleon's Tomb—I mentioned it last night. Then we're off to Notre Dame, where I've organised a guide to show you around. Manuel has lived in Paris for years. His knowledge is outstanding. And then Russo and I leave you to explore for the day, but we will have a pickup at five p.m. if you wish to return to the hotel and freshen up before we visit a cabaret this evening. Alternatively, I've noted the address of the cabaret on your info sheet and you can meet us there. As usual, you can stick with us or do your own thing. The world, or Paris at this stage, is your oyster."

Tables full of people began to disperse before Stella remembered her own plan for the day. "Oh, before you all head off, I'm taking the

Metro to the catacombs after Notre Dame this morning, if anyone's interested in tagging along." Having spoken to Pippy about this last night, Stella glanced toward her to be met with the most horrified expression. Phoebe, on the other hand, grinned from ear to ear, and Stella was sure she wasn't supposed to be turned on by such an openly evil expression.

"St-St-Stella. Stella." Pippy ran toward her, Phoebe in tow. "The c-c-catacombs?" Her stuttering seemed to exacerbate under stress. "You in-in-invited e-e-everyone?"

Shit. Stella hadn't realised Pippy was stupid enough to think she would exclusively invite her little group. She played it down. "Of course. The more the merrier, honey. I'll see you on the coach, okay?" Stella nervously directed her next comment to Phoebe. "You coming along?"

Phoebe played with her knife—ironically, the blade was red, raspberry jam smeared on it—deftly rolling it between her fingers. She caught Stella staring and shrugged. "I wouldn't miss it for the world."

An insane rush of nervous energy exploded within Stella, and she spoke before she could stop herself. "You look at home with a knife in your hand." *Oh, that's right, Stella, make a joke with the murderer about a knife.*

Obviously taken aback by such a bold statement, Phoebe advanced toward her. Stella stood her ground. Phoebe whispered, "Many things look at home in my hands, Stella. You just want to hope that if you're ever in my grasp, I'm in a good mood."

Stella smiled and feigned confidence. "When you have me in your grasp, of course."

"Of course." Phoebe returned the smile. "Look, I've seen Notre Dame countless times. Can I buy you a coffee this morning while the others do their little tour?"

Stella's heart began to slow. Phoebe appeared neither offended nor amused by her poor attempt at humour. "Your charm is outstanding. I suppose, given what you've just said, that I should ask whether you're in a good mood or not?"

"Why, Stella, are you expecting to be in my grasp sometime this morning?"

"Safety first, Miss Lancaster."

"Well, in that case, I think you'll find my mood to be favourable."

"That *is* a relief. Coffee it is then. Maybe you'd like to invite Pippy?" Stella joked, grinning wickedly.

Phoebe gave away the slightest hint of embarrassment before recovering. "Sometimes you find yourself in situations not entirely of your doing," she said.

"I see."

"But then again"—Phoebe winked—"you might find yourself in sticky little situations you wouldn't change for the world."

Stella scooted off while she was certain her legs were still able to carry her.

She remained completely distracted by Phoebe as she hurried the group along in the foyer. The moisture between her legs provided undeniable evidence of a strong attraction, but did Phoebe feel it too? One moment, Stella was convinced she was being played, the next, she'd recall a glimpse of what she considered genuine emotion. It was all too confusing. And then there was the blatant intimidation. Phoebe enjoyed making people squirm, and lately it seemed to be Stella she was focused on. She reminded herself that Phoebe was a free woman, never convicted of murder, but the vision of a shiny knife weaving through long, strong fingers flashed once again in her mind. Logic told her to stay away from Phoebe. Overwhelming adrenaline and lust told her she must be kidding if she thought she could even attempt to deny herself. *I'm done for.*

Under a cloudless sky, while the group—minus one accused murderer—toured the gothic Notre Dame with Manuel, Stella met Louis for a Bloody Mary and collected her fee from the previous evening. Phoebe waited patiently in a café nearby.

On her approach, Stella inhaled deeply. She needed that extra oxygen, the sight of Phoebe lounging in her chair at an outside table, beautiful and looking like she owned the place, left Stella feeling giddy. *Give me strength.*

Phoebe looked up. "I saw you coming. I ordered you a latte."

"Thanks, but how do you know I even drink latte?" asked Stella.

Phoebe grinned. "Why do you think I even care?"

With a shrug, Stella sat. "Well, this is off to a good start."

Phoebe sighed, and Stella observed that now familiar adjustment in attitude. Phoebe's shoulders dropped slightly, and her eyes seemed to soften from high alert to mild amusement. "If you really don't want a latte, I'll buy you something else."

"A latte is fine, thanks."

"Would you like something to eat?"

Stella hesitated. Despite feigning interest in half a slice of cold toast at the disturbing sight of Phoebe and Pippy chumming it up at breakfast, she realised she had eaten very little.

The hesitation was apparently enough to indicate she was hungry. In flawless French, Phoebe called the waiter and ordered for both of them.

Gobsmacked, Stella raised her eyebrows.

"Vegetarian pastries and something sweet," said Phoebe.

Stella shook her head.

"What? You don't eat vegetables or something?"

"You just ordered food for me."

"So?"

"You don't think I'm capable of ordering for myself?" asked Stella.

"On the contrary, I think you're incredibly capable in many areas. But with the adoration of a coach load of imbeciles stroking your ego every day of your life, I thought I'd relieve you of the pressure."

Stella didn't agree to meet only to have her ego and sense of control questioned or tested. "I'm quite sure I can take the pressure."

A broad smile, revealing perfect, polished teeth, spread attractively across Phoebe's face. "What's it like? Having a new bunch of idiots in your charge every month or so?"

"They're not idiots," said Stella.

"Not that you can tell from the lot we have now."

"Well, not all of them, anyway." It was difficult to maintain her stance when she knew this was likely to be her last year. She had to concede, many of them were in fact high maintenance, spoilt rich kids.

"You obviously love your job?"

Before Stella could answer, a waiter arrived with fresh coffee and the food Phoebe had ordered. It looked delicious.

"See? Relinquishing control isn't so bad after all." Phoebe smiled.

Stella met her gaze. "I didn't *relinquish* control; you ordered some food. That's all."

"And how do you feel about that?"

"What?" Stella nearly choked on marinated eggplant. "Are we still talking about food?"

"I doubt there are many occasions, food or no food, when you aren't in control. But back to the original question, you do love your job, don't you?" The teasing expression was replaced with one of genuine interest. "For what it's worth, you're very good at it."

Stella's heart skipped a beat. She had met some remarkable women during her years of tour managing. She had met some damn sexy women with one thing on their mind, and she'd met some intellectually attractive women who could almost talk her into an orgasm. But no one made her feel like she was the only person in the entire universe, like Phoebe was doing right now. Phoebe Lancaster made Paris disappear.

"I enjoy what I'm doing," she said, returning Phoebe's intense gaze. "But I no longer love it. I consider myself very lucky to be paid to do this, though."

"It's a remarkable opportunity, I agree."

"But like everything, it has a shelf life," added Stella.

"And let me guess, you've reached yours?"

"Something like that." Stella knew she shouldn't be having this conversation with a client.

Breaking the spell, she looked around at the famous city of love and spread her arms wide. "Welcome to my office. Europe is my workplace. It sure as hell beats any crappy nine-to-five job I've ever done."

"I imagine your time doing this job has been rather colourful." Phoebe flicked her hair back, and Stella nearly melted. "So in the past you've bedded countless women; you would never have paid rent, bills, or needed to buy groceries; you've effectively lived in Europe—a different country every few days—and you practically have your own personal driver. It must take something pretty special these days to get your kicks."

And didn't Stella know it. Searching Phoebe's eyes for the insulting punch line or inevitable put-down, even she had to admit the bar was set incredibly high. But it wasn't "something special" that was proving to be the source of her kicks. She was rapidly realising it was *someone* special.

"Women and thrills aren't everything, you know?" Stella was disappointed that Phoebe's impression of her might be one of promiscuity. "I know the reputation tour managers have."

"Really?" Phoebe appeared entirely unconvinced. "Maybe I'll just have to find out for myself."

Stella laughed. "Find out if I'm promiscuous?"

"On the contrary." Phoebe beamed at her. "Find out if you're not."

God, what is she trying to do to me?

"I think the group has finished touring the cathedral."

"What?" Stella turned as Phoebe pointed. Half of her group were wandering aimlessly around the entrance of Notre Dame. "Crap. I'd better go. Thanks for brunch." Stella rushed off to round up the strays and send them on their way for the day. She couldn't believe she had lost track of time. *Damn you, Phoebe Lancaster.*

❖

It was a big ask—so much to do in Paris—but several people were interested in the catacombs. The majority opted out when they realised the catacombs were dark tunnels that weaved beneath the streets of Paris, full of human remains, exhumed in 1785 from overcrowded cemeteries. Matt, who was hungover and unable to bear the glare of the sun, tagged along, as did Pippy and her two cousins, a couple from Perth, a pleasant and attractive South African girl called Megan, and confusingly, Phoebe Lancaster.

The part of Stella's brain that screamed at her to stay away from Phoebe was losing out every single time.

Stella had the group moving at a swift pace toward the Metro station, but she was so shocked by the sight before her, she reached for her phone and discreetly snapped a photo before sending it to Russo. Within ten seconds, her phone rang.

"You're fucking kidding me, aren't you?" he bellowed down the line.

"Nope. I knew you'd have to see it to believe it."

The vision Stella had forwarded was precisely what she was staring at with her own eyes. Walking briskly in front of her, seemingly oblivious to the rest of the world, were Pippy and Phoebe, arms linked at the elbows, chatting and laughing in the glorious sunshine. Stella suppressed an urge to vomit, but not before a thick layer of jealousy heavily lined her stomach.

"Something is seriously wrong here, Stells," Russo conceded humourlessly.

"You're telling me."

"I'm not joking, Stella. I mean it. Possibly the most attractive woman on the coach making friends with that ignorant Texan twat? This is too weird."

Stella felt ashamed. Her reason for sending the photo was pure, unadulterated jealousy. "I think Pippy has a little crush. Poor Phoebe."

"Poor Phoebe? I don't care about Phoebe. God damn it. She was accused of murder, Stella. Accused of a murder no one else has ever been convicted of."

"Steady on, Russo. She might not have done it, you know?"

Russo laughed. "Did you see her at breakfast? That bloody knife in her hand? Murderer or not, she's got something going on. If that little display was supposed to be a joke, I missed the punch line."

"Look, Russo, I've spoken to her a couple of times now. She isn't evil, and I doubt that tough façade is the real her. How would you feel if you had been accused of a murder you didn't commit? It would haunt you your entire life."

"I know how I'd feel if I had been accused of murder and I *did* do it. I'd feel bloody happy I got away with it and wonder if I could again, probably."

"Oh, come on, Russo. She's not that bad, and she wasn't even tried."

Russo was silent for a moment. "No, Stella. No fucking way. I know where this is heading, and you are fucking insane if you get involved with her."

Stella was quick to defend herself. "I'm not doing a damn thing with her, so stop worrying."

"But you're attracted to her, right?"

Stella hardly ever kept secrets from Russo, and she felt comfortable enough to discuss this. Hopefully, he might offer an insight into her ridiculous attraction. "No. Yes. Maybe. Look, I really don't know."

"This isn't good. You know that, don't you? I'm a bloke and she scares the shit out of me."

Stella couldn't help herself. "That's just it, Russo. On some level, she scares the shit out of me too, but it makes me…"

"Go on, you can say it," said Russo, resigned.

"She makes me that fucking wet. The feeling is addictive. I'm a dribbling mess when I'm around her, and I know it's wrong, on so many levels. But I just can't shake it. Jesus, I actually think she's nice."

"Oh, Stella. This isn't good."

"I can't control it. It's like this attraction belongs to someone else and is hiding out in my body."

Russo was silent, and Stella knew he was formulating a plan. "Well, she's with Pippy today, so just leave it for now. We need to talk about this face-to-face and preferably while consuming alcohol."

"You're right." Stella felt pathetic and out of control, but maybe Russo was right. Maybe his point of view wasn't tainted with attraction. "We're nearly there. I'll talk to you soon." Stella thought for a moment. "Where are you, by the way?"

"Ah, nothing gets past you, Sherlock, does it? Room 2050 actually." Russo's tone softened, becoming playful.

"This doesn't count as a first nighter, you know?"

"Don't rub it in, Casanova."

Stella laughed, inappropriately proud of her long-standing record. "Remind me who's in that room?"

"Genevieve."

Stella struggled to put a face to the name. "Nope, not ringing any bells."

"Fifth row behind me in the coach yesterday. New Zealand, blonde…"

"Ah, yes. Now I remember. Good work, tiger."

"Thanks, chief. Gotta go. Shower's stopped running."

The line went dead.

Stella refocused as they entered the station. Pippy gripped Phoebe tightly through the crook of her elbow, and although Phoebe stood tall, oozing confidence, Stella sensed she wasn't as relaxed as she might have first appeared. Pippy seemed oblivious, but Stella was convinced Phoebe looked awkward at the touch.

In Paris, time was of the essence, and travel on the Metro was a fast, cheap, and easy solution, but not without its share of problems. "The underground is full of thieves and pickpockets, so be careful," Stella warned everyone. In the middle of summer, Paris, including the underground, was thriving with tourists. "Keep together as much as possible," she said, deliberately eyeing Phoebe and Pippy. "That's right, nice and close, girls," she muttered under her breath.

The instant the vending machines produced their tickets, everyone enthusiastically leapt upon the escalator, descending toward the platform. All except Matt who was incapable of any enthusiastic movement at all. "Wait for me at the bottom," Stella yelled, counting them off to ensure she hadn't lost anyone. Her eyes fixated on Phoebe's tight backside. She wore navy blue shorts, and the fabric was pulled tight as she stood descending the escalator with her hands in her pockets. Stella was attempting to ignore the fact that Pippy's arm was still threaded through Phoebe's, and focus on more pleasant things. When Stella glanced up, her eyes locked on Phoebe's. Phoebe winked. Stella almost died.

The platform was crowded. Stella could spot an inexperienced pickpocket a mile off, but a skilled thief blended in. Conscientiously, she swung her satchel to the front and subtly motioned for the rest of the group to do the same. Stella had never witnessed any violence on the Paris Metro, but as always, she remained alert. The excited group, especially Pippy, cavorted dangerously near the edge of the platform, ignoring Stella's advice to step back. Matt, who was still wearing his sunglasses, was the exception. He was too unwell to mess around in any capacity. The train was on time and only four minutes away.

As the clock ticked down and a hint of draft swelled in the tunnel, the platform began to crowd and Stella motioned to the group to come and stand by her against the wall. They all stepped back toward Stella, but as the waiting commuters grew in numbers, her entourage were jostled closer to the edge, not the wall where Stella waited. Pippy danced around Phoebe, whose expression was impossible to read.

Stella's heart began to race as a group of eight youths surrounded Stella's group. Among the throngs of people, these teenagers appeared to blend in, but Stella guessed by their strategic approach that they were an organised gang of thieves. The draft became stronger as warm air was pushed through the tunnel by the incoming train. Stella yelled to her group, but the din of people surrounding them smothered her voice with ease. It was becoming hot and sticky as the platform disappeared with swarms of commuters.

She knew the drill, and her group were a prime target. When the train pulled up, the young thieves would link arms and push as many people onto the carriage as possible. Surrounded by these thugs, her group would gently, so as not to create panic, become pushed together so tightly they would remain unaware that those nearest the thieves would be pickpocketed and robbed.

The draft became stronger, and Stella rushed forward to warn her group, yelling at them not to board the train, to wait for the next one. All at once, everyone seemed to surge toward the platform edge as the warm wind pumped through the tunnel. Stella struggled desperately to navigate a path to her group, but before she could reach them, a chorus of screams erupted from their location at the front of the platform. A wave of panic rippled through the crowd, and soon everyone was screaming and retreating as Stella forced herself forward. The rumbling of the incoming train and frantic screams filled her ears. As she burst through the withdrawing crowd, she caught sight of Pippy, sprawled on the tracks, her group, stunned onlookers.

It was all happening too fast. The headlight of the train grew threateningly. Then, jolting out of shock and into action mode, one of the thugs rushed past Stella and leapt onto the tracks, scurrying toward Pippy who appeared to be out cold. The train horn blew, long and loud. The deafening screech of brakes pierced the air and filled the cavity. Without warning, the horrific events taking place altered from seemingly supersonic speed, to super-slow motion. Stella watched as the young thug hauled Pippy up, grabbing her under the arms. The muscles on the lean man's arms rippled then became taut and bulging as he lifted the weighty girl. He glanced up toward the oncoming light. Stella followed his gaze. He wasn't going to make it. Pippy was too heavy, and he was running out of time.

With a burst of energy, he almost lifted Pippy into a standing position, poised to propel her toward the safety of the platform. The train was slowing, only a matter of metres away now, but it couldn't possibly stop in time. Some others, including Stella and Phoebe scrambled forward, screaming for Pippy to wake up. Stella willed the young boy to save himself or else they would both die. At that moment, as if the same thought entered his mind, an expression of astonishment spread over his face as Pippy, groggy and clearly disorientated, took some of her own weight and assisted in his last-ditch motion, launching, mid-air, from the path of the train. Stella, Phoebe, and the other would-be thieves all scrambled to drag Pippy and her hero back to the safety of the platform. So close was the scrape, the train struck Pippy's lower leg with a sharp crack on the way through.

Pandemonium erupted. The minutes following the incident were a hazy mishmash of fear, panic, relief, and deafening noise. Stella remained in a state of shock until she sat in a Paris police station, viewing CCTV footage of the accident, surrounded by detectives. The horrified expression upon Pippy's face as she fell backward sent chills down Stella's spine.

CHAPTER FIVE

It was almost seven o'clock by the time Stella climbed into a taxi en route to meet the group for dinner. Janet was on the line the entire journey.

"What the fuck is going on over there? How's that Canadian idiot?"

"She's American, Janet." Stella sighed.

"Same fucking continent. Same fucking difference in my book." Janet laughed at her own perceived wit.

Stella wasn't in the mood for Janet, but the sooner this conversation began, the sooner it could end. "She's fine. Her leg's a mess, though, apparently nothing a couple of months in plaster won't fix."

"And what about the others, the idiots in the tunnel with you, did they get to see *one* fucking sight of Paris?"

It was completely expected that Janet wouldn't give a damn about anyone's health and well-being, as long as the tour continued with as little fuss as possible.

"Maybe. I don't know. They were out of the station by four this afternoon."

"Four? It's seven now, what the hell took *you* so long then?"

"Paperwork and waiting for the all clear to leave." Stella just wanted to go to bed.

"Those French twats. They eat snails. Doesn't mean they have to fucking act like them. Did you tell them you had fifty bloody dickhead tourists to babysit?"

"Yes, Janet. I told them."

Janet mumbled more expletives before continuing. "So, how many have we lost?"

"Just the three cousins at this stage. Depending on how soon Pippy's parents arrive, two may join us again down the track."

Janet sighed. "This tour had better fucking improve, Stella, you hear me?"

"Yes, loud and clear."

Janet hung up.

It had been a long and exhausting day. The police interviewed everyone involved, watched the CCTV footage from all available angles, and concluded, given the evidence, that the cause of the fall was undetermined. No one seemed to know precisely what happened, Pippy included. Through hysterical tears, lasting beyond what was normal human behaviour, Pippy could shed no light on how she fell. She recalled, with ease, the moments leading up to the fall, but could understandably only confirm that one minute, she was upright, the next she wasn't. Megan had her back turned at the time and saw nothing. CCTV confirmed this. Matt was too vague to offer any help whatsoever, and he appeared paler than ever. The couple from Perth, Heath and Emma, were too excited to be going on the underground for the first time, so their attention wasn't on Pippy. The would-be thieves were intermingling with everyone, but appeared too busy positioning themselves for their strategic manoeuvre to even notice Pippy. Only Phoebe remained. Calm, cool Phoebe. She appeared to be the only one not in shock, not intimidated by the police, and the only one Stella wished hadn't been anywhere near the damn accident. Unfortunately, Phoebe could offer little in the way of explanation, but her expression, captured clearly on the CCTV, was disturbing. Unless Phoebe had perfected a look of indifference, verging on smug satisfaction, something felt terribly wrong.

Of course the authorities, upon discovering who she was, singled out Phoebe to question intensely, but the event was available for all to see on the CCTV, and it provided no evidence that Pippy was pushed or tripped. Without a witness, the case was a dead end. A horrible accident. Nobody saw a damn thing.

At dinner, it was only natural the group should be discussing nothing other than the accident. Phoebe, in Pippy's absence, was on her own again, silently reading a book, extracting escargot from their shells like a seasoned pro. Stella felt sorry for her, but now two images flashed before her eyes. The knife in her hand at breakfast, and the look on Pippy's face when she realised a train was coming. Was Phoebe responsible for that?

Russo was sitting next to Genevieve, who appeared slightly put out when Stella slumped in the vacant seat next to him. He protectively rested his arm on the back of her chair. "Rough day, Stella, eh?"

"You can say that again." Famished, she ordered frog legs.

He leaned in close, grinning. "Bit extreme, going to those lengths to get rid of her?"

"Hey," she joked half-heartedly. "Desperate times call for desperate measures."

"Seriously though, how's she doing?"

"Fine." Stella sighed. "She'll be fine."

"So is it all sorted with the cops?"

"Yeah, I think so. We need to call into the police station tomorrow morning so they can take copies of the passports of those concerned, then that should be the end of it for our part."

Russo was keen to change the subject, and while Genevieve was deep in conversation with others at the table, he lowered his voice. "Well, I had a rather pleasant morning, until I came to your rescue, of course." Russo had rushed to the station upon hearing of the accident.

"Did you, now?"

"Hmmm…" His voice lowered to a whisper. "Let's just say, she's not as innocent as she may first appear."

"What were you expecting?"

"I don't know, a little less experience. I wasn't expecting to have to perform. I like it better when they think I'm God."

Stella knew this was a joke, all to cheer her up, and she appreciated it. For all his bravado, Russo was no chauvinist. Coach driving through Europe with a constant stream of girls was his ideal job. He loved women, loved sex, but never took it for granted. He'd given a bloke a blow job once before, mainly to see what it was like, but it wasn't his thing, although a threesome here and there was never to be balked at. When Stella first heard they'd be doing tours together, she marched straight in to Janet and demanded she reconsider. Stella had said she'd rather go on tour with Gary Glitter than Russo. Of course, Janet told her to fuck off, and begrudgingly, Stella and Russo began working together. Fortunately, Stella's opinion soon changed, and she and Russo became best friends.

"Drink?" Russo hovered a bottle of red over her wine glass. He was drinking water, but the rest of the table had ordered wine.

Stella's gaze shot over to Phoebe. "I shouldn't, but thanks."

"That bad, huh?"

She frowned.

He lowered his voice. "I know you, Stella. After a day like today, you need a drink. Other than a failed liver function test, the only other reason you've denied yourself a drink in the past has been because of a woman."

Russo was right.

Stella shook her head. "After what I saw today, the look on Phoebe's face on the CCTV, I'm holding this attraction in check."

"I don't trust her, Stella. I don't think you should either." Russo squeezed her shoulder.

"Maybe. I don't know."

As the group moved on to the cabaret, plied with alcohol, the topic of conversation shifted from the day's events, and for this, Stella was grateful. The return coach ride to the hotel was filled with raucous laughter, and Stella, eager to start the following day completely afresh and without the need to discuss the underground incident, moved through the coach and spoke to those involved.

Megan, while initially rather shaken and teary, was simply grateful Pippy would make a full recovery. Heath and Emma had each other for support and were more concerned about Stella and how much longer she had been required to remain at the police station. Emma had suggested Heath stay with her after all the questioning, but there was no need. Stella took an instant shine to this lovely, thoughtful couple. An exhausted and pasty looking Matt appeared grumpy. Stella detected a hint of annoyance in his moody demeanour, as if Pippy fell to deliberately ruin his day. Overall, they appeared to be dealing with the event rather well, and all declined Stella's offer to organise counselling, although she did mention she would be available to chat anytime, should they need to.

Although desperately wishing she could return to her solitary seat opposite Russo, Stella knew she couldn't ignore Phoebe, who was sitting alone toward the rear of the coach. Resigned to her fate, Stella approached cautiously.

"Hi, Phoebe." Stella's voice failed her, rising in octaves. *Jesus. Why do I react like this?* She coughed and continued. "I was wondering how you were feeling after this morning?"

Stella fully expected a sarcastic response, a snide remark, or both, but Phoebe offered nothing. With darkened eyes, she glanced from Stella to the empty seat beside her and back again. Stella warily sat.

Phoebe adjusted her long frame to face Stella. "I was questioned for almost twice as long as everyone else today. Was that your doing?" Her voice remained steady and without tone. It unnerved Stella.

"No, it wasn't."

"Did you alert them to my history?"

"No, I didn't." It was the truth. Upon being accused of attempting to conceal Phoebe's identity, Stella had argued with the police that there was no need for her to alert every single person she met to the fact that Phoebe Lancaster—a completely free woman with no criminal record—was on her tour and at the train station that morning. "On the contrary, I was accused of obstructing the police investigation by *not* alerting them to your presence."

Whatever response Stella was expecting, it wasn't forthcoming. In fact, nothing further was forthcoming. With her trademark indifference, Phoebe turned away. The conversation was over.

CHAPTER SIX

M uch to Stella's relief, the subsequent days passed without incident. Due to the tour's busy schedule, she saw little of Phoebe, but thought about her almost constantly.

Unfortunately, thoughts of Rebecca Dean's death plagued Stella nearly as frequently. As promised, Janet arranged for some information to be e-mailed, but it wasn't anything she hadn't already learned for herself. Rebecca Dean and Phoebe Lancaster kept a low profile personally. They appeared to avoid the publicity that often surrounded Oscar and his media outlets and there never seemed to be any scandal involving them. They were, it seemed, the perfect couple.

Barcelona, one of Stella's favourite cities, brought with it a renewed sense of enthusiasm. The second day in Barcelona was a free day, and although Stella woke feeling tired and achy, the sun was shining and she had things to do. The group had been armed with an information sheet and were left to their own devices, encouraged to explore the city, eat tapas, and simply relax and enjoy. Stella had been unusually cagey surrounding her movements for the day; she wanted to spend it alone.

That afternoon, at Parc del Laberint d'Horta—the Labyrinth Park of Barcelona—a rare musical performance was taking place, and Stella had secured a ticket months ago. Although it wasn't advisable to detach herself from the group for a whole day, after the trouble in Paris, Stella was looking forward to doing something of her choosing.

Singing, with full band, including a string section, was Keira Hannigan, an Irish folk singer with the most amazing voice. Stella had seen her perform before, but to see her in the beautiful gardens that she'd been meaning to visit for some time now, was an opportunity not to pass up. Tickets had been limited, but some fast talking and two hundred Euros secured her a seat.

It was fascinating, especially for Stella, who loved history, to visit Barcelona's oldest park, and apparently, the most romantic place in all of Barcelona. The locals suggested the park possessed a calming and relaxing aura, which could be felt the moment you stepped through the gates, lending itself to lust, love, passion, and romance. Although she was excited to be attending the concert, the labyrinth maze, set in the picturesque gardens, was also a highlight. Stella enjoyed a challenge and had heard it wasn't as easy to conquer as it first appeared.

Public transport in many European countries was easy to negotiate with a little practice, but Stella wasn't at her best after drinking sangria with lunch. Had she been honest, her cheeky drink had left her feeling a little drunk. Subsequently, she prematurely disembarked the bus at the wrong stop. By the time she hiked the remaining two kilometres in the full heat of the afternoon sun, Stella felt lightheaded and dehydrated. She rued drinking the sangria and chastised herself for forgetting her hat.

Stella arrived in a lather of sweat and barely in time to take her seat before the show began. Huge trees swayed overhead providing intermittent shade, and Stella soon became lost in the music, forgetting the uncomfortable dry heat.

Keira Hannigan was striking. She captivated the audience, performing in a beautiful white flowing dress, framed like an angel against the backdrop of the spectacular gardens. Her rich, deep voice reverberated through the sound system, sending shivers down Stella's spine.

At the conclusion of the first song, Stella felt a gentle tap on her shoulder. She spun around, unsure how she could possibly be obstructing the view for the person behind her. Her breath stalled in her throat.

Phoebe Lancaster leaned forward. "Fancy seeing you here."

Stella forced her breath upward. "I could say the same to you."

"After last night, I hardly considered Keira Hannigan to be your style."

Stella frowned. *Last night?*

Then it made sense. She had taken the group to a nightclub, and despite herself, had actually enjoyed dancing to the throbbing beat. After only an hour, it usually began to grate on her ears, but last night she had enjoyed herself regardless, flirting and getting to know her group.

"I was working last night, Phoebe." Stella smiled. "My job is to ensure people have a good time." Her attempts at reassuring Phoebe her behaviour at the club was work-related apparently appeared unconvincing.

"You seemed to be having an exceptionally good time with Matt and some of the other men."

Stella didn't like where this was going. "As I said, I was working. If my behaviour in some way offended you, I'm sorry." Her apology was genuine. "Phoebe, it's honestly part of what I do."

"I can only imagine."

"Perhaps you felt I excluded you?"

Phoebe rested back and turned her attention toward the stage. Like a good little girl, Stella was expected to turn around and watch the concert. With nothing left to say, that was exactly what she did.

The concert was remarkable, but the heat was oppressive. A gap high in the trees allowed a patch of sunlight to beam directly down, burning Stella's scalp. Sweat dripped down her forehead, along her eyebrows, and eventually down her cheeks and neck. A brutal thirst overcame her, and focusing became difficult. She was overheating, but when she leaned down to retrieve the bottle of water from between her legs, her unpredictable shaking toppled it over, spilling every last drop. She hadn't replaced the lid securely.

For the next hour, Stella, with her head throbbing and body aching, fought desperately to enjoy the music. She could hear Phoebe humming gaily behind her, and a part of her wished she had known she was coming so they could have at least sat together, although she had obviously upset Phoebe somehow.

When the concert was over, Stella couldn't remember anything beyond the conversation with Phoebe. It was all a blur, and her mouth and throat were dry. She was thirsty, so thirsty. Her neck and shoulders felt burnt, but she was sure she'd applied sunscreen. Unsure why she was feeling so poorly, Stella became frightened. She needed to find shade and drink some water. The throbbing, now extending to her temples and eyes, was relentless. She began to stumble toward the tiny kiosk and some much-needed shelter. *Where's Phoebe?*

Stella blinked as objects blurred and distorted. To her dismay, the only thing she could clearly identify ahead was the giant maze—the impressive Labyrinth—her confused, delusional mind told her to keep going and find Phoebe.

After only three turns, Stella was lost and completely perplexed. The sweat trickled from her pores like a dripping tap, soaking her singlet top down to the small of her back. In sheer desperation, she slumped down against the prickly hedge—the only shade she could find. Within seconds, she could see nothing at all.

Although not unconscious, Stella was oblivious to the events that unfolded. When she finally became cognisant, she found herself immersed in the pool of an artificial waterfall. Holding her head only centimetres above the waterline was Phoebe. Stella panicked. *She's going to drown me!*

"An ambulance is on its way." Phoebe's tone was unreadable.

"What's going on?" Stella mumbled, swiping away the hand of one of the gardeners as he dabbed her forehead with a damp cloth.

"Heat stroke."

"You're trying to kill me. Please don't hurt me," pleaded Stella.

"Stella, you're dehydrated. You need to drink." Agitation crept into Phoebe's tone.

Stella was grateful for the water surrounding her, but her sunglasses had been removed, and her eyes felt like they were burning. Confusion engulfed her as people darted between her and the sun, creating frightening silhouettes.

"Please, Phoebe, let me go." Stella struggled with the hands that were holding her upright.

Suddenly, in the confusion and disorientation with the sun appearing brighter than ever, Stella caught sight of Phoebe's silhouetted arm, and in her hand, something glistened intensely. Stella slipped over the edge. "Jesus, she's got a knife. Someone help me please. She's trying to kill me. She has a knife!"

Stella felt a sharp sting on the side of her face and stopped struggling, stunned.

"Stella, it's a fucking drink bottle, damn it!" Phoebe yelled.

"What?" Stella was still recovering from the slap on her face.

"Calm down and drink it, please." Phoebe's tone was laced with disappointment. "The ambulance is on its way, but if you don't drink something right now, they'll put you on a drip all night. Is that what you want?"

In desperation, Phoebe straddled her, placing strong, tanned legs either side of Stella's elbows to constrict her movement. With one hand, she cradled Stella's neck and, tilting her head back, poured the water down, giving Stella no choice but to swallow.

The severe thirst was overwhelming, and Stella soon realised the only thing relieving her thirst was the water Phoebe was offering. She gave up the fight and relaxed, allowing Phoebe to hold the bottle to her lips. She sipped desperately. The rush of cold water slipping down her throat and into her stomach provided a welcomed relief.

Within minutes, Stella was voluntarily sipping a second bottle as the paramedics arrived. With little fuss, she was lifted onto a trolley and wheeled toward the ambulance.

"Hold on," whispered Stella. "Please," she managed, louder this time. "Wait a moment."

The paramedic pulled the trolley to a halt.

"Phoebe?" Stella looked around, searching for the familiar face.

"I'm here." Phoebe stepped into her vision.

"Will you come with me? Please?" Stella didn't want to go to the hospital alone.

"I don't know." Phoebe hesitated. "Maybe it's not such a good idea."

Stella saw the hurt in her eyes. *How could she have killed anyone?* "Okay." Stella was so confused. Her fear felt real, but so did her attraction. In such a fragile state, and far from feeling on top of things, she let it go. "I'm sorry."

The paramedic was drumming her fingers impatiently on the side of the ambulance, and with that natural lull in the conversation, took the opportunity to push the trolley into the vehicle and close the door behind her. With a swift thump on the partition separating the driver from the main compartment, the vehicle slowly pulled away. No sirens, no hurry.

Shit. Stella was all too aware of her responsibilities and rested yet another drink bottle in the crook of her arm and dragged her phone from her pocket. She had to call Russo. The young paramedic pressed a cool, damp cloth to her forehead and quickly intervened. "You must drink. Nothing else, just drink."

Stella smiled, holding the bottle aloft, silently assuring the woman she could do both.

The conversation with Russo was brief and to the point. After the initial shock of hearing she was on her way to hospital, he assured Stella he'd take care of things. She trusted him.

In contrast, the paramedic simply glared at her and said, "Drink."

Stella was wheeled through to the bustling emergency department soon after the ambulance arrived in the designated parking bay. Within minutes, she was hooked up to a drip and left to ponder her disastrous afternoon. After a slow, silent hour, a nurse by the name of Sergio entered the room and spoke in excellent English. "Hello, Stella. You have a visitor."

Stella fought to contain her anger. If Russo was to round up the group and walk them to dinner on time, he'd be lucky to have a minute to scratch himself, let alone visit her in the hospital. She cursed. Her hospitalisation alone was enough to cause Janet to have a coronary. The knowledge that an entire evening had been ruined would likely cause her to drop dead.

"Russo, you shouldn't—" Stella stared in amazement as Sergio stood aside.

Phoebe hesitated before shuffling inside the pale blue curtain. "Hey."

"Hey, yourself." Stella smiled and then reluctantly turned her attention to Sergio who was checking her vitals.

"Another bag of fluids, I think." Sergio smiled and ignored Stella's groan. Lying around while her body absorbed fluids intravenously required no assistance from her. She was bored and worried about the group.

After Sergio quietly snuck through the curtain, Phoebe remained standing, awkwardly searching the room for something to fix her gaze upon. "You can sit on the bed if you like," said Stella.

Phoebe sat as close to the foot of the bed as she could. "How do you feel?"

"Better. Much better, thanks. I think I was delirious back there." It wasn't an outright apology for her appalling behaviour, but Phoebe gave her the distinct impression she didn't want to talk about it.

"Heat stroke is a pretty serious thing." Phoebe refused to meet her gaze.

"How did you know that's what I had?" The small talk was unnerving, but Stella understood her options were limited.

"I've seen it before."

Stella waited for further explanation, but nothing appeared forthcoming. "Was Russo on top of things?"

Phoebe nodded, fidgeting with the hem of her shorts. "I can see why he's usually the driver. He's a bit like a drill sergeant when he has to do your job."

Stella grinned. "Yes, well, he does take bossing groups around very seriously."

An uncomfortable silence settled in the tiny cubicle.

Stella finally plucked up the courage to speak. "Thanks for coming."

Phoebe shrugged. "Well, I wasn't all that hungry, and I had nothing better to do."

"There are loads of things better than hanging around the emergency room while you're on holiday," said Stella.

"It's okay. I've been to Barcelona before."

"I get the impression you've been all over Europe." Stella wasn't fishing for information; it was merely an observation.

Phoebe shrugged again. "Some of it. Maybe."

It was on the tip of her tongue to ask why she was on this tour. In fact, Stella had so many questions for the mysterious Phoebe Lancaster, the most pressing being the most inappropriate. *Are you a murderer?*

Phoebe was clearly uncomfortable, and Stella wasn't entirely sure why. Rebecca Dean's death had occurred five years ago. Had there been someone else since then? Stella fleetingly wondered if anyone else Phoebe had been seeing, or even dating, had mysteriously disappeared. She chastised herself for considering such an appalling scenario. She had to admit though, the more she liked Phoebe, the more ridiculous the thoughts were that kept bombarding her mind. The confusion was sending her crazy. One day she was disturbed by the CCTV vision of Phoebe on the Paris Metro and her seeming indifference to such a tragic event, and the next, Phoebe shows up at the hospital in an act of kindness. *You should leave this alone, Stella.*

Sergio returned to save the day and rescue them from further small talk. "You feeling better?" Stella nodded. "We are very busy and need the bed. The doctor will return soon, and then I'm sure I'll be back to take some blood. If your tests show electrolyte improvement, we'll probably send you home."

"Excellent. Thank you, nurse." That was the best news Stella had heard all night.

He looked to Phoebe. "She must continue to drink."

"I'll make sure she continues her intake of fluids when we leave."

Sergio smiled and disappeared.

Phoebe plucked the chart off the shelf. "Next paracetamol is due in an hour."

"You can read those things?" Stella hadn't looked at a hospital chart yet that she could understand.

Phoebe hesitated, appearing uncomfortable. "A little. It's not difficult."

"Formal training?" Stella pushed.

"Nope."

And there it was again, that familiar lack of information, coupled with an air of coldness. Stella left it alone, feeling an unexpected sorrow for Phoebe perched clumsily on the end of her bed. Who was she to press Phoebe for information she clearly didn't want to give, especially since she had altered her plans to be with her in the hospital? How could she question the attitude of someone who, in the past, had the finger pointed squarely at them for the murder of another human being?

Stella had always been a supporter of the underdog. If everyone hated the new kid at school, she liked them. She cheered for the least favourite team in sport, she would choose the runt of the litter, and she often defended those incapable of defending themselves. But feeling sorry for Phoebe wasn't what had her insides in a twist. Phoebe had arrived at the hospital unexpectedly. Was there a genuine possibility that she felt something too?

Stella sighed. All she had to do now was shake her paranoia. This was proving easier said than done.

Even though the doctor ordered blood tests, and Sergio returned for the sample, it was another two hours before Stella and Phoebe slid into the plastic seats of the first cab on the stand outside the hospital. Stella's clothes had been dried, and despite the dull ache that remained behind her eyes, she felt remarkably better than before. Now she was simply tired. Phoebe had made it quite clear additional paracetamol could not be consumed until she was safely tucked up in bed at the hotel, so there was no point in even asking. Stella stared at Phoebe. She couldn't read her expression, nor form a judgement on her state of mind. It was all extremely frustrating.

The taxi journey was completed in silence. Stella was struggling to pluck up the courage to ask Phoebe if she would sit with her for a while in her room. She soon discovered that not only did she lack the courage, she couldn't find the appropriate words either. Everything she came up with sounded like a pathetic come-on. It occurred to her that she was entirely out of her depth and certainly out of practice when it came to normal relationships. She attempted to convince herself she'd be more at home delivering Phoebe a line to entice her into bed, but it had been so long since she'd done that, she wasn't even sure she could pull it off.

Inside the hotel foyer, ceiling fans rattled and simply pushed stale air around the already stinking hot area. Some hotels had excellent air conditioning, but Le Mediterranean on the Ramblas was run-down and the best her company could secure at a reasonable price in the heart of town.

Phoebe broke the silence. "What room are you in?"

Stella told her, and Phoebe collected the key from the reception desk, taking Stella's hand and leading the way. It wasn't until right outside her door, when the nausea hit Stella.

"I think I need to be sick." She rushed past Phoebe as the door swung open, but didn't make it to the bathroom. Stella vomited water and stomach bile all over the old timber floor. "Oh, shit." She began to sway as Phoebe quickly gathered her in her arms to prevent a fall.

"You need to lie down and drink more." Phoebe's tone was gentle. "Especially if you're going to throw it up again."

"I need to clean up first," Stella protested, aware of nothing but the strong arms surrounding her. Phoebe was an alluring combination of strength and softness, and Stella felt so poorly she yearned to melt into her embrace and replenish her energy.

"I'll fix all that." She helped Stella to the bed. "Here, stay above the covers though."

"You can't clean up my vomit, Phoebe. I'll fix it. This is embarrassing." But before Stella could utter another word, she darted into the bathroom, managing to reach the toilet bowl this time. She felt terrible, along with a churning stomach, her face was on fire again.

"Much more of that and you'll need to go back to hospital," Phoebe called from the main room. "I can't fill you up with water at the pace you're vomiting." She knocked on the bathroom door. Stella sat slumped in the corner, and Phoebe stepped over her to retrieve a towel for the clean-up.

"I think there'll be more." Stella groaned, clutching her stomach.

Phoebe knelt and felt her brow before soaking a face washer and resting it on Stella's head. She smiled. "Try to make the next one your last one." She squeezed her shoulder. "Otherwise I'm calling another ambulance."

Just great. Stella leaned over the bowl again, retching, but thankfully keeping everything down. Convinced she had produced her worst, she hobbled out and slumped on her bed.

Phoebe was by her side immediately, holding out a bottle of water. "Sorry, but you really need to sip this, and at least another three, before you call it a night."

"Damn." Stella sighed. "I just want to sleep."

Phoebe straightened, all business-like again and left to rinse the face washer in cooler water. "I'm afraid that's not going to happen unless you want to be on a drip in the hospital again."

"How do you know all this?"

"Why does it matter? It's standard medical advice in the instance of heat stroke. Call the hospital if you like."

Stella sensed the coldness surround Phoebe again. "I'm not questioning you." She sipped the water. "Don't worry. I won't ask again."

Phoebe softened. "Are you always such a difficult patient?"

"I don't know." Stella shrugged. "Are you always so distrustful of people?"

"Frankly, yes."

"Even me? Even after Calais and after coming under scrutiny from the Police in Paris in an attempt to defend you?"

"You give me no reason to distrust you," confirmed Phoebe.

"Exactly."

"You've given me no reason to trust you, either."

Stella let out a small laugh. "I could say the same for you."

"You *should* say the same for me." Phoebe settled on the chair by the window, indicating with raised eyebrows the water Stella cradled. "Let's not pretend you're not thinking what you're thinking."

Stella's heart beat began to quicken. She was terrified to be talking about this. She quickly changed the subject. "Help yourself to the minibar."

Phoebe shrugged. "I'm only staying until I convince myself you've stopped vomiting."

"You don't think I'll call an ambulance if I need one?" Stella continued drinking, shaking her head. "Nope, we've got this covered; no trust issues in this room."

Indifferent, Phoebe shrugged again.

Stella continued to sip the water until fighting sleep became impossible. Phoebe remained by her side, waking her intermittently to drink until eventually, she felt herself returning to a normal temperature. Any desire to vomit had faded completely.

Not long after midnight, Stella awoke to find the lights off, the curtains open, and Phoebe asleep in the chair. She crept silently to the bathroom; all the water she had consumed was suddenly working wonders at flushing her system. Phoebe stirred, but remained asleep. Although Stella knew she should probably wake her and send her back to her own room to sleep comfortably in a bed for the remainder of the night, she couldn't bring herself to do it. She didn't want to be alone. She recalled Phoebe's arms embracing her earlier in the evening and wondered what it would be like to be beneath her, to have Phoebe lower herself onto her, naked and soft and wanting. She imagined what it would be like to ride her, be deep inside her and take her to the edge and back, time after time. Stella couldn't name the connection she was experiencing, but it was becoming evident she had little control over her senses.

Stella wasn't sure what woke her, she hadn't registered any movement or noise, but just before she allowed herself to slip back into unconsciousness, she cracked her right eye open the tiniest bit.

"What the fuck?" A silhouette loomed over her, a hand close to her face.

Phoebe stood next to the bed, her body silhouetted as the moonlight shone through the window behind her. Her reaction to Stella breaking the silence was nil. She simply lowered her hand slowly. "It's just me."

Stella scrambled away from Phoebe, struggling to maintain composure. "I can see that. What the hell are you doing?"

"I was about to check your temperature." Phoebe stepped away from the bed. A defensive tone had crept into her voice.

"My what?" Stella couldn't calm herself down enough to consider Phoebe's feelings, and although she recognised her flight or fight mode, she could do little to change her response. "Why the fuck would you stand over me in the middle of the night?"

"I wasn't standing over you. I had walked over to you and was about to touch your forehead."

Stella scrambled to switch on the bedside lamp. Phoebe the monster instantly transformed into normal Phoebe again. Although by normal, Stella could tell she was a little pissed off. "Sorry. I'd been in a deep sleep and I woke and there you were." She held her chest as if she could calm her racing heart by doing so.

"It's late. I thought I should go and I just wanted to make sure your temperature was back to normal before I left." Phoebe advanced toward the door. "Good night, Stella."

Before Stella could offer any protest, Phoebe was gone.

"Well, that went well." Stella spoke to her reflection in the mirror when she went to the bathroom. It was nearly four in the morning and besides being hungry, she felt surprisingly better than she had the previous evening.

Stella closed the curtains to darken the room in the hope of returning to sleep, but all she could do was lie awake and think of her reaction to Phoebe standing over her. She hadn't meant to insult Phoebe, but she woke genuinely startled. Okay, perhaps her response could have been a little less dramatic, but regardless of who it was standing there, she would have been startled. The fact that it had been Phoebe just complicated things.

CHAPTER SEVEN

It wasn't the aftermath of the heatstroke that left Stella feeling uneasy when she woke, but the altercation with Phoebe. Janet's PA had sent through some more information. She read the e-mail but discovered nothing new. There had to be more to this story than Stella imagined. Who exactly was Phoebe Lancaster? It was apparent who Rebecca Dean was, or perhaps, how privileged she had been growing up, but it was naïve of Stella to believe everything she read. Some articles talked about Oscar embracing his daughter's life choices, others said he condemned her relationship with Phoebe. One minute they were out of the closet, the next they were in it. There were umpteen photographs of both Rebecca and Phoebe with other women and men, but there was nothing to suggest these people were more than innocent friends. It was becoming apparent that the Internet was useless to in any way assist Stella in concluding that Phoebe was untrustworthy or alternatively undeserving of her loyalty and friendship.

A thumping great knock on the door startled Stella, propelling her back to the present.

"Stells, you all right in there?" Russo sounded worried. "Stella, I'm gonna knock the door down. Let me in!"

"All right, all right. Hang on. I'm coming!"

Stella swung open the door to find Russo flustered on the other side. "Jesus," he said. "The coach leaves in five minutes, babe." Russo gripped his muscular chest. "Don't scare me like that. I thought you'd slipped into a coma or something. Is everything okay?"

"Yeah, it's fine. You barely gave me a chance to get to the door."

"And the heat stroke thing? You all right to carry on?" He affectionately touched her cheek. "You look pale."

"Jesus, Russo, you're scaring me. Keep on like this and I'll think you've gone soft." All the bravado in the world couldn't hide the fact that Stella felt a little off. She didn't doubt she was pale. Reading about Phoebe like she was a stranger, a celebrity lesbian, left her feeling like she didn't know Phoebe at all. And that was true. She didn't.

Russo's breathing was returning to normal. "I'll see you on the coach in five, okay?" He gently squeezed Stella's shoulder. "You sure everything's fine?"

"I'm sure, honestly. We'll talk later." She hadn't seen Russo in person since yesterday morning. "Now scoot. I have to pack." Her phone rang. "And I have to talk to Janet."

Janet, as expected, began yelling immediately. No polite greetings were required with her. Stella listened patiently, albeit with numerous eye rolls and a persistent frown before Janet finally exhausted her rather lengthy repertoire of expletives and hung up. Stella's ear hurt.

A paper bag containing a broad-brimmed sunhat, sunscreen, water, juice, and a banana sat resting on Stella's seat on the coach. A little note in the bag read: *We thought you could use these. Heath and Emma.* Stella smiled. It was these kind gestures that made her job worthwhile and the group cheered as she modelled the hat and took a bow.

The bright sun shone through the expansive windows of the coach, and quiet music played in the background allowing those with sore heads to catch up on sleep. To her great relief, the group had enjoyed the previous day in Barcelona, surviving under Russo's guidance, although according to Matt, Russo wasn't much to look at. The atmosphere on the coach was relaxed, and the drive to the Cote d'Azur was tedious, but worth it. Everyone seemed to be looking forward to the glamour of Monte Carlo. There was no sense of urgency, and again, given her absence the previous day, Stella worked the coach chatting to anyone not catching up on sleep. As usual, Phoebe sat alone, engrossed in a book this time, her MP3 player resting on the empty seat beside her.

Other than Stella's untimely hospital visit, there was some other rather juicy gossip gripping the coach. Sisters, Claudia and Eva, from

Peru, were apparently spotted, by Matt of all people, entering Russo's room at the conclusion of dinner. This revelation, rumour or not, would certainly require further investigation. She waited patiently for the right time.

Stella was hungry after talking with the group for over an hour and settled into her seat to snack on her banana. She glanced toward Russo. He appeared wrecked. For safety reasons, Russo was not permitted to drink late if he was required to drive the following day. Had Stella not been ill, it was she who would have accompanied the group to Port Olympico and directed the group to the bars with the cheapest drinks and best music.

In Stella's absence, Russo, who had given the group instructions and left them to it, was last seen by many perched at the hotel bar with an orange juice, deep in conversation with Claudia and Eva. Matt had returned to his room for some headache pills, although, when excitedly relaying this story, he animatedly used quotation marks as he spoke the words *headache pills*, leading Stella to assume he meant something a little stronger. As Matt rushed from his room, he caught sight of Russo ushering the girls into *his* room. This sort of information wasn't something Stella could leave alone. If Russo had scored two girls at once—and sisters at that—she wanted to know all about it.

After three hours solid driving and only one person reaching for the plastic vomit bags, Russo pulled the coach into a services stop for food and fuel. With everyone on the coach wide awake from the booming wake-up song, which had changed to Mumford and Sons' "Little Lion Man," the group rushed from the coach, desperate to be first in line for either food or the toilet.

Russo and Stella relaxed on the grass in the shade of the parked coach. Russo was the brawn to their pairing while Stella provided the brains. But today he promptly gave Stella a dressing down about looking after herself. He was desperate to hear about Phoebe, although Stella suspected he was simply digging for information to validate his stance on why she should stay away from her. She didn't mention that Phoebe visited the hospital or the subsequent mess in the hotel room. Something told her to keep that to herself for the time being. She hoped to God that decision didn't come back to haunt her.

"Do you know what I think, Stells?" asked Russo, stretching flat on his back.

Here we go. Words of wisdom.

"I think she's damaged goods. I mean, how does anyone recover from being accused of murdering their lover?"

Stella sighed. "Who says she's recovered." It wasn't a question.

"Just imagine what that would be like."

Stella *had* imagined it, probably a million times since meeting Phoebe. How long could you suffer the stares, the snide remarks, the special treatment, and the not so special treatment? How long would your resilience survive? A year, maybe two at the most. It was now five years on. Surely such stressful and relentless circumstances had shaped the Phoebe she knew today.

Or, Stella shuddered at the thought, maybe she *was* a manipulative, scheming, murderous bitch.

Excellent options, Stella. Well done.

Stella was eager to change the subject. "So, it was a good night last night?"

"Yeah, not the same without you, of course, but we all got along just fine."

"And everyone went down to the port after dinner?"

"I suppose. I don't really know. There were a couple of people who stayed behind."

"Were there?"

"Yeah. The sisters from Peru didn't go. Said they were tired."

"Did they, now?"

"Uh-huh. I suggested they lie down." Russo's tone oozed smugness.

"How very thoughtful of you."

"I might have mentioned they could lie down in my room, actually."

Stella sat bolt upright. "So it *is* true?"

Russo was fit to burst his seams, he was so eager to tell. "I've been dying to tell you all morning, but you never came to breakfast."

"I want to know *everything*."

"Can I be frank here, Stells?"

"Please do." If Stella hadn't known Russo so well, she would never have believed half the stuff he told her. Neither of them would ever tell anyone else, especially in the group, about their liaisons, but they almost always told each other. Russo was the only one who'd had anything to boast about recently.

"Well, they were like professionals. A double act. A threesome's never coordinated, just a bit of fun, right?" Stella nodded. "Well, this was something else altogether. And sisters as well. Christ, I'll need a cold shower after telling you."

"Just get on with it, eh? We haven't got all day. If you hurry, you might fit in a quick wank before we head off."

In great detail, Russo described what transpired between him and the sisters. "Honestly, Stells, I thought I'd died and gone to heaven. They were into each other as much as me."

As Russo flopped back, flinging his arms out with a long, deep sigh, reliving his achievement, the group began slowly wandering back toward the coach, revived and jovial.

While everyone remained perky and refreshed from the stop, Stella handed out information sheets for Nice and Monte Carlo, providing a brief rundown on the history and some celebrity gossip. Although she encouraged everyone to soak up the scenery during the long drives, her own intentions were to remain hydrated and rested for the evening ahead. Dinner was at the hotel, but beyond that, the group were free to do whatever they pleased.

Three years ago, Stella had stumbled upon a quirky little bar called The Orange Velvet, a twenty-minute stroll from the hotel. Since then, she had attended on every tour, dragging at least half the group with her. The music was always fabulous, the beer and cider even better, and because she guaranteed patronage, the drinks flowed free for her all night long. Tonight, while advised not to consume alcohol by the doctor and Phoebe, she was looking forward to relaxing.

Stella was beginning to understand the difference between wanting to know something and then actually finding out. She'd never lived in denial concerning her sexuality, and denial had never really been a part of her makeup. Until now. The struggle between being sensible and staying away from Phoebe was difficult when she harboured such strong feelings for her.

On some level, she wished she could boldly come straight out and ask Phoebe if she murdered her girlfriend. But what a ridiculous question. Of all the questions to ask a prospective lover, or friend for that matter, the simple fact that it even included the word "murderer" should be enough to suggest she should walk away. And if Phoebe did murder Rebecca Dean, she was hardly going to come right out with it. "Yep, sure showed her who's boss. You wanna be next?"

It was an impossible question to even contemplate. The question, the answer, it was all swimming around in Stella's mind, never reaching a conclusion she could grasp.

CHAPTER EIGHT

A t dinner, Stella sought out Phoebe and spotted her alone in the corner reading a book that rested beside her relatively untouched plate. Phoebe was wearing a sleeveless black shirt and faded jeans. Even in such casual attire, she looked stunning.

Stella had spent the best part of the last hour pacing her room, struggling with a growing need to be near Phoebe. It was madness, she knew, but when she wasn't working, her thoughts were consumed by her. With the exception of a heat stroke crisis, Phoebe had never really laid a hand on Stella, certainly nothing sexual, but Stella's growing infatuation was already causing her heart to race and her mind to wander. She inhaled deeply and purposefully strode toward her.

"Mind if I join you?"

Phoebe didn't look up. "I'd prefer to be alone."

Stella didn't detect a harsh tone, which provided only slight relief, but the refusal took her aback. "Sure. Sorry to interrupt." She turned to leave.

"No, Stella." Phoebe smiled, almost in spite of herself. "I'm being rude. Bad habit. Please, join me."

It wasn't the most gracious of invitations, but Stella didn't need to be asked twice.

"How are you feeling today?" Phoebe closed her book.

"Better, thanks." She nodded toward a huge glass of water. "Keeping hydrated."

Phoebe smiled and nodded. "And is there anything concerning last night we need to discuss?" Her gaze was intense but calm.

"I don't know. Is there?" Stella winced. Answering a question with a question was usually a dead giveaway.

Phoebe studied her long and hard, and when Stella began to crumble under the scrutiny, Phoebe said, "Well, I guess it comes down to trust."

Stella began shifting a cherry tomato around her plate. Trust. Phoebe had left before things went too far. Last night was history. She had nothing to gain from rehashing something she preferred to forget. Stella cleared her throat. Her desire for reassurance came a poor second to her growing desire for Phoebe. "It's a free night tonight, and as you know, I'm heading to a bar."

Phoebe grinned and visibly relaxed at the change in subject. "Yes. I know."

"Well, I've obviously invited the group, but I wanted to invite you personally." Stella could feel her cheeks redden. "Would you like to join me for a drink?" She straightened. "With everyone else, but mostly with me."

Phoebe remained impassive. "You shouldn't drink."

"Oh, I know. I'm not. I'm on water. Believe me, I have many ways of looking like I'm drinking. Some nights I don't touch a drop— trick is to look like I am."

Phoebe smiled, warm and brilliantly. "Well, it works. I was beginning to wonder how you functioned on a daily basis."

Stella pressed on. "So, you'll come?"

"What about the group? They'll demand your attention."

"I'll ignore them if I'm faced with a greater demand."

"Oh, really?"

"It's not just their free night. It's mine too, and if I want to spend it chatting with you, then I will." She winked. "Plus, I know how to work the group. Ten, maybe fifteen minutes at the beginning of the evening, I'll get round to all the different groups, and no one feels neglected. Trust me. You know I've done this loads of times."

"I don't know anything about you, Stella. I really don't fancy a late night."

"That's okay." Stella hoped she was wearing her down. "I'll walk you back any time you want to leave."

"You'll walk me back?" Phoebe laughed outright.

Stella could feel herself blushing again. *Damn it.* "Yes, as a matter of fact. I'm asking you to accompany me for a drink, so of course I'll walk you home."

Phoebe was nearly doubled over now, laughing. "You'll walk me home?"

"Why is that so funny?"

Phoebe wiped tears from her eyes. "Because look at you. You're hardly an imposing figure."

"I'm not walking you home to win any gallantry awards. I'm walking you home because it's the appropriate thing to do." Stella nodded once, indicating that was all that needed to be said on the subject.

"Really?"

Stella grinned. "I don't want a late night either, and if I know I'm returning with you, I can fend off anyone else who has designs of accompanying the tour manager home."

"You have ways around everything, don't you? You work the group so they'll leave you alone and you hardly ever drink, but appear to. Do you always get your way?"

"Mostly, but you and I both know that nothing is ever really as it seems. Is it?"

Phoebe frowned, but it faded before they both turned their attention to the food in front of them, completing the meal in comfortable silence.

With extra minutes up her sleeve, Stella had time to quickly dash across the road to the late night chemist and stock up on hydration supplements. She took the stairs to avoid the temperamental elevator, and had only descended one flight when a familiar hostile voice gained volume on the level below.

"Don't you dare talk to me about intimidation. You don't know what intimidation is. You know nothing about me, yet you judge me. So, by all means be intimidated, or not. I don't really care. But I warn you, don't stand too close to me at a train station." A door slammed and the bang echoed through the stairwell as footsteps rushed toward her.

She had nowhere to go without looking suspiciously like she'd been listening, so her only option was to drag her phone from her pocket, grasp the door handle, and look like she had barely stepped into the stairwell. Within a moment, she was confronted with a breathless and tearful member of her group.

Stella couldn't remember her name, so pretended to end her call before gently squeezing the upset woman's shoulder. "You okay, honey?"

"Phoebe Lancaster is evil. Pure evil. Did you hear what she just said to me?"

Stella was hopeless at lying under these circumstances, but finally remembered the woman's name. "No, Anna. I've been on the phone. Is there a problem?"

Anna inhaled deeply, swiping tears from her eyes. "Look, just keep her the hell away from me. That's your job isn't it? And I'll be making a complaint to your office back in London. That woman should *not* be on this tour." She brushed past Stella and continued up the stairs.

In the foyer, Stella found Phoebe standing alone, as usual. She firmly grasped her elbow. "Walk with me, please."

"What?" Phoebe stood her ground.

Stella glared and tightened her grip. "It's not a request."

The moment they stepped onto the street, Phoebe dislodged her elbow. "Well?"

"What happened just now with Anna, on the stairs?"

Phoebe was controlling her anger rather well. "Oh, that? Why don't you ask her?"

"Because I'm asking you." Stella marched up the adjacent alley, out of sight from the hotel entrance. Phoebe followed.

"Don't you dare judge me, Stella. She started it. I just—"

Stella lowered her voice. "I know."

"—finished it." Phoebe looked confused. "What?"

"I'm not stupid. How did she bait you?"

Phoebe echoed Stella's words. "Bait me?" She shook her head and began to pace. "I haven't let anyone suck me in like that for years."

Stella figured as much. "Why now?" Phoebe continued to pace, her mind appearing elsewhere. Stella caught her wrist. "Phoebe? Why now?"

They stood only a short distance apart, Phoebe staring down into Stella's eyes. "I don't know. I let my guard down. I was looking forward to our night out, and I guess I just wasn't expecting a confrontation. That girl was out of line. She told me to stick to the lift and stay out of her way. I didn't mean that stuff about the train. I had nothing to do with what happened to Pippy."

"I see."

"I wasn't following her."

Stella moved to entangle her fingers gently through Phoebe's. "I don't want you giving the head office any reason to remove you from this tour."

Phoebe nodded, eyes down.

"Look at me, Phoebe." Stella gently shook their hands. "Please?"

After a long moment, Phoebe's eyes locked on hers. Stella smiled. "You'll want to kiss me soon. When you do, don't fight it." She released their touch and returned to the hotel foyer to assemble the troops. Phoebe silently followed.

❖

Matt's flirting was insatiable; Stella had met her match. Phoebe was sitting this dance out, and Stella was beginning to wish she'd done the same. It was one thing for a single man to pay her so much attention, but Belinda was right there, dancing with them. With absolutely no alcohol in her system, Stella's senses were heightened by sobriety. The only person she wanted invading her personal space was Phoebe, and she was slouched at the bar wearing an unreadable expression, observing Stella's every move.

As the dance floor became crowded and personal space became impossible, Matt slid an arm around Stella's waist, drawing her close. This was the sort of dancing that usually preceded sex, and it caught Stella off guard. Although keen not to offend Matt, Stella attempted to dance away from his solid grip. After all, his actions were inappropriate given he was on holiday with his wife. Her vague moves were met with resistance, although not from Matt. Behind her, sliding right into her backside, was Belinda. Over her head she watched as the pair eyed each other seductively. She became an unwilling participant in their dirty dancing sandwich.

Stella was in the process of formulating a plan to extricate herself when a soft yet strong hand gripped hers and dragged her away. "You looked like you needed rescuing. Sorry if you were enjoying that." Phoebe released her grip. Outside the pub the air felt moist. Rain was on the way.

"Enjoying it? Are you kidding? He had a hard-on." Stella shivered at the thought. "Christ, I hate that."

"Happen often?"

"More often than you'd think."

"Oh, I don't know. You are very tempting." Phoebe flashed a smile. "I think the attraction is there for both of them."

Stella looked toward the sky. A storm was brewing. "I'd prefer any attention I attract to come from elsewhere."

A firm arm gripped her waist from behind. "There's something about you, Stella," whispered Phoebe in her ear before gentle lips brushed her nape.

Before Stella could respond, a deafening thunderclap filled the air, and lightning illuminated the sky, causing them both to jump. Rain began to fall in sheets and the moisture building in her pants was instantly forgotten.

"Come on," yelled Phoebe over the deafening rain. "Let's make a run for it."

Rapidly, the streets thinned of people, and Phoebe led Stella at a steady pace toward the hotel. Although her legs were considerably shorter than Phoebe's, she kept in step, successfully dodging puddles and leaping over strong streams of water that accumulated and travelled at speed down the street gutters. As they passed a section of covered market stalls near the hotel, they both jumped at a crashing noise. Stella swung around, but the rain was so heavy, all she saw was a bin rocking back and forth on its side. A shadow disappeared behind a green canvas cover that was secured to a trestle table.

"Did you see that?" Phoebe yelled.

Stella stopped to analyse the situation. The heavy rain on the tin roof was amplified and deafening. All up, there were approximately fifteen covered tables. In the daytime, the stalls sold fruit and local produce. They were usually a welcoming sight, and Stella had purchased from the vendors on many occasions.

Stella felt exposed and the danger, if any, was unknown. She tugged Phoebe into a squatting position, hopefully out of sight. Just when she'd convinced herself that hiding in a deserted market was a ridiculous notion, wet, sloshing footsteps scuffled behind them. They both heard it and snapped their heads around searching for the source, but Stella saw nothing. Then, two tables away, to their left, a definite shadow darted in front of the streetlight, and clear as day, the silhouette of a person emerged before them. Two scary silhouettes in as many nights and Stella was beginning to wonder if she was jinxed.

They scrambled back on their hands and knees to crouch beside a wooden crate. Another bin crashed to the ground at the northern end of the marketplace, and Phoebe's arm encircled Stella in a protective hold.

If it weren't for her growing fear and the unpredictability of the situation, Stella would have gladly melted into the embrace. One strong arm encircled her entire waist, while the other gripped her hand, holding it to her chest. But there was no room in her emotions to enjoy the closeness. Were they hiding from someone just like them; caught in a rainstorm on their way home, or was it something sinister?

Rain lashed down, and lightning lit up the sky like a nightclub strobe. Although she didn't want to look, Stella peered around the corner in the direction of the noise. Again, a silhouette danced from one side to the other. *Christ-all-fucking-mighty!* The shadow appeared to close in. Every time it revealed itself, it had crept nearer. This wasn't someone lost or seeking shelter.

"Someone's there!" Stella screamed before Phoebe's hand clasped tightly over her mouth.

"Shh," whispered Phoebe, directly into Stella's ear.

Logic told Stella she should have been frightened, terrified even, as her head was forced back onto Phoebe's shoulder by the pressure on her mouth, but it was confusing. She was more frightened of the situation than she was of Phoebe.

Stella calculated that their only option was to make a run for it and pointed to the shelter of a shop doorway across the road. Phoebe nodded, released her grip on Stella, and together they ran.

In the shelter of the doorway, Phoebe yet again protected Stella, as if in her arms was where Stella belonged. This time Phoebe pushed her to the corner and used her body as protection, one hand behind her back grasping Stella's.

Stella's view of the marketplace was obscured. From her cramped corner, she could see Phoebe scan back and forth. Stella pushed her forward, determined to gain her own view. Her eyes, now completely adjusted to the dim streetlight, scanned the length of the marketplace. Other than flapping canvas, she could detect no movement.

"Can you see anything?" Stella asked.

"Nope. Not a thing."

Stella felt Phoebe relax.

"Let's give it a minute. I think we're safe here," said Phoebe.

As quickly as the storm had swirled up and become menacing, the rain subsided to a mere steady drizzle and the wind died down.

"Was I seeing things when I saw something? Someone?" Stella moved from behind Phoebe but refused to release her hand.

Phoebe sighed. "No, I saw it, too." Phoebe scanned the area before pulling Stella out of the doorway, along the street toward the hotel. "Opportunistic, premeditated, or pure coincidence?"

"Pardon?" Stella hurried to keep up with Phoebe's long strides.

"We perceived danger. If, for argument sake, that danger was real, then was it opportunistic—he was in the right place at the right time—or was it premeditated—we were in the right place at the right time—well, for him, anyway."

Stella was beginning to understand. "And if there was no danger, it was purely coincidental, right?"

"Right." Phoebe ushered her through the hotel foyer and into the lift. "What's your gut tell you?"

Stella looked down at herself, grinning at the puddle her dripping clothes were creating on the floor. "My gut tells me I need to get dry." The lift door creaked open, and Stella realised their rooms were in opposite directions. "Minibar?" she quickly suggested.

Phoebe hesitated. "I don't know. It's been a long day."

Stella swiftly closed the distance between them. "I'll only lie awake all night going over this in my head. I'd rather dissect it with you." She reached up to wipe away a series of drips running down Phoebe's cheek. "I'm not ready to say good night to you yet."

Phoebe remained undecided.

"Minibar, bath robes, hot shower, and I can have the hotel dry our clothes overnight." Stella smiled. "Come on. Surely that's an offer you can't refuse."

Phoebe simply nodded.

❖

Stella watched, lazing back on the bed, marvelling at Phoebe's lean and exquisite body. She was a voyeur, staring at Phoebe relaxing under the stream of hot water, the shower door wide open. *My God, you're beautiful. Get on with it.*

Phoebe finally came to her. She tugged at Stella's T-shirt, eventually slipping it over her head. "Let me make you feel better."

After the night they'd had, Stella could think of no reason to argue and her desire was so strong, she would be lucky to form words regardless. She watched as Phoebe slowly and sensually slid on top of her. Stella needed tending to, needed to feed the hunger that surged through her body, culminating in a knot of passion, slowly creeping down from the pit of her stomach to the throb building momentum between her legs. Stella adored the silky touch of Phoebe's naked body, the curves, the soft, lightly tanned skin, and the scent; she adored Phoebe's powdery clean aroma that lingered on her skin and in her hair.

"God, I need this." Stella caressed Phoebe's supple breasts, kissing her until their mouths met. "I need you to fill me."

With an unexplained familiarity, Phoebe's hand explored between Stella's legs, moving to part them. "Shh, just relax." She glided her fingers through Stella's wetness and moaned at her obvious arousal before circling her clitoris and withdrawing altogether. Their mouths met again.

"Phoebe, please," groaned Stella through the kiss, raising her hips, encouraging her hand back to her desire. She wanted Phoebe to take her. Take her in mind and body and make her forget the world beyond the four walls that enclosed them. "Phoebe, I'm begging you, please. I'll explode." Stella became light-headed, convinced her veins were forcing every last drop of precious blood to her groin.

Undeterred, Phoebe took one nipple in her mouth and began gently caressing the other. Stella writhed, beginning to comprehend the fine line between agony and ecstasy. In rhythm to Stella's increased breathing, verging on panting, Phoebe increased the intensity of her caresses pushing Stella to the brink.

"Please, I want to come," urged Stella.

"No, when I'm ready."

"I need this."

"I know you do." Phoebe wouldn't give in.

"Oh, God, Phoebe, I can't take it anymore."

"You can and you will." Phoebe's tone was so loving, so gentle. She released Stella's nipple after one last long, deep suck, then leaned up and filled Stella's waiting mouth with her tongue, her fingers finally seeking out where Stella so longed to be touched.

"Oh, God. I can't last."

"Not yet." In one swift motion, Phoebe entered her and withdrew again. Stella edged even closer to orgasm. "You're so beautiful. When you come, you come for me."

"I will. I promise. Please, just let me."

Stella opened her eyes to see Phoebe relish the power, and she wondered how long she could deny her. She didn't have to wait long, Phoebe slid down her body, licking the inside of her thigh. As Stella clawed at the sheets, Phoebe's tongue circled her clitoris.

"Inside me, *please*."

"Wait." Phoebe's tongue dipped briefly inside before resuming her assault on Stella's swelling clitoris.

Stella had been pushed as far as she could physically and emotionally go and just when ecstasy was on the verge of becoming unbearable, Phoebe entered her with one finger, withdrew it and re-entered with two. She moved inside Stella deeper and faster.

Stella was convinced she no longer had use of her arms and legs. Her entire focus was on what Phoebe was so deftly accomplishing between her legs. The intensity was increased when Phoebe added a third finger. Stella was only seconds away from climax when Phoebe used her whole body to increase the momentum on the thrusting movement.

Phoebe thrust deeply, rocking the bed and sliding Stella upward with every thrust. "Come for me. Come now, baby."

The third finger worked like magic and Stella found the release she had longed for. Her orgasm exploded with a show of light behind her eyes. The muscles still surrounding Phoebe's fingers contracted and relaxed, but the heat inside her tingled down her legs and up through her stomach.

"You're mine when you come." Phoebe smiled triumphantly.

"God. I can't argue with that."

"Your amazing body, in my hands, is all mine." Phoebe edged her tongue back to Stella's clitoris.

"Again? So soon?"

"You're stunning. I'll do what I want with you." Phoebe nibbled on her clitoris.

"Jesus, baby. I don't think I can."

"Trust me, you can and you will."

CHAPTER NINE

S tella?"

Stella was nearing climax for the third time. Why was Phoebe calling her name?

"Stella?"

So close to the edge, all Stella could do was mumble, "I'm coming."

"Stella, you're dreaming." Phoebe's voice echoed in her head, drawing her to awareness.

"What?"

"You're dreaming. You were thrashing around just now. You need to wake up."

Reality began to invade Stella's consciousness. *Dreaming?* She looked around, stretching the cramp in her neck. The clock indicated it was nearing three in the morning. They were on the sofa, her head rested on Phoebe's lap, and she was wrapped in a white bathrobe that was gigantic on her.

"I'm dreaming? You didn't just shower? We didn't just..." Stella's voice faded. She was beyond disappointed. It was all just a dream. She'd just experienced the hottest sex she'd ever had and not one bit of it was real. If ever Stella felt robbed of a prize, this was it.

"Do you always moan like that in your dreams?" Phoebe asked.

"God, I wish." Stella felt deflated.

"What were you dreaming about?"

"Nothing."

"Come on? It must have been good," said Phoebe.

"No way. That's my secret. I could tell you, but then I'd have to kill you."

The words hung in the air for a long, awkward moment. Stella was sure her heart had stopped beating, but before she could recover, Phoebe broke the silence.

"Interesting choice of words."

"Sorry." Stella sat and cupped Phoebe's face in her palm. "I really am so sorry. I wasn't thinking."

Her brick wall now firmly back in place, Phoebe attempted to leave. "It's okay."

With no other way to keep her there, Stella quickly manoeuvred to pin her down by straddling her lap. "No. It's not okay."

"It's impossible to go beyond it." Phoebe's discomfort was obvious, although she made no further attempt to move.

"It's only impossible if you try and fail." Stella could tell her robe was gaping at the chest. She knew her actions were reckless, but she didn't care. She longed to experience the real Phoebe, not just the dream version. This conversation was too important; the lingering effects of her dream drove her onward. "Have you tried?"

Phoebe frowned. "No." She sighed. "It all seems too hard." She grasped Stella firmly by the hips and began to move her away.

Compared to Phoebe's lean, muscular frame, Stella was slight and easy to push aside, but she couldn't let this opportunity pass. Stella seized both sides of Phoebe's head and kissed her. Initially rough and graceless, Stella was driven by an undefined need, and as Phoebe relaxed her grip, Stella sank back onto her lap. Insistently, Stella opened her mouth and began a gentle exploration with her tongue. Phoebe's resistance was half-hearted and although not actively participating, she wasn't fighting the kiss either. Stella interpreted this as permission granted.

Within mere seconds, Phoebe appeared to disengage her head and follow her heart. "You taste so damn good," she muttered into Stella's mouth.

"Don't ever do that again," Stella said.

"Do what?"

"Stop kissing me to tell me I taste good." Stella guided Phoebe's hand beneath her robe and onto her breast. "Don't ever stop kissing me."

What followed was pure bliss. The kiss deepened, as did Phoebe's caress. Stella felt Phoebe's entire hand gather her breast until her thumb and forefinger encased and squeezed her nipple, slow and steady. Her body reacted in the most primal way, and the moisture between her legs sent her squirming with a desire to have her need fulfilled.

In the moment it took Stella to lose herself, it all ended.

"I can't do this." Phoebe pulled away.

"Yes, you can." Stella kissed her again.

"No. Please stop. I can't!" And before Stella had time to protest again, Phoebe was up off the sofa and Stella was on the floor, flat on her back.

Phoebe stared in horror at Stella sprawled and half naked. Without another word, she fled the room. Of two minds whether to go after her or not, Stella gathered herself and rushed out the door. By the time she reached Phoebe's room, the Do Not Disturb sign had been placed on the door handle. She knocked once, but she didn't want to wake up the entire floor, so she retreated to her room.

It was near five by the time Stella finally slept, and there were no more dreams of Phoebe. In fact, there were no more dreams at all. She fell asleep wondering what went wrong.

CHAPTER TEN

With little else to do until the group were scheduled to gather in the foyer and travel to dinner, Stella went shopping. Although swimming in the Mediterranean was fun and she urged her group to embrace the opportunity, it was too hot for her today, and the air-conditioned comfort of the shops won out.

Phoebe had been absent at breakfast. And, yet again, when Stella gently knocked on her door that morning, there was no answer. Stella's mood swung like a pendulum. One minute, she savoured the memory of Phoebe's touches and kisses. In the next, she was frightened she might never experience them again. Her solitary hope was that, at best, she at least had the rest of the tour to try to figure Phoebe out. Beyond that, she might vanish forever.

The hot day was made more comfortable by a gentle breeze and Stella sat at a table outside a café she often frequented. She was really only there for the coffee, but found herself ordering juice and a croissant also. Her stomach churned with apprehension for what might lie in store for her and Phoebe, or perhaps it was unbridled fear that she might have blown her only chance.

"Hi, Stella."

Stella's head snapped up. "Phoebe. Hi." She stood frantically to usher Phoebe into the seat opposite her, and in doing so, sent her own chair careening backward into another patron. Phoebe looked on with a grin as Stella placated everyone involved. "Join me?" Stella said, flustered.

Staring at Phoebe, Stella recalled the *real* version of last night's events. They had dissected, at great length, the calamity in the markets. Both agreed the silhouette was certainly in the form of a person, but beyond that they had nothing to go on. Exhausted, they had fallen asleep on the sofa.

"Did I hurt you last night?" A concerned frown creased Phoebe's forehead.

"What? No. When?"

"When I threw you on the floor." She winced. "I didn't mean to do that. I guess I panicked."

Stella wasn't sure she fully understood, but she wanted to. "Panicked, why?"

"This is going to sound ridiculous, but that was the first kiss since…"

Stella gave her a moment before lowering her voice. "Since what, Phoebe?"

"Since Rebecca."

It was difficult to imagine what it must be like to want to have your deceased lover's lips as the last lips that you kissed. Stella was devastated to have taken that away from Phoebe. "Oh, shit. I see. I'm so sorry, Phoebe. I crossed the line."

Alarmingly, another thought entered her head and she couldn't ignore it. Was this the sick game of a murderer who'd manufactured the perfect crime? Stella shook the thought from her mind, but it seemed the more intense her feelings became, the more she harboured thoughts of fear and dread. Surely one would cancel out the other, but it wasn't transpiring that way.

❖

Stella was determined not to become overwhelmed by her lingering doubts, but she struggled with the most intense attraction she'd ever experienced. She and the group enjoyed a rather pleasant evening in Monte Carlo, but she was distracted and not on her game all night. Phoebe attended the luscious banquet dinner but kept to herself. Stella couldn't afford to be openly attentive to Phoebe. It was an organised dinner, and Stella was, after all, working. But they stole glances and shared affectionate smiles when they could.

Some tension was building between Russo and his harem. Genevieve and the Brazilian girls were embroiled in some bizarre love competition for Russo's affections. In a fashion only Russo could effect, he was reliving younger years, discussing motor racing with some lads from Melbourne, completely oblivious to the infighting. Stella was sure they could all have stripped naked and thrown themselves on a sword before Russo would have glanced up and diverted his attention away from all the car talk.

The ritzy glamour of the casino sucked most of the group in and spat them all out a few euros lighter. Stella could always pick the winners and losers as they returned to the coach. The winners were usually drunk, and the losers simply looked forlorn, in need of a drink. Few ever heeded Stella's advice upon arrival at the casino threshold. Every time, she would warn her group, "The house always wins," and every time, there would be one person who would tell her later that they should have listened.

It was after midnight before Stella eventually trudged to her room. Although not deliberately seeking Phoebe's company, she loitered behind in the foyer for longer than necessary, half hoping Phoebe would hang back and initiate a conversation, but nothing eventuated. Phoebe had obviously retreated to her room after a long day, not unlike the rest of the group.

Silently, Stella showered and slid under the sheet. Being alone was a circumstance she was accustomed to, but feeling lonely was foreign to her. For the first time in a long while, Stella felt lonely. She despised the feeling.

CHAPTER ELEVEN

Travelling down the A11, Florence looming in the distance, Stella received a text message from Ryan, a colleague posted at the Florence campsite. It read: *Two groups here, gonna be a big night. You and your lot welcome. PJ party. Coach collect at 7:30 p.m. Confirm.* Stella read the text aloud to Russo.

"Awesome." He was pumped. The following day was a drive free day, which meant tonight was the perfect opportunity to paint the town red.

Stella grabbed the mic. "Sorry to interrupt." Those catching up on sleep groaned at the intrusion. "But you might be interested in an offer. Our tour company has a campsite on the outskirts of Florence, and tonight there are two other tours in town. We have been invited to join them for a little gathering. It's a free night. Take it or leave it. We won't be taking our coach. Russo needs an evening off, but one of the other coaches will collect us after dinner and deliver us to the campsite. We find our own way back to the hotel via taxis." The group looked keenly interested. "They serve cheap drinks at the site bar, and the music is great. So, if you would like to come along, be in the hotel foyer at seven thirty sharp. Oh, and it's a pyjama party, so dress up, and believe me, they won't let you in if you don't!"

That evening, as dinner concluded, the group dispersed. Amazingly, absolutely everyone returned to the foyer ready to depart at seven thirty, everyone with the exception of Phoebe. Wearing a white singlet top and long black pyjama bottoms, Stella cringed at the sight before her. At least half the men wore satin boxer shorts with T-shirts while the other half looked homeless in worn out track pants or actual pyjama bottoms. One of the Melbourne lads was even strutting about in underpants. The ladies looked only slightly more respectable, many appearing in brand new pyjama sets.

Stella found herself constantly seeking out Phoebe, curious as to what she would be wearing, if indeed she decided to attend at all.

❖

Ryan was Hawaiian—tall, dark, muscular, tanned, and undeniably gorgeous. At only twenty-two years of age, he was one of the youngest cooks working for the company, and he absolutely idolised Stella.

True to form, not one person in the bar and pool area was without either PJs or a swimsuit.

A deep American voice bellowed from across the room, "Is that the sexiest tour manager in the world I see before me?"

Ryan vaulted the bar, rushed over, and swept Stella into his arms. Their size difference was vast, and as his strong arms pressed her close, she deftly wrapped her legs around his waist.

"Hey, steady on, mate," snapped Matt, glaring wide-eyed at Ryan.

Clearly amused, Ryan remained undeterred and winked before lowering her to the floor. "I love the new hair colour. You look more like a rock goddess every time I see you." He kissed her fully on the lips.

"And you look more handsome every time I see you." Ryan was nothing if not good for Stella's ego. "You keeping well?"

"I sure am, sweet thing, but let me finish up in the kitchen. Order me a drink?"

"Your usual?"

"You got it. Oh, and promise me a dance later on?"

"I love it when I'm on a promise to you." Stella pinched his tight backside before he disappeared through stainless steel kitchen doors.

With nearly one hundred and fifty people gathered to have a good time, the evening was destined to be colossal. The pool was in use until ten o'clock, at which time it was deemed unsafe to swim—everyone was way too drunk, or at least well on the way. The rule by no means deterred anyone from jumping in, or being pushed, but offenders ran the risk of exclusion if they persisted.

Russo was in heaven, two new coach loads of girls to hang off his well-sculpted, tattooed arms, and he loved every moment of it. The sisters from Brazil, it seemed, had the same idea. They spent considerable time chatting up brothers from Canada, and given what Stella knew of their double act, she refused to contemplate quite what the new pairing might get up to.

Stella, who had been working the room—dancing and flirting with everyone—was taking a breather and chatting amongst a group who were strangely discussing ballroom dancing.

"It's called the Pride of Erin, I'm sure," one of the girls, an Australian, said, exasperated.

"No way," cried another. "You're thinking of the Barn Dance."

"The Barn Dance? I've never even heard of the Barn Dance."

"Stella?" Phoebe beamed a kind smile that sent Stella's stomach into a spin. "You look like someone who knows their ballroom stuff. Do you know the Pride of Erin?"

"Well, Ms. Lancaster." Stella returned the smile. "I do believe I know *exactly* how the Pride of Erin goes. The question is, do *you?*"

Stella was relieved by this exchange. Although they'd shared coffee the previous morning, the conversation had progressed into neutral territory after Phoebe's confession that Stella was the first since Rebecca. Since then, Stella had been busy with the majority of the group and she'd been unable to give any undivided attention to Phoebe. She was worried things may have deteriorated between them. She also didn't want to come across as pushy or needy. If Phoebe needed time to process the kiss and a growing attraction to Stella, then that's what Stella would facilitate.

"Is that a challenge?" Phoebe seductively slid from her stool and sauntered toward Stella.

"Perhaps it is, but if you don't feel up to it, I'll understand."

"You'd be surprised what I feel up to." Phoebe extended a hand to Stella, pulling her toward the unsuspecting DJ as the group cheered them on.

When the throbbing music stopped abruptly, the sweaty crowd occupying the dance floor booed in disapproval. Everyone curiously watched Stella being led onto the scuffed wooden floor by Phoebe as an extravagant classical piece began. Stella stole a quick glance at Russo, who simply raised his eyebrows and grinned.

"Can you actually remember how this goes?" Stella whispered, awestruck by Phoebe, who looked absolutely stunning in her expensive black camisole top and floral printed shorts.

"Ah, now the truth comes out. You said you knew."

"I'm sure it will all come back to me." Stella winked. "I'll follow your lead. I assume you're taking the dominant male role?"

Phoebe grinned. "I think that would be best, don't you, given your, um, lack of height?"

"Point taken." Stella glanced around at the crowd gathering, all clapping and chanting. "Come on then. Get on with it."

Like a pro, Phoebe twirled Stella so they both faced the same direction and Stella offered up her other hand. They waited awkwardly for the music to restart before she counted them in. Stella had been right, the steps came flooding back, and they completed three rounds of the dance to raucous applause and laughter. On the third waltz, Phoebe held her closer than before, her hand strongly drawing Stella in, firm on her lower back. Having been afraid to do so until now, Stella glanced up to find Phoebe's eyes fixed on hers. Stella's face was merely centimetres away from Phoebe's plunging neckline. A powerful waft of sweet, powder fresh, expensive perfume flooded Stella's senses. Something was pulling at Stella's heart, and the connection caused her to ache.

The crowd whistled, roared, and clapped as she and Phoebe retreated to the bar and the preferred throbbing dance music filled the room yet again. Stella, now rather sensitive to Phoebe's touch, was well aware that Phoebe's hand remained in hers as they waited patiently to be served drinks.

"I knew it." Matt rushed up and cuddled Stella from behind, her hand separating from Phoebe's as he positioned himself between them. "You're gay!"

Stella wasn't sure where this was heading. "What makes you say that, super sleuth?"

"*You*, getting into *her*." He jerked his head toward Phoebe who was now chatting to a girl from another tour. "That is so fucking unreal." He danced away, pleased with himself.

"Hey, Ryan," she called to the hunk propped up at the far end of the bar. "You ready for that dance now?"

"Sure am. I hope you don't expect any fancy shit like that from me."

Stella grinned and gulped her drink, finishing it in one thirsty mouthful. "You know what I expect from you, baby."

There was no longer a defining line where the dance floor began. A mass of sweaty people, all in their pyjamas, or even less clothing, moved in time with the throbbing beat. Stella couldn't help steal a glance toward Phoebe, who continued to converse with the stranger. A pang of jealousy bounced in her stomach.

Stella and Ryan had been doing their dance act for two years now. By her own admission, Stella was no dancer, but she had been a pretty good gymnast in her younger years, and remained rather flexible. Ryan, on the other hand, could move. His hips seemed to have a direct connection to the beat of the music. Stella loved how good he made her look.

Their signature routine began hot and steamy. Ryan's hands found themselves in all the right places, and their moves were nothing short of obscene. Every time they put on their little show, the crowd would yell and scream at them to get a room. Stella was thankful she'd had that last drink. Dirty dancing certainly wasn't something she could convincingly perform sober.

A small group gathered around them, Matt included. As Ryan effortlessly lifted Stella, her legs wrapped around his waist, his head buried in between her breasts, he whirled her around, and she caught glimpses of Matt, an expression of absolute disgust distorting his face. Ryan spun around with increasing speed, supporting Stella's lower back as she released his head from her chest, leaning back until she was spinning at right angles. As the spin decreased in speed, Ryan clutched Stella's backside, and like an expert, flipped her three-hundred and sixty degrees, lowering her to the ground, flat on her back, his foot resting in her groin, arms raised in triumph. The crowd loved it.

Stella needed help up, she was laughing so hard. To her satisfaction, she turned to watch Matt storm off in a huff. Predictably, Belinda dutifully followed.

Ryan lifted Stella to her feet, and the commotion died down. At the bar, they puffed and panted, eagerly topping up with liquor.

"Thanks for the grope." Stella loved Ryan's new touch.

"Sorry." He looked concerned. "Did I go too far?"

"No way. It was just the thing one of my boys needed to see."

"Oh dear, one of those. Do you want me to take you out the back for a good time? That might get him off your case?"

"Did someone suggest going out the back for a good time?"

Stella and Ryan turned to see Phoebe approach. Yes, please, Stella silently pleaded.

"Well, Stella. Our little Pride of Erin was rather tame compared to that." Phoebe ordered a drink.

"Not my fault. You were leading."

"I'll remember that next time."

Stella was disappointed when Phoebe returned to the table, comfortably in conversation with the same girl, although she noted, with a concession to her jealous feelings, that their posture appeared friendly and easy, not romantic and flirty.

"Righto," Stella said, resting her icy beer in the middle of her forehead. "I need fresh air. It's roasting in here."

Dodging the dancers, she weaved her way toward the door. As the old Western saloon-style doors swung back and forth behind her, an arm gathered her up and carried her away from any prying ears and eyes. Stella thought it was Ryan, but hoped it was Phoebe.

It was neither.

"Surprise." Matt beamed at her, high as a kite.

Stella wriggled to break free. "Let me go, Matt."

"How come it's okay for that fucking poofter to manhandle you?" His grin widened. In a singsong voice he added, "I bet he doesn't have any of these." He pulled a stash of little pills from his pocket. "Come spend some time with me and Belinda. See where the night takes us." Matt began singing something about spending the night together whilst skipping around her. If she didn't think he was such an idiot, she would have been amused.

"Matt, I'm really flattered, but I'm not interested." She thought the direct approach might work. "You get caught with those and you're on your own, sunshine." Matt shrugged. "I'm serious. Get rid of them, and don't let me see them again, or you might not make it to the end of the tour. I can't tell you this any simpler, Matt. I don't do men, and I don't do married women if I can help it."

"Well, I'm rather pleased I don't belong in either of those categories." Phoebe stepped out from the shadows.

Stella's knees buckled. More flirting, more innuendo. Sometimes she simply couldn't work Phoebe out. She loved it, but it was so damn confusing. Was it just brazen talk, or was there more to it? She felt like a teenager again.

In a childish and dramatic display, Matt's shoulders slumped. "Oh, man. What chance have I got with you around, Lancaster? How come that big faggot idiot in there gets a turn at you and I don't? This sucks!"

"Piss off, Matt," both Stella and Phoebe said in unison before laughing.

With a huff and a groan, Matt marched inside.

Phoebe frowned. "He's not just drunk is he?"

"Nope. And he's completely delusional."

Phoebe changed the subject. "Thanks for the dance earlier. I think we make a good pairing."

Stella recalled it clearly, although she guessed the alcohol she had consumed since was somehow enhancing the experience. "You handled me well." She sounded ridiculous. "I mean you controlled me well."

Phoebe grinned and raised her eyebrows.

Stella was embarrassed. "You're a great dancer. That's what I actually mean." Stella gently stroked Phoebe's cheek. "I think you're amazing."

Phoebe didn't recoil, but she didn't take it further, and Stella found herself feeling disappointed. "You hardly know me, Stella."

"I know enough."

"Do you?"

"I've been reading up on you. I know you've been hurt in the past. I've no idea what happened with Rebecca." Phoebe cringed at the mention of Rebecca's name. "But although you worry me and scare me a little, you also excite and intrigue me." *God, I wish you didn't.*

Silence lingered between them for a long time before Phoebe finally spoke. "So, what did you find out about me?"

"Only stuff I read on the Net. Newspaper articles, magazine excerpts. I've no idea how much of it, if any, is true."

"You're the first person, Stella, in a long time, who has shown me any interest other than to heckle me, interview me, or photograph me. Most normal people run a mile."

"I can't go anywhere, Phoebe. You're not the only person on that coach. Trust me. If you'd disappeared that first day, I'd hardly have hunted you down to be your friend."

"I concede the first day was fairly rough. But now?" Phoebe appeared hopeful.

Now that she knew Phoebe would have followed, she wished she had escaped the bar hours ago. Excessive alcohol fuelled Stella's courage. "What I want more than anything right now is for you to take me in your arms and dance with me again."

Phoebe glanced down. "These arms?"

"Uh-huh. Those exact arms."

"You'd better step closer, then."

Stella's senses switched into overdrive. Everything began to happen simultaneously, and she couldn't remember the last time a woman had made her feel so alive and sensitive to absolutely every action or word. Her heart raced, her palms became clammy, her stomach flipped, and of all things, her legs began to twitch. The power of her feelings and desires was threatening to overwhelm her.

"Can you hear the song, Stella?" whispered Phoebe.

A throbbing bass-driven track seeped into the night air, and Stella cocked her head to try to recognise it.

"No." Phoebe pulled Stella close until their bodies were mere millimetres away. "Not that song." She gently touched the very centre of Stella's chest. "The song in here."

"It's a slow song."

Phoebe slid a firm arm around Stella's waist. "Correct. Slow and sexy."

Stella suddenly understood the game. "For you to know the beat of my song, my heart should be as close to yours as possible, I think." Stella dragged a finger from Phoebe's waistband slowly up over her stomach until it rested between Phoebe's breasts. "Here."

"Excellent idea." Their eyes remained locked. "Do you understand how important our stance is?"

Stella shook her head. It felt so light, she was fearful it might shake right off her shoulders and float away.

Phoebe continued in a low tone, her voice smooth as silk. "Well, to maintain a solid footing, I think it only appropriate for my thigh to settle right between here." With featherlight touches, her hand glided to Stella's upper thigh, gently cupping her. "Open them wider, please?"

Stella obeyed, and Phoebe replaced her hand with her thigh.

"I'm not at risk of falling now," said Stella.

"Really?"

"Well, not off my feet. Falling for something else isn't out of the question."

"Falling can be dangerous." Phoebe began to sway in time to the imaginary slow song, pressing Stella's head against her shoulder and wrapping her arms securely around her.

"Are you frightened of falling, Phoebe?"

"Not me."

"Are you suggesting I should be?"

"Fear is a state of mind."

"I see." Stella contemplated this for a moment. "Given the state of my pants, and the moisture content, might I suggest that fear is playing no part in influencing my current state of mind. What about your state of mind?"

"I'm not afraid of anything."

"No?"

"That's correct. Nothing."

Stella grinned. "Well, I'm hardly an imposing figure, am I?"

Phoebe's hand slid down the inside of Stella's pyjamas, coming to rest firmly on her bottom. "Hardly."

"So, you're in no way frightened of me?"

"I think you're probably rather tough, but no, you don't scare me."

Stella realised what she wanted so desperately was beyond Phoebe's awareness. It momentarily saddened her. "Physically, I doubt if I'd scare a flea." She moved her mouth to tenderly kiss the very centre of Phoebe's chest, as low as her top would allow, and dangerously close to Phoebe's heart. "But in here, I'm quite certain I have you running scared." Stella felt Phoebe's sharp intake of breath as her lips settled on her soft, velvet skin.

"I have you right where I want you, Stella. In my arms. I'm not afraid."

"So, what if I ask for more? What if I ask you to take me somewhere private now, address the issue you've created in my pants and in my heart?"

Phoebe began to pull away.

Stella gripped her firmly. "No, Phoebe. I'm not playing with you, I promise. But you can't deal with fear when you're refusing to accept it even exists."

They struggled—Phoebe in an attempt to escape and Stella holding on tight like a barnacle clinging to the bottom of a boat.

Phoebe gave up her fight to flee and thrust her hand to Stella's throat.

Stella tasted some of the fear she'd been talking about.

"I really want to kiss you."

"Then kiss me."

Phoebe's lips met Stella's with force, and it was a messy kiss until Stella collected her thoughts and caught up. She opened herself to Phoebe, giving in to her need and allowing the moment to send her flying high. The relief was almost palpable. Stella was strongly aware of the connection between her satisfied mouth and her clitoris. She soared to another level when Phoebe's tongue danced with hers. The kiss was fiercely intense, the only thing left to surpass it was an orgasm, but Stella knew that wouldn't happen. Not yet. It was a remarkable breakthrough for Phoebe to be passionately kissing her, but anything else would have to wait. Stella wouldn't have Phoebe inside her, not tonight.

Just when Stella seriously considered the only option was to touch herself, Phoebe pulled away. "I can't do this." She was close to tears.

"Hang on, Phoebe. Don't run." Stella refused to let her go. "This is the fear I'm talking about. Please talk me through what you're feeling. Please don't run," she pleaded, struggling to hold Phoebe close.

"I need some air, some space. Just back off, Stella." Phoebe was crying.

Stella released her. "Okay, just please talk to me."

"I can't. I never have."

Stella was beginning to think Phoebe might hyperventilate. "Imagine you're in a playground and you're stuck on the roundabout."

Phoebe shook her head, trying to make it all go away.

Stella stood close but they didn't touch. "You're going round and round. You see the same things, the ride never changes and you're alone. No one can get on. You're all alone."

Phoebe nodded. "I need to get off, right?"

"That's right. You'll never get a chance to have fun on any of the other rides if you keep going round and round."

Phoebe looked on the verge of speaking, but obviously thought better of it. "I'm not ready for this."

Stella tried one last time. "I get that. But you'll never be ready for this. You're waiting for a day that doesn't exist. You're waiting for the day when you'll wake up feeling great, like your old self again and ready to tell the world, but I'm sorry, that's just delusional. Understandable, but delusional. The day you feel ready for this isn't coming. Your day of utopia isn't coming." Stella took her by the hands. "But you have today. You have me, and today is a good day to start. *I'm* a good place to start. Trust me, Phoebe. I'm a safe place to start."

"You won't want to hear this."

That thought had crossed Stella's mind and as much as she probably didn't want to hear it, she had to. "Please, give me a try?"

"Rebecca and I had a son."

Son? That was the last thing Stella was expecting to hear. Phoebe Lancaster and the story of her life were more complicated than she could have imagined, but she knew people kept secrets, big secrets. The fact that Phoebe had her own shouldn't have come as a surprise.

"So Rebecca had a child, a boy?"

"No, not Rebecca. Me. I had our son."

Stella knew her eyes bulged open in disbelief, but she couldn't hide her astonishment. The next question didn't bear thinking about. "Did he die?"

Phoebe smiled painfully. "No, he's very much alive. I was the surrogate. Rebecca's egg was implanted in me. We intended to do the same with my egg, but she…well, it never came to that."

"So much for the turkey baster method."

Phoebe shrugged. "It's more expensive, doing it our way, but we wanted to be connected and related. My egg in her, her egg in me. It's not uncommon when you can afford it."

Stella touched Phoebe's cheek. "What's his name?"

"Sebastian. He was beautiful when he was born. Perfect even, but I guess all mothers say that."

Stella's head swirled with so many questions. She focused on the big ones. "Where is he now?"

"Rebecca's father has him. They're in Switzerland at the moment."

"Oscar Dean has your son?"

"I thought I was going to jail. I thought he was going to kill us both, me and Sebastian. I did what I thought was right. Rebecca was dead. If I gave him to Oscar and I stayed alive and out of jail, I at least had a chance to see him again. This is my chance."

"You thought Oscar was going to kill you?"

Phoebe nodded. The words were rushing from her mouth now. "You don't know what it's like. Rebecca had just died. I thought I was doing the right thing. I was scared, I was grieving, and I just wanted to do the right thing."

"And now you've come to see Oscar and get Sebastian back, right?"

Stella thought she was catching on, but the look on Phoebe's face suggested otherwise.

"Not exactly."

"Then what, exactly?"

"Oscar doesn't know I'm here. I signed my child over to him five years ago. I'm not here to see Oscar. I'm here to see Sebastian."

Stella attempted to calculate Phoebe's loss—first her lover and then her son. She couldn't fathom the grief and emptiness that would plague Phoebe every single day. "I'm so sorry, Phoebe. I'm just so sorry."

Minutes of silence passed before Phoebe spoke again. "The day I lost Rebecca, was the day I lost everything. I need to see my son, and I know there are people who will try and stop me, but this trip was the only way I could think of to get close to him and hopefully remain undetected. A bus tour like this is the last thing I'd be expected to do if they knew I was in Europe. She broke down. "God, I miss them."

"I don't know what to say, Phoebe." And Stella didn't. She hadn't expected to discuss any of this. She tried to pull Phoebe close, but she resisted.

"I know what you've been thinking, Christ, who wouldn't, but I didn't kill Rebecca. I loved her with everything I had, and that bastard, Simon Threadbody, took her from me, in front of me, and he walks around a free man. *I* lost fucking everything."

The words Stella had been longing to hear finally rang a sweet tune in her ears. She couldn't explain why she believed Phoebe, but she did, unquestionably, and the relief was immense.

"If Simon killed Rebecca, why didn't you just tell Oscar that?"

"Simon said we'd both look guilty. If he went down, he swore he'd take me with him."

"Jesus, Phoebe. This is big. Real big." Stella had so many questions.

"I'm not nuts, Stella. I'm not really anything. Anger is a hard habit to break. Hardly an improvement on the habit of loss and grief, is it?"

"It's a start." Stella knew it sounded hollow, but there was one thing she was certain of, Phoebe Lancaster was attempting to move forward. Baby steps, yes, but Stella refused to give up on her.

"How will you see Sebastian?" asked Stella.

"Well, that's complicated."

"I'm not sure I like the sound of this."

"Someone I knew when I was a child works for Oscar. She's Sebastian's nanny. She's helping me."

"Can she be trusted?" Stella asked.

"I think so. I hope so."

The commotion of a fray gathering momentum inside distracted them both. It became so loud and frantic the spell between them broke. Stella shrugged at the shit timing before she rushed back through the swinging doors, Phoebe close behind.

"You fucking Yankee faggot!" Matt was being restrained by at least three men, arms thrashing, sweat pouring from his brow, and his face crimson in anger. "Don't you fucking lay a finger on her again, do you fucking well hear me, you arse jabber?" Matt was out of control.

Idiot. How many pills did you take?

Ryan stood in the centre of it all, hands on hips, grinning. Matt was no match for him, in size or strength. Matt's cheerful drug-induced demeanour had now been replaced with a ranting lunatic.

"Wipe that cocksucking smile off your face. I swear to God, if I ever find out you've touched her again, you're a dead man."

Stella was surprised to see Russo and weaved her way through the crowd to him. She thought he may have been otherwise engaged. "What's going on? Did Ryan pull some moves on Belinda?"

"Belinda?"

"Isn't that who Matt's ranting about?"

Russo frowned and Stella recognised his fatherly look of disapproval. "I'm afraid not, Stells. He's talking about you. Was a bit offended by your dirty dancing it seems."

"You're kidding?"

Stella approached the DJ bench, switched off the music, plugged the mic in, and gained everyone's attention with her firm tone. "Can someone get him out of here?" She was referring to Matt, and more men joined in to drag him outside. "Unless you have a very good reason to stay, can my group please follow Russo to the front gate? Cabs are on the way, and please, whatever you do, don't speak to Matt and wind him up further." She disappeared into the crowd, urging everyone to leave.

Ryan scooped her into a tight, caring hug.

"Thanks for having us, honey. Sorry about my idiot crew member."

"Don't worry. Clients are like family. You can't choose them, but you have to put up with them." He touched her cheek. "It's good to see you. Keep in touch. And don't worry. That dickhead will settle down when he's not so high."

Stella wished he could get higher, but only if it were through her foot connecting with his stupid arse.

CHAPTER TWELVE

Stella slept in. Not that it mattered. Almost everyone else did too. Unfortunately, this resulted in a mad dash at nine thirty. Under heavy and vocal protests, Stella practically had the group jogging to meet Antonio, a young, energetic guide who would amaze them with his charming tour of Florence.

In a small café just metres from the famous Uffizi gallery, Stella savoured her first real coffee of the morning and rested the side of her weary head in her hand. Fearful of falling asleep, she thought it best to stay awake by people watching. Behind the darkness of her sunglasses, she watched the hordes of tourists negotiate cafés, galleries, and boutiques. Of all the countries in Europe she visited, it would be Italy she'd miss seeing on such a regular basis.

As if trained to do so, her eyes fixated on Phoebe weaving her way through the crowd from the far end of the street. Phoebe was undeniably stunning. Her poise, her aloofness, and her sheer beauty turned Stella to mush. She had given up fighting the attraction. Seeking Phoebe's company at breakfast, lunch, and dinner was fast becoming normal. Wanting, with unbelievable desire, to speak to her, touch her, and be inside her were sensations she was beginning to enjoy. Since last night, she was no longer alarmed by the intensity of her feelings, nor how her fantasies developed a life of their own, often leaving her feeling like she was merely along for the sexually explicit ride.

A warm smile of recognition spread across Phoebe's face as she caught sight of Stella. Now moving with purpose, Phoebe smartly weaved through the people, and within moments was gently placing a kiss on each of Stella's cheeks.

"Imagine, just the lady I've been looking for, sitting staring into the crowd as if looking for me."

Stella could have sworn her heart completely deflated before inflating again to double its original size. Phoebe, in that solitary moment, had taken her breath away. Stella was lost for words by such a brazen public display of affection. A simple hello eluded her.

Phoebe smiled, clearly pleased with Stella's response. "More coffee?"

"You read my mind," said Stella.

"So, I've been thinking," said Phoebe, when the waiter departed with their coffee order.

"Go on."

"Your name typed into a Google search doesn't reveal anything, unlike mine." She shrugged, as if even Google had beaten her. "I don't really know the first thing about you, other than the fact you're a tour manager, of course. I think it's only fair we even up the scores a little." The cheeky wink that accompanied this last statement sent Stella's heart racing.

"What do you want to know?"

"Let's begin with your age."

"I'm twenty-seven."

Phoebe sighed. "And? Come on. Spill."

"I was born in Hong Kong. My mother was in finance. We moved back to England when I was two. She had a nervous breakdown because my father, whom I've not laid eyes on for twenty-two years, shagged both the maids in Hong Kong, resulting in two pregnancies. He visited for a day when I was five. I've not seen nor heard from him since. I can play the bass guitar, badly. I smoked too much pot when I was fifteen, and I realised I was gay early in my teens. My last long-term girlfriend hit me once because I like to flirt. You're an easy target when you're so small."

"This woman who hit you, can we talk about her?"

It had been a lesson well learned, but a short, uneasy laugh escaped Stella. "Sure, I guess."

"Why did you go out with someone violent?"

"Well, I certainly didn't know she was violent to begin with. She cared for me, loved me, protected me, but in the end, all it amounted to was control. She was a police officer, working shifts. Dedicated, like they all are. Coordinating schedules can be difficult under those circumstances. I, on the other hand, was dedicated to clubs, pubs, music, and drinking. I'd regularly go out with friends while she was working, or at home sleeping. We constantly fought over my behaviour. I'd toe the line, but eventually, it would happen all over again. The first time she hit me was the only time. It resulted in a black eye, nothing serious, but enough to make me know it wasn't worth it. *She* wasn't worth it. Usual story though. I flirted, I danced, I didn't know she was there watching me, and then she dragged my drunk ass home. We fought, she hit me. End of story."

"I'm sorry."

"I'm okay. As I said, it only happened the once." Stella took the opportunity to change the subject. "Can we talk more about you? Is it true Oscar Dean was appalled to discover his only daughter was a lesbian?"

"Sounds like a line from a trashy magazine, but I'd say he was more disappointed than appalled. Opposition media outlets liked to talk it up a lot."

"He must have hated you."

"Not so much hated, tolerated is a better word I think. Until Rebecca told him she was a lesbian, they had an excellent relationship. Up until that time, he had been a model dad."

"And it all went tits up at that point?"

Phoebe laughed. "You could put it that way. He became very difficult. Oscar Dean is a powerful man, a powerful criminal. The reason criminals become powerful isn't purely money. They make threats and they carry them out. You soon command attention when people go missing or end up in hospital black and blue. He had his fair share of legitimate business dealings, but he also liked to be the hard man sometimes. By the time I came on the scene, he'd cleaned up his act, but a reputation like his stays with you forever. That's the way he liked it."

"I assumed he might have been manipulative, but an outright criminal, I had no idea."

"I suggest you don't go singing it from the mountaintop. Oscar doesn't take nicely to people tarnishing his name."

The waiter delivered more coffee, and Stella, still feeling unwell from the night before, ordered pizza.

"You met when Rebecca was nineteen?"

Phoebe nodded. "Oscar found it increasingly difficult to keep tabs on her. He threw eligible bachelors, including Simon, at her all the time. I can't even begin to describe his frustration when she rejected them all, but on a day-to-day basis he just let us go about our business. He certainly wasn't out and proud about his baby girl."

"Did you really believe he was going to kill you?"

Phoebe's face saddened. "In the moment, I did. His threats certainly seemed real. I guess I'll never know."

Just as Stella was about to broach the subject of the circumstances surrounding Rebecca's death, the loud scraping of chairs and tables diverted her attention. They both turned to see Matt charging toward them.

"How are my two favourite lesbians today, then?" He cuddled Stella.

"You're awful chirpy today for someone who over-indulged last night," said Stella.

"Well, you know what I always say; the best way to avoid a downer is to stay up."

Stella should have guessed. "Do you at least remember how much of an ass you made of yourself last night?"

He threw his arms in the air. "Hey, I'm only human. We all make mistakes."

She wasn't convinced he had any recollection of his appalling behaviour. "Where's Belinda?"

"Funny you should ask that." A mischievous grin spread from ear to ear. "She found a little shop that sells some toys we might like."

"Excellent," Stella replied sarcastically. "Perhaps you should go find her."

Matt wasn't listening. "When I say 'we,' I mean *we*, Stells. All three of us." He turned to Phoebe. "You're welcome to join us. The more the merrier."

"Piss off, Matt," barked Stella and Phoebe in unison.

Not in the least bit offended, Matt shrugged. "Jesus, do you two practice that or something?"

Phoebe and Stella couldn't help but laugh after he'd trotted off.

Yet again, Phoebe insisted on paying the bill. "He's nothing if not persistent," she said.

"He's an idiot, that's for sure."

"Uffizi?" Phoebe cocked her head in the direction of the famous gallery. "I've been before, and I presume you have too, but it might be a nice way to spend the morning."

Stella nodded, encouraged Phoebe wanted to spend time with her, but the moment had passed for further in-depth discussion. They strolled tantalisingly close, hands lightly making contact every so often, to join the substantial queue awaiting entry. Even though Stella had perused the famous gallery many times, she was certain experiencing it with Phoebe would add a new dimension. After all, Phoebe Lancaster's presence was adding a new dimension to nearly every aspect of Stella's existence. She craved her like no other. In fact, she couldn't remember ever feeling this consumed by another human being. Absolutely everything reminded her of Phoebe. Every daydream revolved around her, every dirty thought—and there were many—involved her. Stella was unnerved to feel so impulsive when it came to Phoebe. And considering Phoebe was dominating her thoughts, Stella was beginning to tire of the continual need to draw her focus back to her job.

"A penny for your thoughts?" Phoebe gently nudged Stella with her hip.

Even such a small, probably meaningless contact stimulated the butterflies in Stella's stomach. She grinned awkwardly.

"It's the Uffizi isn't it?" Phoebe closed her eyes. "I love Florence, and I love this place."

"How did you know I was thinking about that?" Stella lied.

"Just a hunch. You were a million miles away," said Phoebe, smiling.

"You have a beautiful smile." Stella blushed and so did Phoebe. "I'm sorry. I swear that was a silent statement in my head."

"There's no need for apologies. Actually, I wanted to talk to you about something." Phoebe cleared her throat. "The other night in Nice, I enjoyed your company. And last night, talking as openly as we did, well, that was certainly intense. And special, don't get me wrong.

I'm glad we talked and did…you know…other stuff. I think it's been good for me to…um…spend time like that with someone."

What exactly was Phoebe suggesting?

"Well, not just someone, but you," Phoebe continued.

A faint sheen of sweat appeared on Phoebe's brow.

Is she nervous?

"And, well, anyway," Phoebe clumsily continued. "It's difficult to spend time alone with fifty other people around, and let's face it, you *are* at work," Phoebe was talking so quickly Stella could barely keep up. "So I was wondering how possible it would be for us—if you agree of course—to perhaps share a room. No, I mean like a two-bedroom room, not the same bed or anything. Well, not yet. Or ever if you didn't want to—"

"Phoebe?" Stella interrupted. "Slow down and breathe. You'll haemorrhage something soon."

Phoebe inhaled slowly and deeply. "It's been a while since I've done this. I'm sorry. I shouldn't be putting you on the spot, but I really enjoy your company. It would be nice to chat, have a few drinks, and not have to go back to my own room."

Stella's thorough thought process, one she prided herself on in times of stress and crisis, had abandoned her. This request really was out of the blue. Although she was deliriously happy, words abandoned her.

Faced with only silence, Phoebe struggled on. "I think I like you. I *know* I like you. I'd like the chance to explore what has begun." Phoebe shrugged, embarrassed. "Please? Can we get to know one another without prying eyes?"

Stella remained speechless and, like a mute cartoon character, could only nod her approval.

Phoebe kissed her cheek. "Excellent. Thank you."

CHAPTER THIRTEEN

Day ten, Florence to Rome, was always an exciting day. Stella loved Rome, its history, ancient buildings, gelato, and of course St. Peter's.

She was in the mood to torment the hungover members of the group after many of them danced the night away until the early hours of the morning. Almost dead on their feet, she and Phoebe had reluctantly gone their separate ways at three a.m. that morning, knowing it would be the last time they would have to occupy separate rooms. Stella was amused to be surrounded by so many tired and cranky clients. Although it wasn't in her nature to be cruel, she selected a thumping dance track to keep them on their toes while Russo skilfully negotiated the streets of Florence. In bright sunshine, heading along the open road toward Rome, Stella felt a sense of renewed energy.

Her elation was short-lived, however. Whispering, so details remained private, she leaned in close to Russo and informed him of her new sleeping arrangements.

"*What?* Are you insane?"

"There's no need to yell."

"I'm not yelling out loud. I'm whisper-yelling. And honestly, Stells, I think there's every need."

"Can't you just trust me on this?"

"No, frankly, Stella. I can't. Her girlfriend was stabbed to death."

"Not so damn loud!"

"I'm not being loud. You're being ridiculous."

Stella opted for the truth. "Russo, I really like her and she didn't kill anyone. She deserves a break, and frankly, I think I deserve her."

He shook his head. "In a few weeks, she'll be gone, your crush will pass, and some other leggy blonde will wander into your sights. Why risk this? Why with her?"

"She didn't do it."

Russo momentarily threw his arms in the air, and the bus swerved a little. "Yeah well, what if she did?"

Upon arrival in the ancient city, Russo delivered them safely to the Colosseum where a local guided the group through the ruins. The spectacular Roman Forum would remain unexplored until the following morning, but this afternoon, Stella would guide her group from one magical sight to the next. She loved showing the Pantheon, Trevi Fountain, Spanish Steps, and no matter how far she walked, most people never tired of the amazing ancient city. At dinner time, she left them to source some traditional food near Piazza Novona. Stella had kept an eye out for Phoebe, but she failed to show up at the designated meeting place. She wasn't the only one of course. Many people took the chance to explore and get lost.

Stella was ridiculously nervous. Her anxious teenage years, spent in eager anticipation of that first kiss, first date, or first time sex, bore no resemblance to the apprehension or rush of excitement she was experiencing at the prospect of sharing a hotel room with Phoebe for the first time that evening. After the frank and open discussion in Florence, not to mention the passionate kiss, Stella should have felt more confident with the situation. The reality was she felt quite the opposite. Insecurities plagued her, and she couldn't help but wonder would Phoebe have been as willing to explore as far as she did had neither of them been so drunk? It was true that the kiss had drawn them closer together physically, but Phoebe's openness and honesty drew them closer on a much deeper level.

Even the simple task of booking the room had triggered the now familiar butterflies that so often bombarded her stomach. They acted as a subliminal reminder of how special Phoebe had become and how no other woman on the planet had stimulated such a strong reaction in her. Ever.

Stella dined alone. It was only natural that she would wonder and worry about Phoebe's absence, but Rome was an amazing place to get lost in. Still, she couldn't help feel a little anxious given Phoebe's reason for being on the tour. The more she thought about the frightening night in the Nice markets, the less she was inclined to dismiss the notion that it was something innocent.

Stella returned to the hotel. Rome was expansive, and there were too many people to wander aimlessly in the hope of bumping into Phoebe. She was left facing an evening alone to complete paperwork, and the thought was hardly appealing.

She opened the sliding doors to reveal an amazing view of Rome. A warm breeze circulated air through the expansive room.

Stella begrudgingly spread her paperwork all over the small dining table. The next stop was Corfu in Greece, and although it was the longest stay—three nights—and in the most luxurious resort they frequented, Corfu always required meticulous organisation. Stella fastidiously booked scuba diving and island cruising, water skiing, parasailing, and fishing. It was relaxing upon arrival, but the planning could be a nightmare. Tonight, she would e-mail her requirements, then tomorrow evening, she would call everyone to confirm. Everything in Corfu required double-checking.

❖

"Wow." Phoebe scanned the fancy room. "Nice place."

Stella was often upgraded to deluxe rooms, and this two-bedroom suite was spacious and modern.

"I tried to get back to you for dinner, but I went exploring farther than I anticipated. My phone battery died." Phoebe held her dead phone aloft before plugging it in to charge.

Stella attempted a nonchalant demeanour, but she was so pleased to see Phoebe, she only managed to come across as awkward and goofy. She went directly to the minibar. "Can I fix you a drink?"

"Sure, vodka if there's any." Phoebe disappeared into the smaller of the two bedrooms.

Stella's heart sank. She wanted to believe Phoebe was merely using the room to store her suitcase, but she couldn't be certain.

She pushed the disappointment from her mind and concentrated on preparing the drinks. One thing was certain: she couldn't rush Phoebe. Her disappointment was selfish. The pace of their relationship should be dictated by Phoebe, she knew that.

"That night in Nice, what do you think really happened?" Stella realised she was so relieved to have Phoebe back safe, she needed to know if Phoebe was in danger wandering alone through European cities.

Phoebe stood in the doorway of the bedroom. "You're worried because of what I told you the other night, right?"

"I know you're on this tour to stay under the radar, but what if they know you're here already?"

Phoebe took the drink Stella offered and they both sat on the couch. Comfortably close, but not touching. "It may not just be Nice."

"What? Has something else happened to you that I don't know about?"

"Oh, you know about it." Phoebe waited but continued when Stella offered nothing. "Paris and Pippy?"

"Holy Jesus." Stella relived the horrible morning at the Metro station.

"It was heaving with people and it was noisy. I didn't see the footage, but I'm not convinced those thieves were in that station and on that platform by chance."

"But it was the thieves who ultimately pulled Pippy to safety. Why push her then save her?"

Phoebe waited for Stella's brain to catch up.

"Because they knew it wasn't you. Because they pushed the wrong person." Stella paced the room. "Fucking hell, Phoebe, they tried to kill you."

"Or scare me. Either is possible."

"This is big, Phoebe. The police couldn't establish who pushed Pippy, so if they had pushed you and you died, your murder would have looked like an accident."

"You know what they say. One incident is generally just that; an incident. Twice is a coincidence, but three times suggests you're being played."

"So at the moment, we're at coincidence, right?"

Phoebe hesitated.

"We're not at coincidence? Why are we not at coincidence? Did something happen today?"

"I thought I was being followed today."

"And when on earth were you intending to mention this to me?"

"I didn't want to worry you. I thought I kept seeing the same person. Always from a distance, but I just can't be sure. It was just a feeling I guess."

"That's why you're so late isn't it?" Stella hated putting two and two together and ending up with four. She realised she wasn't prepared for an *actual* threat. She'd initiated the conversation to be reassured, to have Phoebe smile and pat her on the hand and tell her it was all in her wild little imagination. She felt like an idiot. The problem was real. The threat was real, and it was all much bigger than she had originally anticipated.

Phoebe touched her knee. "Honestly, I don't know for sure, so let's leave it at coincidence for now, okay?"

Stella nodded and glanced at her watch. If Phoebe wasn't sure, she wasn't sure. Unfortunately, the little voice in the back of her mind said that Phoebe probably *was* sure. *Damn it.* She changed the subject. "Foot massage?"

"I thought you'd never ask. Can I jump in the shower first?"

"Of course," said Stella. What she really wanted to say was "can I join you," but it was too forward and Phoebe should really be the one to offer. She didn't offer.

Stella paced back and forth on the balcony, her imagination switching between Phoebe naked under a steady stream of water and Phoebe being followed by a nut case. She preferred the shower option but couldn't shake the other.

Four drinks and four massaged feet later, Stella couldn't stifle her yawns any longer. It was late. The issue of the sleeping arrangements was yet to be resolved. "We really should go to bed."

Phoebe nodded, seemingly lost in her thoughts. Stella realised she would have to do all the talking around this subject. She took the direct approach. "You're welcome to share with me, but I realise you may not want to. If we keep our doors open we're at least technically sharing the same space." She shrugged. "Might be a good place to start?"

"I think it's a very good place to start." Phoebe smiled. "Thanks for giving me space but still being here at the same time."

Stella smiled and kissed Phoebe good night on the cheek. "Sleep well."

Phoebe grabbed Stella by the front of her top. "I hardly think that pathetic effort will make the grade. Want to try that again?"

Stella was happy to give it another go. This time her lips lingered near Phoebe's, but before they touched, she whispered, "Is this better?"

It obviously was because Phoebe's arm encircled Stella's waist and they kissed sensually. There was no urgency, just a little tongue, and definitely a bucket load of sexiness.

"Much better." Phoebe gently patted Stella's backside before leaving.

Parting to sleep in separate rooms left Stella feeling incomplete. She pushed her door wide open in the hope of convincing herself Phoebe was only a matter of metres away, but it was hardly the same as sharing a bed.

Thoughts of their conversation that evening darted back and forth in her brain. She rarely found it difficult to sleep, but tonight she tossed and turned, listening to every noise and creak in the hotel. Twice she jumped out of bed and snuck into the lounge room, convincing herself someone was there. On the second occasion, Phoebe emerged from her room.

"Can't sleep either?" Phoebe yawned.

"You heard that noise, too?"

"What noise? I need a drink of water." Phoebe gulped the water like it was her last drink.

Stella sighed. "I thought I heard a noise, that's all."

"Are you frightened?"

"No. Of course not." It was mid-summer in Europe and Stella was shivering. "Maybe just a little."

"The door to the hall and the balcony is locked. I checked earlier. No one can get in."

"I know. I guess I'm just more worried than I care to admit."

"I've thought about this, Stella. I think you're perfectly safe. No one at the hotel knows we're sharing a room, and to be honest, hotels have security cameras everywhere these days. I don't mean to frighten you, but if we are being targeted, we're safer here than out on the streets where there are people everywhere and where every other CCTV camera is probably broken."

Stella hesitated. "It's not just me I'm worried about. Actually, it's not me I'm worried about at all." Tears filled her eyes. She hated the type of crying that snuck up on you, and this was one of those moments.

"Oh, come here." Phoebe drew her into a firm embrace. "Please don't cry. We don't know for sure if anything's going on, but we'll be vigilant, we'll look out for each other, and we'll take it day by day."

"Should we go to the police?"

Phoebe seemed to weigh up the suggestion. "I can't see it helping at this stage to be honest. The police are investigating the Pippy incident regardless, and the other stuff would just be put down to my paranoia." Her eyes saddened. "Plus you saw how I was treated at Calais. I'm not banned from travel, but I'm a person of interest. I don't want to risk being held up."

Stella knew Phoebe was right. Without a criminal record, it was unlikely Phoebe could be refused entry in any country simply on the grounds of suspicion of murder, but somehow her name had been flagged on the French immigration system. Someone in Australia wanted to keep tabs on her, and Stella hoped to God it was the right people.

"Maybe we'll both sleep better in the same room." Phoebe kissed the top of Stella's head.

Stella nodded. If Phoebe was right there next to her, it would be one less thing playing on her mind beyond the walls of her room.

Stella, in nothing but a singlet, and Phoebe in her little pyjamas, silently crawled into Stella's bed. Both were exhausted.

"Good night," said Stella.

Phoebe reached for Stella's hand. "Good night, Stella. Try not to worry."

Stella mumbled acknowledgment, surprised to find she had already relaxed enough to let sleep begin to take her over.

What felt like hours later, Stella stirred. She relaxed immediately, unconcerned about Phoebe's whereabouts. She was right beside her.

Their embrace wasn't such that they were entwined in each other's bodies. On the contrary, Stella had rolled over into the foetal position, tightly hugging Phoebe's arm. With nowhere else to go, Phoebe's hand rested gently on Stella's knee. She smiled to herself. Awareness of the contact and connection between them electrified her. Phoebe squeezed her knee and sighed. Stella knew she was still asleep, but the simple fact they remained physically connected, seemed magical in the early hours of a new day. Contented, she allowed her eyes to close.

CHAPTER FOURTEEN

A sliver of light slowly passed over Stella's forehead annoyingly creeping across her eyes until the pestering glare penetrated her eyelids. She flung her arm up to provide shelter with the crook of her elbow, but it was too late. The spell was broken and the night was over.

For a few moments, Stella lay blissfully unaware, caught in those comforting moments between slumber and full alertness, not focusing on any particular thought. Then, as if a shot rang out, she was fully conscious. Facing her, fast asleep and snoring lightly, was Phoebe. With another controlled movement, she gently craned her neck to peer downward. Entangled in her feet, was the bed sheet, and she was naked from the waist down. The stubble of her Brazilian waxing glistened in yet another sliver of radiant sun. Stella was feeling a little exposed. They had agreed to take it slowly; if Phoebe woke now, it would embarrass them both.

Slowly and delicately, Stella edged off the bed.

"Morning." Phoebe spoke through a yawn as Stella reached the doorway.

You're one for great timing, Lancaster.

Stella turned only her head to meet Phoebe's sleepy gaze. "Good morning. Did you sleep well?"

Phoebe remained silent for a moment then whispered, "You're beautiful."

Stella was caught off guard and her stomach lurched. She loved how Phoebe's words caused such a physiological reaction in her, but she was uncertain how to react. She had been convinced she would know when Phoebe was ready to take things further, but it seemed her head and her heart were failing to communicate. Common sense prevailed. "That's a lovely thing to say. I appreciate the compliment, Phoebe, thank you."

"You making coffee?" Phoebe's tone wasn't malicious, but all tenderness had evaporated.

Stella shrugged. "Sure. After I shower." She continued toward the bathroom.

"Why do you do that?" Phoebe had followed her into the living room.

"Do what?"

"Ignore me?"

"I wasn't ignoring you. Honestly, I appreciate the compliment. It's just that you seemed to regret saying it afterward. I understand. Well, I think I do. I realise none of this can be easy for you."

"I'm sorry." Phoebe entered her bedroom, the one that lay vacant for most of the night.

Stella sighed. She was sorry, too. She had wanted to go to Phoebe, *wanted* Phoebe, but she was frightened of reading the signals wrong. So much had happened in such a short time that she simply felt unable to read the situation clearly. She leaned in the doorway of Phoebe's room nervously pulling her top down to her mid thigh. "I'm sorry, too. You complimented me, which is lovely, but I guess I really don't know where we stand beyond that."

"Where do you want to stand?"

"Well, preferably not in your doorway feeling like a lustful, hormone-driven teenager." The smile this brought to Phoebe's face was comforting, but the awkward pause that ensued seemed to go on forever.

"Why don't you take your top off?" Phoebe finally whispered.

"Pardon?"

Phoebe inched closer. "I've seen the bottom half of you naked. Please show me the rest."

"Is that a good idea?" Stella couldn't believe what she was saying.

Phoebe held Stella's gaze without falter. "I've no idea." She took Stella by the hand. "Let's find out."

Phoebe undressed them both before guiding Stella face first into the barely warm water, firmly pressing her against the white tiled wall.

Stella flinched when her breasts met the cool tiles. She groaned when Phoebe's hands slid from behind to cup her breasts, her thumb and forefinger teasing her hardened nipples. Although their height difference appeared magnified in the shower, Stella relaxed, allowing her head to rest between Phoebe's breasts. This encounter had been Phoebe's choice, and Stella would enjoy the seduction, patiently awaiting her turn. She desperately wanted to face Phoebe, wrap her legs around her waist, and be taken over and over again, but Phoebe, zealously exploring Stella's body, remained steady against her as she began kissing the nape of Stella's neck, sending shivers down her spine.

"Jesus, you're beautiful." Phoebe nipped hard on Stella's ear.

Stella was hungry for Phoebe's mouth. Again, she attempted to turn and face her.

"Don't struggle. I promise I won't hurt you." Phoebe crossed Stella's wrists above her head. With one strong hand, she clamped them against the tiles and resumed fondling with her free hand.

Stella groaned. The seconds it took Phoebe to restrain her hands felt like agony to her abandoned, sensitive nipples.

"Please, Phoebe, please." Days of tension bubbled to the surface as Phoebe's hand began to caress lower. Stella writhed at the sensual touch and held her breath as Phoebe explored, brushing over her clitoris and into the source of her heat. Stella gasped, and her legs became weak. Phoebe's hand gently rubbing between her legs seemed to be the only thing holding her upright.

"You're ready," Phoebe whispered.

It was an understatement. Stella had been ready for days, and now she was on the verge of orgasm.

Abruptly, the stream of water stopped, and Phoebe withdrew her hand from between Stella's legs.

"No!" Stella begged, grinding her backside into Phoebe, urging her to continue.

Phoebe released Stella's arms and grasped them in the same fashion behind her back. Dripping wet, she guided her to the bedroom.

At the foot of the bed, Phoebe kissed and gently nibbled Stella's neck and shoulders. Her voice was husky, and she sounded breathless. "Promise me you'll do as I say?"

There was little doubt Phoebe was in control, but Stella sensed a hint of hesitation, and she felt Phoebe stiffen behind her, her composure possibly wavering.

Stella moaned in agreement.

"I need to hear the words." Phoebe reached around to find Stella's swollen clitoris. Gently, she rubbed it, causing Stella to sink her full weight back into Phoebe. "Stella, the words?"

"Jesus, yes," she whispered. "I promise. Please, Phoebe, I can't take much more of this."

Phoebe released her and cleared her throat. "Lie down. On your stomach."

Stomach? Stella briefly glanced at Phoebe, hoping she'd made some kind of mistake, but her gaze never faltered. Obediently, Stella assumed the position. This was nothing like the dream she so vividly cherished.

After briefly sliding her hands down Stella's still moist back, Phoebe left the room and called over her shoulder. "Don't move and don't speak. I'll be right back."

Stella remained on her stomach but slid her hand down between her legs. This wasn't some bondage scene that Phoebe had set. There were no rules, but she needed to touch herself, touch *something* until Phoebe returned. Her clitoris was beyond sensitive. Even the pressure of lying on her hardened nipples shot currents of arousal down to her centre. She dipped her fingers further. *Christ*. She was so wet.

"Need a hand with that?"

Stella snapped her head back to see Phoebe leaning in the doorway, lust and a glint of apprehension in her eyes. "You told me not to speak."

"Yes. So I did. You'll do well to remember it." Phoebe knelt on the bed. "Take your hand away, please."

Stella complied. She remained still and silent.

"Leave your head down and spread your legs a little."

The calm, yet calculated orders were sending Stella into a heightened state of arousal, although now, Phoebe's air of authority was waning. Stella's entire body craved Phoebe's touch. It yearned to be satisfied, and she was willingly at the mercy of Phoebe Lancaster.

A short squelch of lubricant confirmed Stella's suspicion that Phoebe would use a dildo. One she suspected she carried with her for personal use. When finally Phoebe's fingers touched Stella, she flinched, her breath catching in her throat, every muscle in her body constricted in anticipation.

Gently opening her, Phoebe nestled the head of the dildo in Stella's centre. "I know you're ready, but relax, okay?"

Stella pushed back. She didn't want to relax, couldn't even if she tried. The head slipped inside her. It was sizable, but certainly not the biggest she'd taken. Her relief at finally being entered was instantaneous. She felt her whole body flood with indescribable warmth, and as she was slowly filled, her orgasm neared.

Slowly and deliberately, Phoebe slid in and out, responding to Stella's body and her urgent moans of encouragement before finally gaining the speed and momentum Stella desperately desired.

Stella was close, and her frustration nearly boiled over when Phoebe slowed to a standstill, remaining inside her.

"Your silence is impressive," whispered Phoebe.

Stella wriggled in protest; the response of her body gave away her impatient need to orgasm. They played this game—Phoebe bringing Stella to the brink and pulling back—many times.

Stella screamed for her to finish. "Please, I'm begging you." The desperation in her voice was unmistakable. "I need this. Please let me come."

Phoebe gripped the back of Stella's neck, thrusting harder and faster—the bed shaking—deeper and deeper, until, with a loud cry, Stella finally climaxed. Waves of glorious orgasm pulsed through her and tears of relief streamed down her face.

They were the first to arrive at breakfast. It had been dawn when the streams of bright light had first crept through the curtains earlier that morning. Even after sex, and the awkward aftermath, they had arrived at the dining room before anyone else.

Stella finally plucked up the courage to speak. "Do you ever use your fingers?" She remembered the sweet sexiness of her dream and compared it to the detached Phoebe she had just experienced.

"Excuse me?"

"During sex. Do you ever use your fingers?"

"Of course. Who doesn't?"

Stella waited, but Phoebe offered nothing further.

After another long silence, only broken by crunching muesli and slurping coffee, Stella attempted a different approach. "Thank you for this morning. I enjoyed it."

Blushing ever so slightly, Phoebe smiled. "You don't have to thank me."

"We had plenty of time, you know." Stella glanced around at the empty dining room. "I could have taken a turn. I would have enjoyed touching you. I think you're stunning," she added a little shyly.

Phoebe dropped her spoon. "That's what I hate about all this lesbian business. It's not about *turns*, Stella. Just because I do you, doesn't mean you have to do me."

A tone of indifference had crept in, but Stella ignored it. "I'm well aware I don't *have* to do anything. But this morning, I wanted to touch you." She lowered her voice. "I wanted to fuck you, too."

Phoebe shrugged, refusing to meet her eyes. "Maybe next time."

Stella laughed, almost choking on coffee.

"What?" Phoebe asked.

"*Maybe next time?* Who are you kidding?" Stella was hurting. "Why won't you talk to me? Trust me just a little, and I promise I will prove to you that I won't let you down." Tears threatened to fall. "You wouldn't even let me look at you this morning. Do you have any idea how much I like you?"

Phoebe simply stared at her breakfast. Stella wanted to believe her silence indicated she was upset or a little frightened, but unfortunately, she knew she could easily have been angry, insulted, or threatened.

"I want to help you—"

"You can't help me." Phoebe cut her off.

Stella lowered her voice. "Try me," she said gently.

Phoebe remained silent, and with the lines of communication clearly severed, Stella returned to the room to finish preparing for the day.

Twenty minutes later, Phoebe returned and sat silently studying her Roman fact sheet. The silence had grown oppressive. "No more than fifteen minutes before Rebecca died, we made love." The words were spoken quietly, and Phoebe refused to make eye contact.

Phoebe continued. "I've not been with anyone since…"

Stella sat next to Phoebe on the sofa. She didn't want to force Phoebe to face her, but she wanted to show her support with a physical presence. She remained silent until Phoebe found the strength and the words to continue.

"…since Rebecca died." Phoebe released the most enormous sigh.

"So this morning was a big step?"

"Until this morning, I never wanted to be with anyone but Rebecca."

"And now?"

"Things have changed."

"Did you feel anything while we were…you were…you know, this morning? Were you turned on at all?" Stella stumbled over her words, hardly remembering a time when she was this nervous.

"Stella, you're the first person I've cared for since Rebecca. You must know I'm attracted to you?"

Stella knew that even this brief conversation would take its toll on Phoebe emotionally. She doubted if Phoebe had spoken of this at all since Rebecca died. "Thank you for sharing this with me." She lightly placed a reassuring hand on Phoebe's knee. "I appreciate your honesty. I know talking about Rebecca isn't easy for you."

"It's not. I'm sorry."

"This morning, did you give me something you regret giving?"

"*What?* No!"

"Did I take something you weren't ready to give?"

"No." Phoebe looked directly at the floor. "I wanted you to feel good. I guess I'm just not ready to have that reciprocated."

"Is that all?" Stella sensed there was something else.

MICHELLE GRUBB

Phoebe nervously tugged at the hem of her shorts and Stella patiently waited.

"I feel so guilty," said Phoebe.

Stella tried to fill in the blanks. "Are you feeling guilty about wanting me or wanting me to want you?"

"Sorry." Phoebe smiled awkwardly. "I know what Rebecca would want."

"Phoebe, look at me please?"

Phoebe slowly raised her head.

"I understand this is difficult, but I think I know what you want. I have no intention of placing any pressure on you. I'm not in a hurry. I'll be right here when you finally reconcile what you want with what you can live with, okay?"

"Will you help me?"

"Of course."

Phoebe placed her hand atop Stella's and squeezed gently.

CHAPTER FIFTEEN

While the group toured the Roman Forum in the sweltering heat, Stella waited with takeaway latte in hand, smothered in sunscreen, reading information that had been reported in Australia about Rebecca Dean's murder. She couldn't put Phoebe through another question and answer session, so she read the information for herself. Apparently, Rebecca Dean was stabbed, but there was no knife. When the police arrived at the scene, Simon Threadbody and Phoebe were both there, but neither of them saw or heard anything. Both Simon and Phoebe claimed their innocence and concluded that there must have been an intruder. There was no physical evidence to suggest either Phoebe or Simon killed Rebecca. Rebecca was found lying in a pool of blood with one single entry wound from a large kitchen knife. Stella had seen enough police shows to know there had to be blood on Simon and she assumed his clothes and Phoebe's were taken for forensic testing. She wondered how they had gotten away with it. Then, after realising what she had just pondered, she felt terrible for thinking that Phoebe had somehow gotten away with murder. She hadn't; she knew that. And she felt awful for thinking it.

Rectangular in shape, the Roman Forum was an impressive plaza surrounded by the ruins of Roman government buildings. It never ceased to amaze Stella how some of her group would inevitably moan about walking through the ruins. She personally found they could take her back to ancient times where the forum was the hive of life in Rome. From her vantage point on a grassy knoll, her group were easy to spot. Fifty tourists following a guide holding an orange flag certainly stood out. When Stella guessed that Phoebe could easily spot her, she speed-dialled her number and observed her pull the phone from the pocket of her army green designer brand shorts. Phoebe quickly glanced at the number and answered.

Pure velvet purred down the line. "Hey, you. What's up?"

The smoothness of Phoebe's voice sent her imagination right back to the hotel room that morning. She had been thinking a great deal about their intimacy. If she were to rate sex on the intensity of an orgasm, Stella had experienced amazing sex that morning. If, on the other hand, she were to rate sex as a coming together of two people, a connection, a mutual desire, then Stella had experienced nothing more than a meaningless, empty encounter. As it stood now, Stella was soaring high from an exceptional orgasm, but it was the result of the emptiest sex she had ever experienced. Confusion was an understatement when it came to how Stella was feeling. She focused on the task at hand. "Can you see me?" Stella asked.

"What? Weird time to play I spy, isn't it?" teased Phoebe.

"I'm sitting on the hill, about one hundred metres directly in front of you. I can see you. I'm just wondering what you had planned for the rest of the day?

"What did you have in mind?"

"I don't know. You, me, coffee, lunch and maybe some wine later?"

"Sounds like a busy day."

"So you'll join me?"

"Of course, I'd love to." Stella watched Phoebe put her hand on her hip. "Have you been spying on me?"

"Guilty. It seems that my eyes are magically drawn to you."

"Oh, you soppy romantic."

"What can I say? Italy turns me into some crazy Casanova."

"Now I know you're full of rubbish. I can't make you out. Remind me what you're wearing again?"

"Really, Phoebe? After this morning, you can't even remember what I'm wearing?"

Stella watched Phoebe turn away from the rest of the group and cover the handset for privacy. "You weren't exactly fully clothed when I was paying you so much attention this morning."

"I'm wearing a white tank top and black shorts." Stella watched as Phoebe scanned the hill in her direction.

"Okay, got you now. And now that you've brought it to my attention, I think I like you better as you were this morning."

"Phoebe!"

"Sorry. See you soon."

Stella accessed the Internet and planned her day with Phoebe. She knew Rome inside and out, not like a local, but more intricately than a tourist. She reserved a table for lunch at an upmarket restaurant and selected a few quirky little tourist attractions to visit. If they made good time, she would be able to fit it all in before work commitments monopolised her attention before dinner.

From across the grassed area, a voice called Stella's name. She glanced over to see Russo holding his arms out by his sides questioningly.

Shit! The group had finished the tour already. She searched for Phoebe, and she gave a quick smile. Stella leapt up and raced over to the group, reverting instantly to professional tour manager mode.

After everyone clapped and thanked Lucia, their tour guide, Stella addressed the group.

"I know you're all keen to cool down in the shade, or better still, air conditioning, so I'll be quick. Rome has so much to see and do, as I'm sure you've all discovered. Today is the day to do all the things you couldn't fit in yesterday." Stella knew some of the group had visited the Vatican and St. Peter's yesterday, while others shopped and wandered the city. "Because there is so much to see, nothing is organised as a group, but I know of a wonderful restaurant, with air conditioning, that serves the most amazing pasta. I'll be dining there myself tonight, so if you're about, feel free to join me. I'll meet you at the Trevi Fountain at seven. Right now, I'm off to get lost myself. Go, team. Away with you."

Keen to do their own thing, everyone rushed off, mostly in the direction of the Vatican, but others wandered toward the shopping precinct. Phoebe remained behind.

"So, what's in store for me today then?" Phoebe eyed Stella from head to toe. "You look amazing today."

Stella blushed.

"Plus I know exactly what's under those clothes."

"Stells. Hey, Stells."

It was Russo again, and Stella counted to ten before she turned around to watch him approach with one of the girls from the tour.

He glanced at Stella, then Phoebe, but hid the developing frown well. "Sorry to be a pain, but Kerry here has lost her passport."

Stella's heart sank. The little blond Australian girl was probably only in her early twenties. She looked stressed. Sorting out a new passport would consume Stella's entire day. But it was her job to help Kerry, and it was Italy after all. Someone always seemed to lose something in Italy. "It's definitely not in your luggage somewhere?"

"No. I'm so sorry about this, but we've turned my room and my luggage inside out. It's not there." Kerry looked genuinely remorseful.

Stella turned to Phoebe. "Sorry, maybe a rain check? This could take a while."

Phoebe smiled, and with nothing else to do, she and Russo headed in one direction, while Stella and Kerry made their way toward the Australian embassy. With Kerry beginning to tear up, Stella gave her a gentle squeeze and assured her she wasn't the first, nor would she be the last tourist to lose her passport, but either way, the problem would be fixed somewhere around dinner time.

CHAPTER SIXTEEN

Stella sank into the corner of the sofa and patted her lap. "Come on. Come and take a load off." Phoebe had trekked all over Rome and looked exhausted. Stella, on the other hand, had sat idly in the Australian embassy for hours and had energy to burn. Phoebe smiled. "Now, there's an offer I can't refuse." With a movement so natural it even caught Stella off guard, Phoebe settled her head in Stella's lap, pulling Stella's arm down to rest on her middle. "So, the embassy was outstanding fun?"

"Riveting. I'll take you one day."

"You sure know how to show a girl a good time." Phoebe adjusted herself so she could see Stella's face. "You really do have the most incredible blue eyes."

"That's one of the nicest things you've said to me."

"I'm shy." Phoebe winked. "But I thought it the first time I saw you. I knew I shouldn't be tempted, but I couldn't help myself."

"Why not be tempted?"

"To protect you." Her eyes lowered. "And because I wasn't sure I was ready for any of this." Then she smiled. "But just looking at you now, I had no hope of resisting you."

Stella fidgeted slightly, uncomfortable being scrutinised under Phoebe's gaze.

"Have I made you nervous? Only this morning you were complaining about my lack of eye contact."

"Well, that was different," said Stella.

Phoebe grinned. "Or maybe it's just that the unfailing and highly desirable tour manager isn't the cool cat she would like everyone to believe."

Stella linked their fingers together. "Or perhaps, being a highly desirable tour manager to one person in particular is all said tour manager needs to focus on."

Phoebe sat up and faced Stella, appearing ever so slightly short of breath. "This is where you kiss me, tour manager."

Stella leaned in, inhaling Phoebe's fresh shower scent.

The tenderness of their barely touching lips felt exquisite. Many moments were spent establishing a rhythm and exploring, ever so gently, the sensation of being in such close proximity with only the merest touch. An awareness Stella had never experienced before consumed her; Phoebe's weight across her lap, the shallow and delicate breath that lingered between their mouths, not to mention the burning desire that was intensifying in her deepest places. This kiss was nothing like their first kiss in Florence. Something told Stella that whatever Phoebe indicated she might want tonight, tender exploration and genuine openness was all she should give. Some things were bigger than the moment, and this moment heralded the beginning of an unknown world.

It was Phoebe who caved in first. Her hand slid up to Stella's neck, indicating without doubt, that a sense of urgency had taken over.

Stella allowed Phoebe to edge her lips apart. The grip on the back of her neck tightened, and the very tip of Phoebe's tongue found Stella's bottom lip. Stella was in a heightened state of arousal. Experiencing the sensation of Phoebe wanting her was magical. Stella pulled back.

"What's wrong?" asked Phoebe.

"I want to set a boundary tonight."

"A *what*?"

"A boundary. You know? A limit to where this should end."

"You're kidding, right?"

Stella was perfectly serious. She manoeuvred out from beneath Phoebe. "Do you have feelings for me?"

"Pardon?"

"Simple question." Stella sat safely beyond Phoebe's reach and temptation. "Well, do you?"

"Of course I do. You know I do."

"Good, then that's all I need to know. The next time we are together, I will be making you feel exceedingly good indeed. Until you're ready for that, for us, we need to set a boundary."

Phoebe sighed, but a cheeky grin turned the corners of her mouth. "Okay, Mother Teresa, what's your plan?"

"Kissing. And maybe some heavy petting."

"*Heavy petting*? Do people actually say that anymore? You've turned into a nun. What have you done with Stella, my sexy tour manager?"

"I'm right here, but I'm not wrecking something that could be amazing, not just for a cheap thrill."

"You did last night!"

"Very funny. And that was this morning, and it wasn't all that cheap. But it won't happen again until I can give as good as I get."

Phoebe playfully pushed Stella off the sofa and sat astride her. "Don't for one second think you can give as good as me."

"And don't *you*, for one second, think you're giving me anything more than some sexy snuggling and kisses tonight."

Phoebe's expression turned serious. "Thank you."

Stella stared deep into the eyes that, for the first perceptible time, portrayed a glimmer of true feeling. If eyes were the window to the soul, Phoebe Lancaster's damaged soul was buried deep beneath pain and sorrow. "Kiss me, please."

❖

The insistent light of dawn began to slowly brighten the bedroom. Naked, Stella lay cradled against Phoebe's body, and she felt the arms enveloping her twitch and stir. Last night had been deep and sensual, but there had been no orgasm or penetration. They had talked, touched, and explored each other mentally and physically. It had been so intense, Stella had never quite found the best time to ask Phoebe why Simon wasn't in jail for Rebecca's murder. But now she realised a window of opportunity was available before work consumed her and she must again dedicate her attention to a coach load of tourists, not solely the incredibly gorgeous client snuggled behind her.

"Phoebe? Are you awake?" she whispered.

"What if I said no?" mumbled Phoebe.

Stella inhaled deeply. "Why didn't you tell the police Simon killed Rebecca?"

Stella felt Phoebe stiffen but was relieved when the taut muscles relaxed back into her.

Phoebe cleared her throat. "We were both there, it was his word against mine, and we bargained on each other's silence. It was his bright idea to suggest there had been an intruder. It was a hot day, the doors to the pool and deck area would have been wide open so there was no need to assume there was a forced entry."

"How did you convince the police that an intruder killed her while you were both in the house? Come to think of it, why were you both in the house? I mean, why was Simon there?"

"Both Rebecca and Simon worked for Oscar. Their business dealings rarely crossed paths, but Rebecca had found a string of dodgy transactions."

"Simon was cooking the books?"

"Not exactly. He had made a mistake and was trying to fix it. It required some creative accounting and Rebecca called him on it. He said they argued about it, he lost his temper, and threatened her with a knife. He said she went for him, and in the tangled mess, she was stabbed."

"An accident? Do you believe that?"

"I don't know what I believe anymore. She died and he held the knife."

One question played on Stella's mind. "Where were you when it happened?"

Phoebe stared at Stella with pleading eyes. "Please, I really don't want to talk about it anymore." She began to cry. "I didn't protect her and I should have. I wake every morning and relive that day. It never goes away."

"But you couldn't be by her side all the time, Phoebe. It's not your fault."

Phoebe wiped her eyes. "We were grilled for days by the police, but we both stuck to the intruder story. I was sure he was going to drop me in it. The police tried everything in the book to trick me, but I had a story and I told it. After all, I was pregnant. It's amazing what can motivate you to repeat the same story over and over again. In the end, without a motive, the police couldn't put forward enough evidence to form a solid case to take to the prosecutor. Alone or together there was just no proof. We heard nothing, we saw nothing, and we only discovered Rebecca's body after she went to fetch a drink and some food and didn't return."

"But surely they could have prosecuted you both. I mean I'm glad they didn't, but it just looks like you both conspired to kill her and were covering it up." The moment Stella said the words, she knew the answer. "Oscar."

Phoebe nodded. "He's not powerful enough to ensure a conviction in court. When it gets to that stage he has no control. Even Oscar Dean can't threaten an entire jury. But he had some connections in the police and within the Department of Public Prosecutions."

"That's when you gave him Sebastian?"

"Yes. I signed Sebastian over to him and he did whatever he had to do to squash the police investigation."

"An heir is more important than you going to jail, right?"

"Correct. To this day, I've no doubt he thinks I really did kill Rebecca, but our son was more important to him than my punishment." Phoebe looked exhausted. "I've never talked about it like this to anyone before."

Stella cradled her head against her chest. "Thank you."

CHAPTER SEVENTEEN

Day twelve, Rome to Corfu, was really a travelling day, the highlight being a trip to Pompeii. Only a handful of people fully understood the magnitude and devastation that the eruption of Mt. Vesuvius caused back in 79AD. Although Naples itself was nothing to write home about, only slightly interesting because of its colourful Mafia history, Stella never tired of discussing the fate of Pompeii with those few who were interested enough to listen carefully to the guide.

The long drive to the port of Brindisi was the perfect remedy after a big night out, and although Russo knew Stella's mind was elsewhere, he insisted on chatting endlessly, to the point where Stella was convinced he was making stuff up to keep her from snoozing.

On only one other occasion was the ferry ride from Brindisi to Corfu rough. It was now two occasions. After dinner, Stella played cards with some of the group, but retired early to find Phoebe already tucked up in bed reading.

"Is it just me, or is the boat rocking more?" asked Phoebe.

Stella laughed. "This ferry is no more a boat than our coach is a bus, my dear."

Phoebe patted the bed next to her. "Can you please hurry up and get in here? I feel like I haven't seen you all day."

Stella stripped and headed for the shower. "If you weren't so antisocial," she called through the running water, "you could have joined us for cards and spent hours in my company."

Phoebe appeared in the doorway. "Now, tell me the truth. If you had the opportunity to avoid cards, you would have, right?"

"You've got me there." Stella winked. "Care to join me?"

"I've not long had a shower, thank you anyway. But if you don't mind, I'd like to stay and chat."

"You mean stay and watch?"

Phoebe sat on the closed toilet seat, resting her chin in her hand, staring. "That too."

The conversation flowed easily before Stella finally shut off the water. "Can you pass me a towel, please?"

Phoebe reached above the vanity and selected a towel, holding it outstretched for Stella to step in to. "You really are stunning."

"I'm glad you think so."

"I'm sorry I'm not as generous with my nakedness as you are." Phoebe blushed.

"Or perhaps you're sorry you're not an exhibitionist like me?"

"You're comfortable with your body. Your confidence is an attractive quality."

Stella dropped the towel and stood before Phoebe. "And one day, you'll be comfortable with both our bodies."

Phoebe closed the distance between them. "I'd like to start acquainting myself with your body right now if you have no objections?" Her hand lightly touched Stella's cheek, her thumb brushing the corner of Stella's mouth.

Stella nodded feebly.

"Come to bed with me?"

"An offer I can't refuse."

Phoebe slid into bed, pulling Stella into a straddling position over her hips.

In the moments it took to move from the bathroom to the bedroom, Stella was already wet. "I should have finished cards earlier." She writhed as Phoebe touched her, but made no attempt to reciprocate the gesture.

Phoebe's eyes moved from Stella's breasts to between her legs. "I wanted to message you to return sooner, but I couldn't make any promises about what we would do when you arrived. I didn't want to get your hopes up."

Stella leaned down to slowly kiss Phoebe, her naked hips grinding in a circular motion on Phoebe, nothing but thin fabric between them. "You're safe with me. I haven't forgotten our boundaries."

Stella sensed an increasing desire within Phoebe as their hips began moving in time. Their kiss became so intense, Stella suppressed the urge to force Phoebe's fingers inside her. Phoebe grasped Stella's hips, encouraging the movement.

"You're delicious, Stella." Phoebe moved to kiss Stella's nipples. Stella hesitated.

"Please, surely that comes under the category of heavy petting?" said Phoebe.

"You're impossible and hopeless at boundaries."

One by one, Phoebe took Stella's nipples in her mouth, paying close attention to not only the nipple, but also to the sensitive tissue surrounding them. It wasn't long before Phoebe's hands began exploring further, and Stella realised she was holding Phoebe's head to her. The next sensation Stella experienced sent waves of electrifying pleasure pulsing through her body. Phoebe's fingers were softly caressing Stella's clitoris.

"Phoebe, baby? What about the boundaries?" she panted through moans of increasing ecstasy.

"Can you come this way?"

"What?"

"I'm not inside you. I'm so sorry. I'm not ready for that. But I really want to make you come."

Stella's orgasm was building.

"Don't make me stop." Phoebe closed her eyes.

"I won't. Please, if you're ready for this, just do it."

Phoebe increased the pressure and speed.

Stella straightened and braced herself against the wall. She rode Phoebe's hand harder and faster, no longer craving penetration, just release.

"Come for me, baby. Let it go, now."

Stella pushed down harder, tipping herself into that amazing world of oblivion. As the orgasm ripped through her, she flopped on top of Phoebe, panting and allowing the delightful convulsions to fill her with warmth before eventually subsiding. "That was amazing."

Phoebe smiled. "I'm glad you liked it."

Stella cupped Phoebe's face. "Would you tell me if there was anything I could do for you?" Stella hesitated. "I know you don't like the idea of taking turns, but I just wanted to ask."

Phoebe pulled the covers over them both. "I appreciate your thoughtfulness, but just now you gave me exactly what I wanted."

Stella snuggled close, her right leg draped over Phoebe, her right arm under Phoebe's top, resting on her stomach, and her face buried into her neck. The ferry rocked from side to side, but Stella didn't care.

At nearly two a.m., as they evidently reached the midpoint of the journey, and the middle of the Adriatic Sea, the movement of the ferry began to resemble a washing machine. Within twenty minutes, a booming announcement crackled through the public address system. It was expected that the rough going would last for at least another two hours and all access to external decks had been restricted. The message briefly addressed some simple safety advice, but the upshot of it was to remain in your cabin, preferably in bed.

Dozing lightly, Stella and Phoebe silently lay in each other's arms, riding out the storm.

❖

It was difficult to believe, when gazing out over the idyllic calm water as the ferry began docking in Corfu, that the sea had been so unfriendly earlier that morning. Corfu was bathed in bright sunshine, and the mere sight of it filled Stella with delight.

First stop upon disembarking was the hotel. It was certainly a treat—the rooms were lavish, the dining area had wonderful views, and the pool area, including the cocktail bar, shone like a beacon for every guest. As predicted, there were the usual hiccups when checking in, but overall, the process was uneventful. This first day gave the group time to explore and relax. Tomorrow, things heated up with planned activities.

Stella's room was always an upgrade. They looked after tour managers well in Corfu, but upon entering she noticed Phoebe was yet to arrive. Come to think of it, she didn't recall handing her a swipe card during the check-in process, and thinking back, she couldn't place Phoebe since disembarking the ferry.

She dialled Russo's number. "Hey, did you see Phoebe earlier this morning?"

"Nope. Why?"

"She's not in my room."

"Wow, you two sure do like to keep track of each other."

"You're not amusing, Russo."

"Is her luggage there? Maybe she's gone out exploring?"

Stella had already checked, but she found herself looking again. "Nope, no luggage."

"Did you do the head count?"

Stella had forgotten about that. "Yes. I counted exactly fifty."

"So she must be here somewhere." Russo's tone sharpened. "I'm sure if you'd come up with forty-nine and the missing party was Phoebe, I'd have heard about it."

"Okay, quit with the attitude."

Russo sighed. "Just call her." He hung up.

Of course Stella had thought of this, and of course Stella had already tried Phoebe's number countless times. Each time, she heard Phoebe's request to leave a message.

The first day in Corfu, although relaxing, still left Stella with some organising to do. Water sports dominated the following day, and after reconfirming arrangements, she scanned through the participation list. Phoebe's name wasn't on it. A chill rippled through her. Phoebe hadn't checked in, nor had she booked activities for the following day, nor, upon further investigation, had she booked a seat at the famous Greek feast on the final evening of their stay. Alarm bells rang, but what was she to do? On the first day of the tour, she openly encouraged her group to get lost, but after what she and Phoebe had been sharing, the intimate moments as well as the ordinary moments, Stella couldn't believe for one second that Phoebe had simply gone off to do her own thing. If Phoebe hadn't shown up by dinnertime, she would alert the authorities and register her as missing.

After a final double-check, ensuring absolutely everything was booked, confirmed, and reconfirmed, Stella changed into her black bikini and slipped on a stylish black tank top. Although she looked the part, the last thing she wanted to do was mingle and act chirpy with the group. Almost everyone from the tour was gathered by the pool, and she copped a multitude of wolf whistles as she discarded the tank and dived into the glistening blue water. Sitting on the edge and baking red raw in the sun was not her thing, nor was covering up her body. Her scant bikini barely covered her, but this was Greece, and she found her adventurous approach always encouraged others to forget their insecurities and simply enjoy the moment. As expected, within minutes of her diving into the near empty pool, the number of swimmers swelled. Within no time at all, her group occupied the entire pool with beach balls, volleyballs, and tennis balls flying everywhere.

"Hey, Stella?" She turned, dodging a tennis ball. It was Megan. "Where was Phoebe off to this morning?"

"Pardon?"

"Wasn't that her climbing into a taxi down at the dock?"

Stella motioned for Megan to follow her into the cocktail bar. "Was it definitely Phoebe?"

"I'm one hundred percent sure." Then she added, "Plus, I'd recognise her expensive luggage anywhere. The old bloke driving the cab struggled to haul it in the boot."

"What colour cab was it?"

"Yellow. Bright yellow."

Stella had a lead she felt compelled to act upon. "Can you excuse me, Megan? I seem to have left my phone in the room."

Stella hurried to reception. "Hi, Sophia." Sophia was almost one hundred years old, but was always good to Stella. "What's the name of the cab company that has bright yellow taxis?"

"Yellow Taxis." Sophia smiled.

"Yes, the bright yellow ones."

"That is what they are called, Stella. Yellow Taxis."

"Oh, makes sense. Do you have a number for them?"

In the privacy of her room, Stella phoned the taxi company. Realising they had no obligation to help her, she put on her most professional tour manager tone, although it did little to hide the worry in her voice. After being handed to several different people, each with varying degrees of English, Stella finally spoke to a young lady who advised her that Spiro, their most experienced and honest driver, picked up a young lady and delivered her to Corfu Kapodistrias Airport. She advised Stella, more than once, that Spiro would have charged the correct fare. Stella thanked her for the information and hung up.

A taxi to the airport didn't appear to be the action of someone working on impulse. She phoned the airport. A flight had departed that morning for Athens at ten thirty. It would be fruitless to try to find out if Phoebe had been a passenger. In her heart, she knew Phoebe had been on that plane. Disappointment gripped her. *What the hell is going on?*

The afternoon dragged, and Stella struggled to concentrate on anything or enjoy herself. She just hoped Phoebe knew what she was doing. Still, the fact that Phoebe hadn't found the courage to confide in her stung.

At dinner, Stella announced the resort was hosting a poolside cocktail party exclusively for the group. The catch was everyone had to gather into groups and prepare a scene from their favourite movie. The incentive—cheap prizes and free cocktails.

Stella constantly switched from being worried about Phoebe, to being annoyed with her. Predominantly, she hoped she was safe. She missed her beyond what she imagined was possible so early in a relationship. She also wasn't even sure if what they shared *was* a relationship. Whatever it was, she wasn't ready to let it go.

Russo noticed she was struggling and was helping organise activities. At one point, he rested his hand on her arm and smiled uneasily. She knew it was his unspoken way of reassurance, but nothing could ease the anxiety that threatened to overwhelm her. Why couldn't Phoebe simply call?

Even Stella had to admit the movie scenes were hilarious. The best one, requiring Stella as a prop, although completely inappropriately dressed, saw the Melbourne boys re-enact the singing bar scene from *Top Gun*. "You've Lost That Loving Feeling" echoed throughout the whole of Corfu as the entire group joined in.

In their nightlife party element, it was also the Melbourne boys who amazingly convinced some of the group to play spin the bottle. The rules were that there were no rules! The bottle would be spun twice, and the two people it stopped on—male or female—were to enter the centre of the circle and kiss on the lips. Initially, this met with some resistance from the men, and most opted out quick smart.

The first six spins saw three pairs of girls enter the circle and kiss. By this stage, those not participating had gathered to watch.

Those involved were drinking frantically to gain courage. The men were awestruck. The kisses weren't long or passionate, a quick peck on the lips, but the entire scene oozed foreplay. The first two men to kiss were Simon and Gez. Their horrified expressions were priceless, but neither could back out now—pride was on the line. With purpose, chests puffed out, both men strode into the circle, grabbed each other by the shoulders, and then kissed, lightning fast, on the lips. A cheer erupted and their arms flew triumphantly in the air.

As the game wound down, the last kiss of the night fell between Stella and Megan. A chant of "snog, snog, snog" rang out and the crowd looking on suddenly grew. Stella wished she hadn't joined in the damn game, but she had a job to do, and in true showmanship style, she took the challenge. Stella circled Megan, revving up the crowd, drawing every ounce of tension into the centre of the circle. Through deafening cheers and applause, she leaned in to kiss Megan. Stella's lips pushed Megan's apart and her tongue entered her mouth. The crowd roared. Stella felt Megan's hands grasp her buttocks, and she forced her mouth wider still.

It was then Stella remembered her kisses with Phoebe. The intimacy they had shared the previous evening had been magical, certainly nothing she had experienced in such a long while. It was in this moment that she realised Phoebe was the only girl she wanted to be kissing. Abruptly, she ended the kiss, and the crowd continued to chant. Megan knew something was wrong. There was a split second when she looked longingly at Stella, but must have realised the moment had passed. Playing to the crowd, Megan dramatically fell back on the lawn. The bartender turned up the music, and everyone who didn't jump into the pool was thrown in. In Greece, no one cared if you were drunk and swimming.

CHAPTER EIGHTEEN

Stella woke with a headache. She needed the protection of her sunglasses, regardless of the weather. At least half the group were enrolled for water sports, while the others went fishing and sailing. Some, the smart ones, preferred to sleep off their hangover poolside at the resort.

"So, Stells, no word from Phoebe?" Russo pulled another soft drink from the cooler and passed it to her. They were reclining on lounges under the shade of an expansive umbrella, watching the group energetically frolic in the sea as they patiently awaited their turn to ski, parasail, banana ride, and jet boat.

Stella shook her head. She had convinced herself Phoebe would have made contact by now, and disappointment filled her. "No, nothing. Other than a useless call to the police, I don't know what else to do."

"Useless?"

"They checked the records of the flight. She was on it."

"So according to them she's not missing?"

"Nope, just on holiday it would seem."

"I honestly think she has issues. Maybe things are working out for the best."

Enough was enough. "For Christ's sake, Russo, will you just leave it alone? I know what's best for me, not you. I know how I feel. I know how she makes me feel," said Stella.

"Okay, okay, steady on. I'm—"

"No, Russo. I will not steady on. I've had it up to the eyeballs with you and this bullshit. No more. Do you hear me?"

In a show of surrender, he raised his arms. "You got it, chief. I'm sorry. I'm just worried, that's all." He left it a while before continuing. "Do you want to hear what I got up to?"

Stella sighed. She never could stay mad at Russo for too long. "Go on."

"In light of spin the bottle, Simon asked if I'd kiss him, for real, not just a peck." Russo grinned.

"Let me guess, you turned him down?"

"I did turn that down, but not the bit where he blew me in the gardens." Russo was grinning from ear to ear.

"What?" He'd gained Stella's full attention. "You're kidding, right?"

"I made it clear I wasn't into blokes and I wasn't going to reciprocate. It was his first time. He's pretty sure he's gay. *I'm* pretty sure he's gay. He wanted to stay the night. *That* was when I really turned him down."

Stella sat up straight. "You said no to a simple kiss, but you let him suck you off?"

"I'm not gay. I don't want to kiss a bloke."

"Whatever. Trivial details. But you let him do the other?" Russo nodded. "And now he thinks he's gay and *then* you send him back to his own room. You're a harsh man, Russo."

"Hey, I'm a hero. I gave him some pointers, so the way I see it, I've done a community service. Now, next time, with a bloke who actually wants more, he'll know precisely what to do." Russo looked decidedly chuffed with himself.

"You gave him *pointers?* He's got his own equipment, you know."

"Yeah, I know, but he bothered to stop and ask. I told him what I liked. Did you know men have rather large mouths, and very, very strong lips?"

"I've heard it all now," Stella muttered under her breath as one of her crew approached and the discussion ended.

Dinner that evening was free choice. As on previous occasions, Stella and Russo remained noncommittal and vague concerning their plans. It was the only evening during the entire tour when they refused to include any members of the group. As usual, they booked a table at Corfu's most expensive restaurant—although cheap by European standards—where clients rarely ventured. It was the safest place to dine unseen. They often sat on the balcony, overlooking the beach, watching members of the group wander obliviously below them.

As expected, dinner was amazing. They occupied the corner table at the far end of the narrow balcony. George, the owner and chef, promised fresh seafood every time, so there was no need to order. He simply served them.

Russo slowly placed his napkin on the table. "You really like Phoebe, don't you?" he asked sincerely.

"I can't put my finger on it," said Stella. "I can't tell you why."

"You don't mean to tell me this could be—"

"Don't you dare say it."

"—the L word?" He whistled loud and long.

Stella slouched back in her seat. "Whatever it is, I think I've got it wrong. She couldn't even tell me she was nicking off."

Russo turned deadly pale.

"Are you all right?"

"No. Jesus." He wiped his brow with his forearm. "I didn't give it a second thought on the ferry. *Shit*, I'm such an idiot!"

"Russo? What the hell are you talking about? Is it Phoebe? You're not making sense."

"Look, Stells, honestly, I didn't think—"

"For fuck sake, just spit it out," said Stella. He was scaring her.

"There was a bloke on the ferry. He came up to me while I was playing cards. Kind of to the side, you know, so I didn't even really look at him. He asked had Phoebe Lancaster boarded the ferry. I didn't think anything of it."

Stella was almost speechless. Almost. "You didn't think anything of it?"

"Well, he was kind of wearing a uniform, like a member of staff on the ferry."

"Kind of?"

Russo looked confused. "Well, now I think of it, maybe not an exact uniform."

"Well, what then?"

"Maybe just something nautical looking, I guess."

"And this didn't seem odd to you?" She rested her head in her hands and attempted to count to ten before she spoke again. She reached three. "What the fuck, Russo? Have you suddenly developed shit for brains? You'd better tell me everything you remember and you'd better damn well remember it all."

As it turned out, there wasn't much to remember. Russo had barely looked at the man. He could have been in his forties, but then Russo reckoned George was only forty-ish and Stella knew for a fact he was pushing sixty. Sure, Russo could tell if a girl was legal or not. No bother there. But a middle-aged man between the ages of forty and sixty and Russo hadn't a bloody clue.

Stella Googled an image of Oscar Dean and proceeded to shove her phone in front of Russo's face. "Did he look like that?" He shook his head, muttering that if Oscar Dean had spoken to him on the boat, he'd know who he was. She was doubtful. Next she found an image of Simon Threadbody. "What about him?"

Russo looked longer and harder. "It could be. But I'm really not sure. That's probably closer to the age of the bloke." He skipped through some alternative images of Simon. "I guess it could be him."

Stella was losing patience. "So, let's just say your ever-diminishing little life was on the line here, big guy. Would you say the man you saw was Simon Threadbody?"

Russo looked forlorn. "No, I couldn't wager my life on it."

Stella had had enough. "Come on. Let's go." She was becoming increasingly worried for Phoebe.

The fifteen-minute walk back to the hotel was entirely uphill, and after an indulgent dinner, it was the last thing either of them felt like doing. Russo attested that on every occasion, Stella complained the entire journey. Tonight she was too angry to complain, and she knew Russo preferred their banter to her silence, but tonight wasn't Russo's night.

Russo's phone rang, startling them both. "Hello. What? Hang on. Simon, calm down and start again."

"What is it?" Stella straightened. Tour manager mode kicked in.

Russo's full attention was on the conversation with Simon. "Where are you? Okay, stay there. I'm about five minutes away." Russo's tone became authoritative. "Simon, pull yourself together. It's not the end of the world." He hung up.

"What's going on?"

"Simon told Gez he's gay. He thought Gez might be too. Turns out he's not. They've had words. Gez told him to fuck off and now Simon is upset. I'll go talk to him."

"Fine. Good idea. Maybe keep his mouth off your dick this time, though."

Poised to offer a rebuttal, Russo thought better of it and jogged back down the road in the direction of the port.

Above her, Stella could see the lights of the hotel. Annoyingly, the road weaved back and forth, climbing gradually, so the actual distance travelled was twice the distance required. She sighed. She was alone, worried about Phoebe, and annoyed that bloody Russo possessed a brain the size of a gnat. She wanted to be in her room tucked up in bed, and she wanted Phoebe to call. She half-heartedly hoped Phoebe might have turned up by now, but in the back of her mind, she knew that wouldn't be the case.

Stella remembered a cut-through Russo had shown her once. It went in a straight line directly up the hill, through the bushes, avoiding the windy road. She was rarely dressed appropriately enough to go trekking through the overgrown track, but tonight she didn't care and searched for the opening in bushes.

Bingo! Stella left the smooth bitumen of the road and, on all fours, climbed up into the thick bushes. Thongs weren't the most ideal footwear for traipsing through the undergrowth, but she was being careful. When she stopped to catch her breath, she heard a twig snap behind her. She listened intently, and her heart rate increased slightly but there were no more sounds. Probably a feral cat, she told herself. Corfu was full of them, roaming the streets and living off restaurant scraps. She pressed on, and within minutes, finally reached the road.

Stella was determined to conquer the fast route and walked directly across the bitumen, hoping the opening to the next section of the track would be visible. It was, and again, she hauled herself up out of the narrow ditch and into the bushes. Even wearing flip-flops, she quickly found her stride, weaving through the overgrown trees and shrubs. She was making good time but wished she'd not had that last glass of wine. It sat heavy in her stomach making her feel a little queasy. The exercise was proving a good antidote for Russo's stupidity.

Stella guessed she was about halfway when the sound of rustling branches, a thud, and a grunt saw her drop to a crouching position. She immediately told herself she was being ridiculous, but she stayed down regardless.

"Russo, is that you?" Her tone was nothing short of irritated. "I've had about as much of you as I can take tonight. Scare me out of my wits some other time."

Silence.

She waited.

Another twig snapped.

She ran.

Driven by instinct and not willing to wait around and be the punch line to one of Russo's practical jokes, Stella fled. She held on to the hope it was a joke. In fact, she knew it could be nothing at all, but she also feared it might be a threat. A real threat. She scrambled up the hill, desperately holding her arms outstretched, fending off the sharp, jagged pricks of dried tree branches. It was impossible to hear if she was being pursued. Her breathing was laboured, the trees swished past, and her heart pounded as if it were a bass drum. The dissecting road wouldn't be far away. There she would wait and see if Russo showed his face. There she would berate him so much the whole of Corfu would know he was an asshole.

The moment she reached the road, escaping the claustrophobic bushes, Stella stopped running. She stood with hands on hips waiting for Russo to emerge.

Russo didn't emerge. Instead, Stella heard footsteps. Loud, twig cracking, thumping footsteps. Someone was in the bushes, and if it wasn't Russo, who was it and were they following her or simply minding their own business, oblivious to her increasing fear?

She decided not to find out.

Stella turned left and followed the road. Her thongs were a hindrance, but fragments of broken glass glistened in the dim street lamplight, so removing them seemed pointless. Panting, unable to draw enough oxygen, she slowed to a jog as she reached the second to last tight bend in the road. The lactic acid build-up in her thighs burned like fire, and eventually, she had to stop.

This was a mistake. All the wine she drank at dinner gurgled, and as her body convulsed, great volumes of vomit spilled from her. She glanced around, wiping her mouth and expecting to hear the sound of footsteps rapidly closing in. The pounding of her heartbeat filled her ears, and her eyes darted back and forth but she could detect no movement. Even Russo wouldn't string a practical joke out this long. She saw nothing move. Not even a tree swaying in the breeze.

She was beginning to wonder if it were all her imagination. Even more determined to reach the solace of her room, Stella brought her weary legs to life and continued up the hill. As her pace quickened, her feet tangled beneath her, and she fell hard on her hands and elbows. She felt ill again, and it occurred to her that perhaps it wasn't the alcohol, but fear. She couldn't be sure that Russo or anyone else was following her, but with everything that had happened so far on the trip and with everything that Phoebe had said, fear gripped her insides. The tears produced when vomiting turned into tears of despair. Again, she paused and remained quiet long enough to reassure herself no one was following. *Why aren't any of the others around? Where's Russo?* Stella brushed off the gravel, slightly comforted by her close proximity to the hotel, and forced one foot in front of the other.

Common sense told her that the middle of the road was the safest place, so with heavy legs protesting every step, she trudged up the hill. Stella glanced nervously over her shoulder, and every time she saw an empty road, her pulse slowed. There was nothing there. *Please tell me I'm not going insane.* Halfway to the final bend, Stella began to relax. In the distance, she could hear the faint throbbing bass of the poolside sound system. She guessed most of the group was back at the hotel, dancing or swimming while the bartender produced deadly cocktail concoctions.

Without warning, out of the darkness, something smashed into Stella's side, propelling her through the air. She landed awkwardly and with force, stunned, but before she could orientate herself, gather her thoughts, or even fight back, she was set upon. She knew it wasn't Russo, not a violent act like this. Whoever it was scrambled the length of her body, and with a pain she had never before experienced, her neck snapped back from the force of a fist connecting with her jaw. A punch like that, she guessed, was only the beginning. Her brain bounced back and forth inside her skull, causing her eyes to roll upward and briefly impair her vision. Stella fought to remain lucid.

She covered her face and attempted to roll onto her stomach. All she could think about was escape, and now that something terrifying was actually happening, her mind snapped back to the incident in Nice, then on to Phoebe and Simon Threadbody. One event, shit luck. Two, coincidence, and three, this was number three and Stella was convinced this was no random attack.

Her legs were so heavy from running, she willed them to function, but whatever had hit her was on them, on her, and her legs had been rendered useless. Stella lashed out with arms and fists of her own; she refused to take this beating without a fight. She attempted to scream, but she had bitten her tongue when the first blow struck her head, and it swelled so that her scream was barely audible. When eventually she connected with something, it winced and hit her again. This time her arms provided some protection, deflecting the contact.

Unexpectedly, she felt enormous relief on her legs, and as they became free, she thrashed them about too, again connecting with something. But her win was short-lived. Within moments, agony forced her to withdraw into the foetal position. Her side, centimetres above her hip, stung with sharp, piercing pain. She felt the full force of someone's foot smash violently into her ribs. Some kind of fabric was forced deep into her mouth and tied behind her head. She could barely breathe. Before the pain could even begin to take hold, Stella was scruffed by the back of her shirt and lifted onto unsteady feet. Her head throbbed, and she was defenceless against her assailant who wrenched her head down. In one easy move, her upper body was rendered immobile by a powerful headlock.

She knew a little self defence, but not one tactic or manoeuvre entered her mind. Stella improvised, lashing out again. This time her foot connected with a leg, and she remembered one strategy was to stomp with all her power on the top of the foot. With as much effort as she could gather after positioning her body and attempting to calculate where her attacker's feet might be, Stella raised her foot and drove it down hard and heavy. Once, twice, then on the third go, she connected forcefully. The grip around her head tightened, forcing her face toward her attacker, almost smothering her.

Stella realised they were still on the road, but she was now being dragged toward the bushes. A new and heightened wave of terror struck her. In the bushes, no one would hear her or see her. As the idea came to her to grab her attacker's crotch and rip their bollocks off, she was released from the headlock, only to be thrust in front, her arm painfully forced up her back, her shoulder joint millimetres from dislocation. Now at arm's length, Stella was powerless to grab any part of her attacker's body. She had missed her opportunity.

As they approached the scrub on the opposite side of the road, a strong hand grabbed at her hair, forcing her forward and up into the overgrown bushes, propelling her deeper into the undergrowth. Again, branches and twigs scratched at her face as she was forced facedown onto the ground. Her shoulder burned in agony. Her attacker sat on the middle of her back. She flayed and bucked, but a swift jab to the ribs put a stop to that. The gag was momentarily removed, but to her dismay, a pitiful cry was all she could manage before it was quickly replaced. To make matters worse, the gag now appeared connected to whatever was holding her arms up her back. The more she thrashed, the tighter it pulled her arms. Stella was completely immobile, defenceless.

The possibility that she might die became a horrible realisation. But the likelihood that she would be raped was a near certainty, and as hands grappled beneath her to unbutton her shorts, her worst nightmare was quickly becoming a reality. The burning pain shooting through her shoulders was immense as she fought to keep her shorts on, but it was hopeless. The bastard on top of her knelt on one ankle while he removed her shorts from one leg then the other. She felt hands claw mercilessly at her underwear. They weren't removed as such, but ripped from her. Unable to comprehend what was surely about to happen, Stella braced herself for the penetration. *Christ, please help me. Get it over with.*

She might survive. After it was over, after he was satisfied and having not seen the face of her attacker, she might be abandoned in the scrub. He might not be a killer, just a cruel, sadistic rapist. She lay exceptionally still. If she let him rape her, let him see that she was no longer fighting him, that her pathetic resistance had ended, he might spare her life. The rape was inevitable. Her death wasn't. Not yet.

Unexpectedly, like a siren in the still of the night, Stella's phone rang. Her volume was always set to maximum so it could be heard over the coach sound system. The clangour echoed through the trees. The phone had been in her shorts pocket and must have fallen out. It was in the bushes somewhere, and out of reach of the monster on top of her. By the time her cursing attacker found it and shut it off, Stella could hear her name being called in the distance.

"Stella! Stella! I heard your phone. Where are you. Stella!" Russo's voice grew nearer, but because he had no idea she was in danger, his tone portrayed no sense of urgency.

Never in her life had Stella been so pleased to hear Russo. Fear told her to remain calm and hope he stumbled upon her. She was terrified that if she moved a muscle, her attacker might flatten her skull with a rock.

"Stells? You there?" Russo sounded like he was on the road.

So close.

Stella detected a burst of activity out of the corner of her swollen eye, and she braced herself for the worst, but the second it began, it ceased. Then silence. The darkness was oppressive and although she was unable to confirm it, she thought she might be alone.

"Stella! Can you hear me? This isn't funny, you know."

Stella groaned. In her mind, it was a full-blooded scream. It was dismal, but enough to attract Russo's attention.

"Stells, was that you?" He burst through the scrub. "Holy-fucking-Christ." The bright beam from Russo's phone lit the entire area. He rushed toward her, untied her arms, and removed the gag. "Jesus, Stella. What the hell happened?"

CHAPTER NINETEEN

When Stella woke, she hoped everything was finalised, completed somehow, but she knew it wasn't.

Her body was naked under only a sheet and the room was dimly lit by cracks in the blinds. She ached all over and struggled to open her tired eyes. She at least determined it was her room at the hotel, and she faintly remembered Russo being by her side earlier. Anxiety settled in the pit of her stomach, and without looking she knew Phoebe still hadn't turned up. If ever a moment had arisen when she needed Phoebe, this was it. A wave of overwhelming sadness seeped through her for wanting what she couldn't have.

Her swollen body protested as she pulled herself upright on the pillows and attempted to survey the damage. Her legs were stinging, but seemed to move without hindrance. The scratches all over her body appeared superficial and would hopefully fade within a week or two. Her shoulder, ribs, and jaw were another story. The painkillers on her bedside table were testament to the severity of her beating, and she awkwardly reached over and swallowed a little pill.

The events of the previous evening came flooding back. Her body responded to the flashback, coating her in a thin film of sweat.

She pieced together some of the conversations she had either been a participant in, or had overheard at the hospital—people talking about her as if she wasn't right there. She had wanted to give them Simon Threadbody's name, but what would she say? "Oh, by the way, can you check this bloke out because I think he's been stalking Phoebe and me? Yes, Phoebe is the girl that I wanted to report missing. No, I don't know him. I've named him because he killed her girlfriend five years ago?" The list went on and Stella kept her mouth shut.

More often than not, the suspect in sexual assault cases was known to the victim. Other than Matt's appalling behaviour at the bar in Florence, no one else flagged red to Stella. As it was, Matt had an alibi for the entire evening. Russo had provided the Greek police with the names of those on the tour. They had checked with the federal police, and none of them had previous convictions for sexual assault.

The police believed she might simply have been a random victim, in the wrong place at the wrong time. There really was nothing to suggest she was known to her attacker. They did what they could at the crime scene, but Corfu was constantly bursting with tourists. The chances of finding the culprit appeared slim. One officer went so far as to say that they'd have a better chance apprehending the perpetrator if she *had* been raped. DNA was like a currency these days. Russo politely told him to fuck off.

It had been a long night. Stella had been rushed to the barely adequate Corfu Emergency Room, swabbed all over for possible traces of her attacker, and then cleaned up. Against his better judgement, Russo watched Stella discharge herself. In between the procedures, the police recorded her statement. She read and reread what had been written, altering sections lost in translation, but everything seemed so jumbled and blurry. It all happened so fast, but excruciatingly slow at the same time. *What's missing?*

A gentle knock at the door startled her, and it took Stella a few long moments to rise and pull on the hotel robe. Her blood pressure dropped, and she had to sit down again. "I'm coming," she croaked out.

It was Russo, balancing a tray laden with food sent by the concerned kitchen staff. It wasn't Phoebe, and Stella ignored the twinge of disappointment.

"What time is it?" Stella moved aside for him to pass.

"Half six. Are you hungry?"

"Is it that late?" Stella recalled slumping in the shower for over an hour after her return. It had been midday by the time she disrobed and gave in to exhaustion. She checked her phone. Nine missed calls from Janet. Nothing from Phoebe. She refused to leave Phoebe another message.

"How are you feeling? Rested?" he asked softly.

"I am hungry, actually." Her mouth and jaw were a little tender, but a sizable slice of moussaka steamed alluringly toward her. She slowly began to nibble away at the edges.

Stella's phone broke the silence when it vibrated gently on the coffee table. Her boss wasn't known for her patience. Russo cringed but sat back on the sofa to listen.

Stella cleared her throat and slid the bar to answer. "Hi, Janet."

"Fucking hell, Stella, you sure know how to give a fat woman a scare. I'm heart attack material, you selfish shit."

Stella smiled. "Yeah, sorry about that."

"How are you doing?" This was possibly the first time Stella had heard Janet speak with a calm voice.

"I'm not too bad. Nothing broken."

"Russo said you weren't, you know, raped. Is that true?"

"Yeah." She glanced fondly at him. "He found me just in time."

"Want me to send a replacement?" Janet was matter-of-fact.

Stella had already thought of this, but it was the easy way out. Calling it quits now was tempting, but she had never failed to finish a tour, and what would she do, occupy the sofa in her room feeling sorry for herself? It wasn't her style. And what about Phoebe? If Stella left the tour, Janet would insist she return to London. That was simply out of the question. She knew if circumstance saw her having to push on right that minute, she couldn't do it. But she needed to convince Janet to leave her on. She quickly selected her strategy.

"Can I think about it?"

"What is there to think about?" Janet wasn't being difficult. "Where's the Lancaster girl?"

The Lancaster girl. A deep longing for Phoebe panged in her lower abdomen. Where *was* Phoebe? She hated hearing Janet refer to her in that tone. How could she reconcile her desire and growing fondness when everyone around her was implying she was an evil murderer?

"I don't know where she is."

"Does this have anything to do with her?"

"No. Nothing." It was only a partial lie. If it had been Simon Threadbody who'd attacked her, he had everything to do with Phoebe, but Phoebe had nothing to do with her attack.

"How long do you want?"

"Can I make the decision en route to Venice? We leave in the morning."

"I don't know, Stella."

"Sailing up the Adriatic doesn't require a tour manager. I'd like to see how I feel when I'm off this fucking island. By six tomorrow night, I promise to give you my decision."

"Four, not six. If I don't hear from you, I'll be sending your replacement. Okay? I can't be any fairer that that. Now stay out of trouble." Janet hung up.

The following day, a taxi collected Stella and delivered her to the ferry well before her group. It was clear and crisp, and Stella sat on the balcony of her cabin watching the island fade over the horizon.

Four o'clock loomed, but she waited until the last minute to call Janet. Although not entirely convinced Stella was up to the task, Janet requested she obtain a doctor's certificate to confirm she was fit for work before allowing her to continue. That suited Stella. The ship's doctor was young and hungover, and she looked Stella up and down only once before scribbling favourably on a certificate.

CHAPTER TWENTY

Off the shelf makeup was only effective to a certain extent when it came to hiding bruising, and it remained obvious the following morning that Stella had been beaten. Regardless, she greeted the group at breakfast with her usual chirpy grin, determined to uphold her professional air. Like everyone else on board, she stood at the bow of the ship and watched Venice pass to their immediate right, bathed in brilliant sunlight.

First stop was a trip to Verona where everybody rushed to re-enact the famous scene from *Romeo and Juliet*. The group would then slowly dissipate and begin their idle wanderings, stopping for lunch and taking advantage of the shops in the Roman Arena.

Stella indulged in an enormous pasta lunch under the watchful eye of Russo.

"So, how are you feeling?"

"Good." Stella filled her mouth, making up for her poor appetite of recent days. "Besides my ribs, I feel one hundred percent."

"Have you heard from Phoebe?"

She shook her head.

He leaned forward, his features strained. "She may not turn up, you know?"

Stella refused to contemplate that. Their connection had been real, and Phoebe had not only indicated it was important to her, but Stella was convinced she had implied there was a future for them. It seemed impossible to consider Phoebe had been deceptive about that. She was desperate to know the truth. Where had Phoebe gone and why? Was it Phoebe's intention to make her experience the pain that currently paralysed her heart? She yearned for Phoebe and wanted her to return because, quite simply, she missed her.

❖

The open air Taverna, only minutes from their accommodation, was uncharacteristically empty for this time of year. The low drone of the relaxed group and the intermittent death of buzzing mosquitos flying to a sizzling end in the purple light traps was finally an indication that the group was okay.

Stella had only drunk two beers, but it amplified the effects of her medication, and Russo took her back to the hotel. She had been unstable on her feet, and when she told him that she was seeing double, he left his near full drink and helped her home. Nothing Stella did relieved her desire for Phoebe.

"Fancy some company tonight?" Russo winked, but his offer was no joke.

"Why, Mr. Coach Driver, are you not entertaining some damsel this evening?"

"Because I'd rather act all gallant and macho around you."

"You tried to pull, but failed. Am I right?"

"Something like that." Russo shrugged. "Nightcap?"

"Yeah, why not?" She slid the key into her door. "Mine might be water though. Alcohol and painkillers aren't working for me anymore." Russo smiled knowingly.

After swinging the door open, Stella knew something was wrong. Both she and Russo, whose hand rested loosely on her shoulder, stopped dead in their tracks.

The room was lit by the two bedside lamps, and a familiar expensive suitcase lay propped against the bed, and on the side table sat a key to the room—she had forgotten the room was booked in two names, with two keys.

Dressed in a black singlet and underpants, toothbrush in her mouth, Phoebe emerged from the bathroom.

The shock was too much for her system, Stella rushed past her to throw up. Phoebe attempted to follow, but Stella quickly locked the door before falling to her knees. Somewhere, beyond the tiny white bathroom, she heard Phoebe ask Russo what was wrong. He offered no reply. Emptied of everything she'd consumed that day, Stella joined the uncomfortable pair in the bedroom.

Phoebe was clearly concerned, but stopped short of touching Stella when her advance was met with hesitation. "Stella, what's going on?"

"You tell me, Phoebe. What's going on?"

Russo coughed, reminding them both he was still there.

Stella's makeup was all but gone after sweating and vomiting and wiping her face. The aftermath of her beating in Corfu was on full display.

"Stella, what happened to you?" This time Phoebe took Stella by the elbow, but withdrew when Stella recoiled at the touch. "Honey, talk to me?"

Russo stepped between them. "I don't think that's wise," he said.

"When did this happen?" Phoebe edged closer.

"As if you don't know!" barked Russo.

"Russo. Leave it," snapped Stella.

"What the *fuck*?" Phoebe's voice raised an octave. She glared at Russo. "You think *I* was responsible for this? When did it happen?"

"Corfu. I was assaulted in Corfu."

"Who did this to you?"

"I don't know."

Russo rolled his eyes.

The penny dropped. "So, because I wasn't there, you think I did it? Jesus. Give me a fucking break."

"No, Phoebe, he doesn't think it was you. We both know you weren't in Corfu." She turned to Russo. "You're not helping."

Stella was rapidly feeling like vomiting again.

Russo took control of the situation. "You're coming to stay in my room tonight. You two can discuss this in the morning, at a reasonable time and in a reasonable state."

"Stella?" Phoebe reached for her hand.

"She's not well. Just leave it for tonight, okay?" Russo led Stella from the room.

Within minutes, Stella lay curled in a tight ball in bed next to Russo. Tears from her silent sobbing saturated the pillow, and she needed to throw up again but was forcing it back down. Vomiting felt like a knife twisting in her already tender ribs.

She dozed intermittently, but it was no use.

❖

Sleep was impossible. Russo was snoring like a freight train, and Stella could think of nothing but Phoebe. She crept from Russo's room and padded down the hall.

"Can I come in?" Stella let herself in—it was her room, after all.

"Honey, of course." Phoebe pulled back the covers, imploring Stella to join her.

"I think we need to talk." Stella was straight to the point.

"Okay, but you're shivering. Can you at least come to bed?"

"In a moment. I really want to discuss the three days when you went missing." Stella longed to fall into bed next to Phoebe. She longed to be held safe in her arms, but most of all, she longed for a good reason, a very good reason, why Phoebe had disappeared.

"That's certainly fair. You'd better shut the door."

Stella closed the door but remained only inches inside the threshold. "So, where were you?"

"I have a good reason for leaving Corfu."

"I hope you have a good reason for not uttering a word to me." Stella choked back tears, and she began to sway.

Phoebe jumped up, quick enough to catch Stella before falling. "I'm sorry I didn't talk to you about it, but I thought the note explained I had something important to do."

"Note? What note?"

"I left you a note on the ferry. You didn't think I'd just leave for days and not tell you?"

Stella remained silent.

"Stella? I would never leave you to worry like that. You have to believe me."

"What about the messages I left? Didn't I sound frantic enough?"

"I thought you sounded annoyed because I'd left a note instead of talking to you. It never once occurred to me that you'd thought I'd just disappeared."

Stella hadn't seen any note. She had been rushing to the group to organise disembarking the ferry. She simply grabbed her bag and rushed out the door. "I didn't see a note. I was worried sick. I called the police. I tried to find you."

Phoebe knelt before Stella. "I'm sorry you thought I'd just left you. I can only imagine how terrible that must have made you feel." She touched her face. "And on top of all this."

"I think Simon did this. Well, if not Simon, someone he sent to do his dirty work."

"Tell me what happened?"

"No, you first. Please tell me, where did you go?" Stella was desperate to piece it all together.

Phoebe kissed her forehead. "I'll show you." Phoebe removed a paper bag from her suitcase. Inside the bag was a box, similar in size to a jewellery box. It appeared to be made from strong cardboard. Also inside the paper bag, wrapped in protective plastic, was a postcard. Phoebe read aloud.

Dearest Phoebe,

I have deviated from my holiday to visit the island of Santorini. It is the most wonderful place. The rest of the world doesn't exist here, just me and the sunset. Oh, and the smelly donkeys, too.

When I return, I promise to bring you here. Just you and me. My father will go mad not knowing where I am, and he'll never find us here. Santorini is heaven on earth. I will buy us a villa and we'll live here until we are old and grey. I miss you.

All my love,

Bec

XX

"Rebecca's ashes were in this box. I've kept them for such a long time. I wasn't sure if I could let her go." Phoebe gently rewrapped the box and card and returned it to the case.

"I'm sorry. That must have been difficult for you."

"It was. But it felt like the right time. It's probably been the right time for a while now, but Santorini seemed like the best place for her to finally be at rest, away from Australia, away from Simon and Oscar."

Phoebe touched Stella's bruised face. "I'm so sorry this happened to you. It's my fault."

"No, it's not. But I don't think it's a coincidence, do you?"

Phoebe shook her head. "Number three."

"My sentiments exactly," agreed Stella. "This was no random attack."

"Simon?"

"Who else?"

"We have to stop seeing each other." The statement was so out of the blue, Stella barely registered it. Phoebe continued. "I'm putting you in danger and I won't have that."

Stella snapped her eyes wide. "Hang on a minute, that's a ridiculous idea and completely too late. We're in this together now. The damage has already been done." She was beginning to lose control. "Don't you dare tell me we can't be together, not now and not ever. Do you hear me?" Stella closed her eyes to hide the tears.

Phoebe took her hand and led her to bed, pulling Stella under the covers and adjusting their embrace until Stella was comfortable. "I'm sorry. It was a dumb idea. I won't mention it again."

Stella shook off the unimaginable thought.

"You have to understand though, that if either Simon or Oscar knows about my rendezvous in Switzerland to see Sebastian…" Phoebe couldn't finish. "Well, I shudder to think of the consequences."

Stella knew what those consequences could be. "Phoebe, you can't put yourself in danger like that. It's suicidal. Do you really want to die?"

"I didn't have a preference either way until three weeks ago."

"What changed three weeks ago?"

"I met you. I didn't want to like you. I felt like I was betraying Rebecca. Especially given I've had her ashes in my suitcase the whole time. I hated myself for liking you at a time when I was preparing to say good-bye to her."

"I'm so sorry."

"On the day I was released, Oscar's lawyer came to see me. He offered me a deal. Oscar would ensure my release, and I would sign my unborn child over to him. I was to remain under his care until Sebastian was born, a prisoner in Oscar's house. I was ordered to have a caesarean section to avoid any complications during birth. Sebastian was taken from me immediately. I was permitted to hold him just the once." Phoebe wiped away tears. "He paid me substantially, effectively buying my silence. He made it perfectly clear to me that my freedom, and indeed my life, was of little concern to him. He accepted, rather quickly, the loss of Rebecca. Sure, he could have waited until the child was born, taken him, and left me to rot in jail, but he wasn't prepared to risk anything happening to his precious heir. Securing my release was a small price to pay for ensuring his grandson was delivered safely and in good health."

"So now you plan to see your son and risk your life?"

"I have lived immersed in grief and loss for so long now. I need to see Sebastian. He is Rebecca's flesh and blood, my flesh and blood, he came from my body and I need to see him. I don't care what the consequences are. Well..." Phoebe said, smiling awkwardly. "I didn't until now."

Stella tentatively snuggled closer to Phoebe, needing to feel the warmth of her body and the protection offered by her strong embrace.

"Where's Simon Threadbody supposed to be now?"

"Oscar's in Switzerland. I presume Simon is supposed to be there, too."

"Has he ever threatened you before now? Assuming it's him that's making our life a misery at the moment."

"Not directly. The threat is implied with men like him. I know how dangerous he is. There's no need to threaten me. He knows that."

"A man was asking after you on the ferry to Corfu. He spoke to Russo. Russo remembered the conversation the day after, but other than to identify the man as middle-aged, he couldn't pinpoint any features." She shrugged. "You know Russo. He was probably somewhat preoccupied at the time."

Phoebe sighed and leaned back. "Simon."

"Would he do his own dirty work?"

"I wouldn't put it past him."

Something was troubling Stella. "Do you think he really would have raped me if Russo didn't show up?"

Phoebe pulled her closer. "I honestly don't know. Simon is many things, but a rapist. I don't know, Stella."

"You want to tell me about it?" Phoebe whispered gently. "About what happened that night?"

"Not really."

"Please? I'd really like to know."

Stella succumbed to her emotions, and the need to share her story with the one person she was beginning to care about above all others. Sobbing, she recounted the events of Corfu.

Phoebe gently kissed and comforted Stella.

Stella simply cried and let it all out.

CHAPTER TWENTY-ONE

Venice to Vienna was a long but spectacular drive through the
Dolomites. Even Russo enjoyed the change from chaotic
Italian roads to the orderly and scenic Germanic countries. Vienna,
the home of Mozart and Strauss, guaranteed the evening would be
filled with schnitzel and classical music. Those not enjoying the local
culture usually found themselves in the cheesy Australian bar where
the only thing resembling Australia was the overpriced beer that no
one dared drink back home.

After the initial excitement of travelling into the beer guzzling
countries, the coach noise lowered to near silence, many taking the
opportunity to catch up on much needed sleep. Stella had confirmed
activities and taken another call from Janet who seemed to be checking
up on her with alarming regularity.

Stella loathed the classical show everyone else seemed to love.
She had seen it a hundred times or more, and after the second or third
time, she simply couldn't rouse any excitement. In fact, she often
made excuses to leave halfway through or earlier. Regardless, on this
particular evening she had been invited on a date.

Two-thirds of the group attended the classical dinner and show,
while the majority of the remainder, as expected, settled into the
Aussie bar. Some had been there all afternoon.

Stella's only obligation was to deliver the group to the show,
so upon commencement, she snuck to the back of the room before
ducking out completely. Russo was staying on. Not for the show, but
because he was back in favour with the Brazilian girls, and with the

coach parked up for a day, he had grand plans for spending most of the evening in bed.

In light of everything that had happened recently, Stella remained on edge. But troubling her was Phoebe's proposed meeting with Sebastian and the danger that might put her in if Simon was indeed the cause of recent events. The world Phoebe had described, in which Oscar Dean was a man to be feared, was a world Stella couldn't fully comprehend. Would Oscar or Simon harm, or indeed kill Phoebe if they ever found out she had schemed to meet her son? This might be a moot point regardless. Simon could be plotting to cause Phoebe harm irrespective of her plans. Was such action a slight possibility or a high probability? And would Phoebe's feelings for Stella alter her actions?

Stella checked the address Phoebe had given her and waited as instructed under the Café Ruàne sign that flashed emerald green when open. Her smart black trousers and revealing shirt had gone unnoticed by the group; everyone had dressed up that evening. But now, fifteen minutes beyond the time Phoebe had said she would collect her, Stella was beginning to worry. Being tall, beautiful, and blond, Phoebe was easy enough to spot in a crowd, but Stella saw no sign of her. Then, slowly, as if in a funeral procession, a shiny black limousine pulled up. Stella expected Phoebe on foot and ignored the car until the driver opened the rear passenger door and ushered her in.

"Stella, it's me." Phoebe leaned over reassuringly.

Stella smiled and jumped in. "Thank goodness it's you. After everything that's gone on, I wasn't ruling out abduction in an expensive limousine."

"Sorry. I didn't think of that." She smiled awkwardly. "We were caught in traffic and I forgot my phone."

"I was beginning to think you'd stood me up." Stella relaxed until she noticed Phoebe's stunning black dress. "I'm underdressed, aren't I? You look amazing."

"You're not underdressed at all. Don't be silly. You look incredibly sexy. And anyway, it doesn't matter what you're wearing, as long as you enjoy yourself."

"So, where are we going?" Stella didn't recognise the streets they were slowly weaving through.

Phoebe reached for Stella's hand, smiling broadly. "You'll just have to wait and see."

"You do *know* where we're going though, don't you?"

"What? Of course I do. Have a little faith."

Phoebe popped a bottle of champagne. "Drink, my dear?"

Stella couldn't refuse although the bubbly champagne did little to settle the nerves in her stomach. She couldn't remember ever being invited on a date like this. She peered beyond the dark tinted windows, leaving Vienna behind and was thankful she had given up on the painkillers. She could tell they were heading northwest, or thereabouts, and within the hour, they arrived at the picturesque town of Krems.

Dinner was in a private room at the exclusive Old Station Spa. Once a place of disrepute—among other things—the inn was now a lavish destination spa with a hefty price tag to match.

Stella's main course of duck had been delicious. The conversation had flowed easily, but now she found the courage to seek answers. "Would Oscar or Simon really hurt you if you saw Sebastian?"

Phoebe inhaled deeply and steadied her hands, fingering the edge of her cloth napkin. "Two years ago, when I discovered what childcare facility Sebastian attended, I began watching the entrance gate morning and afternoon, trying to catch a glimpse of him. After a week or so watching, there was a knock on my front door, and the next thing I knew I was in hospital nursing a broken jaw, broken wrist, broken ribs, bruised kidneys, and a face that was black-and-blue. The same man who did this to me, visited again the day I returned home from hospital, suggesting if I ever attempted to see my son again, I'd be dead."

"I'm guessing he wasn't joking."

"It was a pretty serious beating."

Stella hesitated. "I don't mean to sound rude, but to hire a limousine to Krems and dine at this place isn't exactly a cheap exercise. Oscar must have compensated you well."

"Back then, my death would have looked suspicious if he had indeed followed through with his threats. Too many questions would have been asked. His lesbian daughter is killed, so is her lover, and he becomes guardian of his heir. No, he couldn't afford that much scandal, but he could afford to buy my son and my silence. I've not touched a cent Oscar gave me. Rebecca had money in all sorts of places that Oscar didn't know about. Lots of money. I live more than comfortably off that."

The real prospect of losing Phoebe before their relationship even had the chance to begin, gripped Stella. "This is insane. What if Oscar finds out? Will he, you know? Hurt you? And what about all this stuff with Simon?" Stella's mind was struggling to keep up.

Phoebe reached across the crisp, white linen tablecloth, stroking Stella's hand. "Well, I'm not intending to interrupt them at breakfast and ask to speak to Sebastian. I have been planning this for some time now. I've no intention of getting caught, but I have to be willing to suffer the consequences if it goes wrong."

"And you're willing to suffer the ultimate sacrifice?"

"You make it sound so dramatic. It may not come to that."

"Damn it, Phoebe, it is dramatic! It's insane." Stella hadn't planned to become an emotional wreck, but watching the woman she was falling in love with talk about her own life with such disregard was painful. "Don't you think it would have been safer to see Sebastian back in Australia? Over here, you'll just be another murdered tourist. Back home, you'll be Phoebe Lancaster, the murdered girlfriend of Rebecca Dean. Surely Oscar wouldn't kill you there?"

Phoebe smiled. "Back home, Oscar has eyes and ears everywhere. I could never execute this in Australia. Over here, he has less security, and his mind is consumed with dodgy business deals. My contact, Sebastian's nanny, has a responsibility to ensure he is looked after, educated, and has a good time. I can handle this."

Stella sighed, exasperated. "So, it's simply a meeting, an hour or so?" She knew she was only convincing herself.

"Correct."

Stella shook her head. It wasn't adding up. "What you're telling me is that you'll meet with Sebastian for an hour or so and then that's it? You'll just walk away?"

"On this occasion, yes." Phoebe held back tears.

"What about long-term?" Stella squeezed her hand, but she needed to know how this would pan out.

"Long-term I need to find a way to convince Oscar that I didn't kill Rebecca. I need to convince him that Simon did. Showing him I'm not a murdering monster is the next step."

"And you are hoping that eventually Oscar will let you have access to him, or even some custody?"

"Something like that."

Stella waited, she sensed more was coming.

"I've seen lawyers about this, good lawyers. The contract I signed is watertight, and the fact that I signed it under duress is his word against mine. I could just have easily been saving my own skin with that deal. It's ambiguous either way you look at it."

"And this so-called friend of yours, would she double-cross you?"

"I hope not."

"You *hope* not? Jesus, Phoebe, is hope enough? This could be a matter of life and death."

Phoebe forced a smile and dabbed the napkin to her eyes. "Please try and remain calm, and keep your voice down."

Stella felt the tension drain from her shoulders, and she sucked in a deep breath before gulping the remaining champagne. Nothing more could be said until the waiter, who had appeared out of nowhere, refilled her empty flute.

"So, what's the plan for the meeting?" Stella asked the moment they were alone.

"The plan is well thought out and can be aborted at any time. I have inbuilt strategies for reassessment and recalculation. If anything goes terribly wrong, I'm hoping I have an out."

"Excellent. But what, where, when, and how?"

"You don't need to know that." Phoebe rang the little china bell, summoning the waiter again.

"*What?*"

Phoebe raised her hand, signalling for Stella's silence, as she handed over her credit card. "I'll rephrase. It's not that you don't need to know. It's more that I don't want you to know. Keeping you in the dark is the only way I know to protect you. I've already put you in danger by informing you of my intentions."

"More danger than Corfu?"

"My point exactly."

"But surely I can help?"

"Surely nothing." The waiter returned, and Phoebe discretely placed fifty euros in his hand.

"Look, Phoebe." Stella was serious as they settled back into the limousine. "There must be something I can do." She couldn't believe what she was about to suggest. "An extra pair of eyes and ears has to be useful?"

Phoebe put her finger to her lips. "This discussion is over, Stella."

"Says who?" Stella couldn't help but allow her petulant child tone to creep into her words. "I'm not in the least bit happy about not knowing the details."

"Do you always get what you want?" Phoebe grinned.

"Mostly, yes."

"Then allow me to open your mind." Phoebe leaned seductively close. "We have an hour confined to the back of this car. Completely alone. Do you want to spend the entire journey moaning to me about this?"

Stella pouted but grinned. "I'm sure I could attempt to redirect my focus elsewhere."

"Good girl." Phoebe produced a bottle of tequila, salt, and lime wedges.

The arousal Stella had so desperately kept at bay broke through the barrier. "I'm very selective as to where I place my salt."

"Really?"

Stella nodded.

Before anything was poured, Phoebe pulled Stella close as her hand crept up her body, over her breast and around her neck. "You seem to be my undoing, Stella-Tour-Manager."

"You're only human, after all." Stella's breathing shortened as their mouths found each other. The kiss was burning, and the throbbing in her trousers required urgent attention. With her tongue feverishly exploring Phoebe's mouth, and Phoebe opening generously to allow it, she recalled with sadness what transpired in Rome. A flash of disappointment passed through her. Any time now, the kiss would end, she would be turned away, and although she knew her lust would be satisfied in one way or another, it wouldn't be enough. Facedown in the back of a car was not what she wanted. Mutual touching, making love, that was what she craved. Stella pulled away, moving to place an uncomfortable distance between them.

"What's wrong?" Phoebe asked, breathless.

"Nothing. How about we wait a while?" Stella unscrewed the tequila, in desperate need of a shot to dull her senses.

"Stella?" Phoebe was hurt, her tone defeated. "Please tell me what just happened? Do you trust me?"

Stella turned to Phoebe. "I trust you, I really do, I just—"

"Shit." Phoebe finally understood. "Fucking Rome."

"Rome was fine. Great, in fact. Let's just not go there again right now." Stella quickly poured two shots.

Phoebe rested her head in her hands. "It was far from fine, and it certainly wasn't great. I shouldn't have done that to you. Not like I did, anyway." She took the shot Stella offered and drank it down, holding her glass out for a refill before downing that, too. "Now's the time to fix what I did to you in Rome, Stella."

"There's nothing to fix. Honestly. We made progress on the ferry. Maybe we should leave it at that for the moment." Stella attempted to make light of the situation. "You made me come. Jesus, what more could a girl want?"

But Phoebe was shattered. "What more? Anything more, I should imagine. If it was so good, Stella, why are you afraid of a repeat performance?"

Phoebe closed the distance between them. "I'm sorry. Don't answer that. I know why."

Stella cupped Phoebe's face, forcing her to listen. "I don't want you to just fuck me, okay? If you don't want to call it making love, then that's fine. We can fuck each other. But I want to do whatever we call it, together. I want you to want me just as much as I want you. You don't need to *fix* what happened in Rome, just—"

"But I want you to fix *me*." Phoebe moved to kneel between Stella's legs, staring into her eyes. "I love that you want me. The mere thought of you touching me is driving me insane." Phoebe seductively rose and buried her head in the crook of Stella's neck. "I want you. I promise. I want you."

Slowly, before Stella could either accept or decline, and in a manoeuvre that caught her off guard, Phoebe's hand began massaging between Stella's legs as she kissed and nibbled her ear. Stella completely forgot Rome and was back to square one—totally aroused.

It was useless. She couldn't fight this now, even if she wanted to. Regaining some composure she reversed the situation by forcing Phoebe back against the seat. If Phoebe was truly ready, she would allow Stella to be inside her. "This stops anytime you want, okay?" Stella reassured her.

Phoebe nodded. "Right now, though, I think I'll kill you if you stop."

"Really?"

"No. Bad choice of words. But I want you. Please, believe me?"

Stella lifted the black dress over Phoebe's head to reveal a gorgeous body without underwear. "Jesus," Stella muttered under her breath as she commenced the slow and sensual seduction of Phoebe Lancaster.

Phoebe's breasts were delicious. Her dusky pink nipples hardened at the slightest touch, and as Stella took one, then the other, in her mouth, Phoebe's back arched, and she moaned. Again, their mouths met. This time it was Phoebe who plunged her tongue deep into Stella, her hands clawing to find the buttons of Stella's shirt. She struggled to even unclasp one and yanked the shirt impatiently, sending buttons flying everywhere.

"I'll have them fixed, I promise," Phoebe mumbled as she unclasped Stella's bra and roughly groped her breasts, moaning in approval. "Lose the pants."

Stella obeyed and quickly removed all her clothing.

She knelt between Phoebe's legs and caught her breath. Before her, naked and beautiful, was a woman ready to be taken. Stella pulled Phoebe toward her until her backside rested on the edge of the leather seat. Without breaking eye contact, she reached for the bottle of tequila and poured two shots, handing one to Phoebe. Stella held a slice of lime, and she licked her wrist before sprinkling salt all over it. On Phoebe's inner thigh, high up her leg, she also licked and sprinkled salt.

"You lick my wrist and suck the lime in my hand on the count of three, okay?"

Phoebe nodded. "But where's your lime?"

"Trust me, I don't need lime." Stella winked. "One, two, three."

The tequila disappeared, and Phoebe grasped Stella's wrist, licking the salt at precisely the same moment Stella's tongue glided up her thigh. As Phoebe bit into the lime and sucked the bitter juice, she let out a gasp. Stella was sucking something else altogether.

Entangled in each other's arms, both finally satisfied, Stella's fingers remained inside Phoebe. She wasn't willing to give up such an intimate connection yet. The experience had been tender and beautiful. After initially taking Phoebe with her tongue and then gently penetrating her with two fingers, Stella watched her take that last leap of faith and let herself go, let herself orgasm at the hands of someone other than her beloved Rebecca. Stella made love to Phoebe patiently and encouragingly. The only permission required was the permission Phoebe granted herself.

Passion that had remained dormant for so many years erupted in Phoebe. Now free from years of self-imposed celibacy, she allowed Stella to continue, tenderly and lovingly. Stella observed Phoebe struggle with the realisation that Rebecca was no longer her last lover. Stella had slowed, allowing Phoebe time to process her emotions, before whispering in Phoebe's ear that she wanted to make her feel safe, that she adored her, and that above all, she wanted to make her feel wanted and amazing. With a little help from her fingers lightly pulsating on Phoebe's G-spot, she required only gentle persuasion. In little time, Phoebe needed to come, just as much as Stella needed to take her there.

Stella was grateful to have been allowed to make love to Phoebe, not that either of them had uttered those words, and although she was aroused in a way she couldn't recall experiencing with past lovers, she understood Phoebe might not yet be ready to reciprocate. She was wrong.

With silent tears trickling down her face, but clearly experiencing a sense of joy, Phoebe had asked Stella to lie down and allow her to explore every inch of her body. As her fingers slid effortlessly through the slick moisture between Stella's legs, the astonishment on her face caused Stella to laugh. Phoebe appeared amazed to have been the catalyst of such arousal. Stella had reassured her with a smile that she fancied the pants off her. Phoebe held her breath as she nestled her fingers in Stella's opening before finding the courage to push them deep inside. Stella had cried out in relief, and after the initial shock of penetrating someone other than Rebecca, Phoebe focused all her attention on bringing Stella to orgasm. It took less than thirty seconds, and it caused them both to smile. When Stella had adequately recovered, she touched Phoebe again and suggested they try it together. Simultaneously bringing each other to orgasm was the icing on the cake.

Content in her arms, Stella sensed Phoebe crying. "Are you okay, baby?"

"I'm fine." Phoebe sniffed loudly and Stella frowned. "I'm fine, really. I feel free. I was terrified that making love to another woman would erase everything about Rebecca. But it hasn't. I'm so relieved to know that nothing I do," she glanced down to where Stella's hand disappeared between her legs, "or you do, can ever change the way I feel about her. Coming over here and scattering her ashes was all about letting her go. But it hasn't been her I've needed to let go of. It's me. *I* needed to let go."

"Well, you did that all right."

"Shut it, you." Phoebe peeked out the window. Vienna was materialising in the distance. "So…better than Rome?"

"Hey, I liked Rome."

"Liar. I know even the fumbling on the ferry was better than Rome."

Stella kissed her forehead. "I liked looking into your eyes when I came."

"You have a selective memory, Stella. If you remember correctly, I wouldn't allow you to come *until* you opened your eyes."

Stella shrugged. *That's right, and it was as sexy as hell.* "You sure are good with your hands." Stella slipped out from Phoebe's warmth to straddle her, grinning. "Those long, probing fingers you drive so deeply into me are certainly worth the wait."

"You mean these ones?" Phoebe entered her again.

"Uh-huh. That would be them." Stella bit her bottom lip, longing to draw out the sensation by holding back her orgasm. She rode Phoebe's hand until the edge neared.

Phoebe reached up to encircle Stella with her free arm. Stella held on for dear life, forcing Phoebe's head and welcoming mouth to her aching nipples. "Come for me, baby," Phoebe demanded.

"Deeper...God, please..."

Phoebe forced her fingers deeper, firmly massaging Stella's G-spot.

Stella cried at her release, her entire body convulsing as the orgasm, yet again, left her world spinning.

CHAPTER TWENTY-TWO

Even the calming chimes of Stella's phone alarm sent her head spinning. She hadn't arrived late to a meeting with her group ever, and she wasn't about to start. But she didn't remember ever feeling so utterly spent. She and Phoebe had finished the bottle of tequila in their room and continued to make love all night. They had slept intermittently, but nothing substantial. Stella felt old.

Showered, but barely progressing any further, she sat staring, head in her hands, at the instant coffee and dissolving bubbling energy tablet before her.

"You're keen." Phoebe emerged from the bedroom naked and pale.

"We have to meet in the foyer in fifteen minutes. Get a wriggle on." Stella could only produce a raised eyebrow in response to Phoebe's nakedness. She cursed her throbbing temples.

"*We?* I don't think so, honey. Room service and bed is in store for me."

"You're going back to bed?"

"Yep. Once I order some real coffee."

"Give me strength." Stella sipped her coffee and winced at the bitter, strong liquid.

It was mid-afternoon before she began to feel human again. She wasn't alone. With the exception of a handful that went home early complaining of an upset stomach, almost everyone who had been drinking the previous night was feeling sluggish and a little under the weather.

As a treat, Stella ordered pizza. A cure for those feeling seedy while wasting the afternoon on the banks of the Danube, lazing on the lawn, watching the world pass by. She raised her face to the warm sun and lay outstretched amongst some of the more amiable members of her group. Stella could almost feel the greasy pizza soaking up the alcohol sitting stagnant in her stomach. Thankfully, she had nothing else planned for her crew, and regardless, everyone seemed intent on resting up for an evening organised by Russo.

Always a little left field, Russo knew of this quirky underground bowling alley that served cheap schnapps and great burgers. It only housed six lanes, each one glowing under ultraviolet light while classic eighties rock pumped through the sound system. It was a surprising treat and it was Russo's baby, so Stella entrusted the organising to him. She relished the one evening on tour where she could direct all questions his way.

There was no way Stella and Phoebe would touch more than one or two drinks; they were still feeling a little ill from the previous night, but almost everyone else seemed determined to try every flavour of schnapps on the list.

The stamina of some people.

"Can't we use our time a little more effectively?" Phoebe was looking bored.

"I have to be here. I'm sorry."

"I hate this music."

Stella raised her eyebrows. "You can't possibly. It's the eighties. Everybody loves the eighties."

"Okay that's true, but I hate it when I could be doing other things."

"Like what?"

"Like you."

Stella knew Phoebe had come along because it was the only way of spending time with her. Unfortunately, Stella couldn't dedicate her attention entirely to Phoebe, and they were sitting at a small retro table that was growing in numbers. "Fancy some crisps?" Stella addressed the group surrounding her.

Predictably, the response was unanimously in favour of more food. At the bar she waited to be served and chatted with Megan and some others. Every now and then she snuck a peek at Phoebe, pleased she was playing her part and participating in the conversation at the table. Phoebe was adorable when she was sulking, but Stella knew she wouldn't be moody in front of the group. Stella trusted her to uphold their "just friends" charade. In fact, Stella trusted her more than she cared to admit. Phoebe was embedding herself within Stella's psyche, and it was beginning to feel like she'd been there forever.

The moment Stella slid off the stool and her feet hit the ground, the entire place was plunged into darkness. No windows, no lights and even the exit signs were out. This wasn't the type of darkness you stumble through to make it to the toilet in the middle of the night. No, this was oppressive, suffocating darkness. Stella immediately thought of Phoebe. Then she thought of Simon. But before she could melt into full panic mode, girlish screams and grunts of "What the fuck" filled the room.

It was amazing how, in a matter of seconds, chaos could completely reign. Stella had seen people use night vision on the television before. She knew if someone was there, someone who shouldn't be there, like Simon Threadbody, they would see the bedlam as clear as day. And they could also see Phoebe as clear as day.

Stella grappled for her phone with no plan other than to find Phoebe. She wasn't the only one thinking quickly. Some other members of her group, the ones who were happy to carry a phone and pay exorbitant international call rates, also switched on their phones. Dots of light danced in the vast room.

"Phoebe!" Stella didn't care that she was singling out one person in fifty. Although she knew she was probably disorientated, she began to run in the direction she guessed Phoebe may be. After only five steps, her phone light flicked off and she collided with something small, perhaps a stool. Unable to right herself, she tumbled down. Her body was still tender from the beating in Corfu, and landing with a thud and a face full of stale alcohol soaked carpet, Stella flinched at the pain and the hopelessness of the situation.

The sting of her ribs sent her arm up to hold them protectively while in her other hand, Stella fumbled with the phone again. "Phoebe, where are you?" Why wasn't she answering? "Phoebe!"

Stella was escalating from frightened and concerned to terrified and anxiously worried. The darkness and its claustrophobic oppressiveness frustrated her. Just when she was about to scream again, a familiar hand groped in the dark behind her.

"Is that you, Stella?" Phoebe patted her down like she was playing a hands on game of blind man's bluff.

"Why didn't you answer me?" Stella felt like vomiting from sheer relief.

"I called for you, but so did half the group." Phoebe pulled Stella down onto the carpet and used Stella's phone to illuminate a path to the bar. They scrambled behind it.

Stella had to admit she could barely hear herself think.

"This can't be a coincidence, surely," said Phoebe.

"I have no idea how to get out of here. I feel like a sitting duck."

"Whatever happens, Stella, don't let go of my hand, okay?"

Stella nodded then realised Phoebe couldn't see her. "I won't. Trust me. I'm shitting myself right now."

Phoebe grabbed a near empty schnapps bottle off the shelf and, holding the neck, smashed the base of the bottle on the edge of the bar, leaving her holding a jagged edge. "Stay close behind me." She held what remained of the bottle pointing downward in front of her and took Stella's trembling hand. "Let's get out of here."

The very moment Stella rose to her feet, determined just to get out of the damn place, the lights flickered back to life. Other than a few scattered stools and upturned tables, not to mention Phoebe standing with a glass bottle weapon, nothing looked out of place. A member of the bowling alley staff came bursting through the door.

"I'm sorry. The entire building has had a surge. Our generator has only just kicked in. I apologise. Is anyone hurt?"

Stella looked around. Simon or anyone thug-like was nowhere to be seen. She and Phoebe looked at each other. Stella approached the man.

"So it was just an accident?"

"Yes. I'm so sorry. I'll arrange for your group to have a free game."

Stella wasn't worried about that. "And no one switched off the lights or anything like that?"

The man stared at her. "No, ma'am. I've just come from the control panel. I can assure you a surge tripped the system. It's happened before. It's an old building with old wiring on some floors."

Phoebe held the broken bottle aloft. "This must have fallen or something," she lied. "I picked it up so no one would get hurt." She handed the bottle to the grateful man.

Stella's heart raced, and by the look on Phoebe's face, hers did too. The rest of the group, in contrast, found the whole episode hilarious and had righted the tables and stools and was going about their business carefree.

"We jumped to conclusions, right?" Stella and Phoebe sat at the nearest vacant table.

"No, we had every right to be cautious."

"Cautious? I was on the verge of heart failure." Stella leaned in to whisper. "I had Simon in night vision glasses hunting you down, that's how far I let my imagination go. Jesus, and all because the bloody power surged."

Phoebe smiled.

"What?"

"You watch too many movies, Stella."

"Yeah, well, thanks to television and movies, I'm handy with duct tape and I'm pretty sure I can defuse a bomb in less than a minute."

"Really?"

"Of course. It's always the red wire." Stella thought for a moment. "Or is it the blue?"

Phoebe leaned in and her smile faded. "I want to take you back to the hotel."

"Why, Miss Lancaster, I do believe you've made me blush."

Phoebe ran a finger up Stella's inner thigh and winked. "I can make you do more than that."

CHAPTER TWENTY-THREE

Day twenty-one was typically an emotional seesaw. Visiting Mauthausen, a Nazi labour concentration camp, was undoubtedly confronting. Usually, until this point, the crew would have been riding high, but with the ups and down of the last three weeks, this group had already had their fair share of demanding experiences. Stella was dismayed at how this tour could be the best and the worst, all rolled into one.

The incident with Pippy and Stella's two hospital visits, all faded into insignificance next to the atrocities that occurred in concentration camps during World War II. Mauthausen acted as a not-so-subtle reminder to everyone just how lucky they all were.

The majority of the group had coped amazingly well with the tour's little hiccups, but there were some hard nuts to crack. There were always going to be those clients who were never happy, and it was around this time when sleep deprivation and the long succession of hangovers took their toll; tolerance began to wane and tensions were high. Without fail, Mauthausen provided the behavioural readjustment many needed.

The camp was an emotional experience for everyone, but especially for those who were Jewish or who had direct links to World War II. The apprehension was palpable as they neared the site. Stella gave a brief talk on how visiting the camp was emotionally challenging and draining.

Returning to the coach after the tour of the camp was always a sombre affair, but Stella had a job to do. Rightly or wrongly, after some quiet time for reflection, it was her job to rev the troops back up for the tradition of the Munich beer halls.

The hotel in Munich was smack bang in the middle of town, and after leaving her group to shop in Marienplatz, Stella headed to the most expensive Internet café she could find in the hope that her movements would remain undetected. She settled at a computer in the far corner, and opened her newly purchased notepad. Phoebe Lancaster wasn't as smart as she made out if she thought Stella was going to sit idly by while she risked her life. Stella began work.

Her first search was on Oscar Dean. Born in 1953, Oscar continued to disappoint her. Short, with a full head of stark white hair, the formidable man was far from spectacular. Stella sent picture after picture to the colour printer.

Secondly, she researched Simon Threadbody. It was the most thorough search she had undertaken on this man, and she was surprised to find little information about him other than his impressive business and financial credentials. Not surprisingly, there was nothing to suggest he was a thug or a criminal.

Consequently, she trawled through hundreds of photos, searching for any that included brutish looking bodyguards. There was no guarantee the same men would escort Oscar or Simon on overseas jaunts, but Stella was thorough. She needed to cover all bases.

Finally, she searched for pictures of Sebastian, a rather difficult task. It seemed Oscar went to great lengths to protect him from the public eye. After searching fruitlessly for over half an hour, Stella eventually struck gold. Oscar had paraded Sebastian in front of some photographers at a fundraising function for the Sydney Children's Hospital. Not only did Stella now know what Phoebe's little boy looked like, she also had a picture of a woman, possibly his nanny—Phoebe's inside contact.

Three hours and fifty euros later, Stella packed pages of printed photos and information in her satchel and headed to Café Universe, her favourite café in all of Germany. She ordered food and coffee and began piecing together the information, preferring to write down, in her own words, the bios she had printed. In no time, she had filled pages of written scribble with information about Oscar, Simon, Sebastian, and their bodyguards. Age, height, pastimes, etc.

Everything she thought she should know. She noted Oscar's and Simon's keen interest in hunting, fishing, and how, even though Oscar was nearly sixty, he still enjoyed keeping fit, probably something to do with Sebastian.

Stella's phone beeped and she checked a message from Phoebe: *Where are you? Fancy a lay down?* Stella smiled. She had almost finished, and although she had been concentrating on building a portfolio of Oscar's entourage, she had developed a niggling throb in certain parts of her anatomy, desperate for that sated feeling only Phoebe could provide.

So now, with the prospect of a matinee session, Stella's spirits lifted dramatically. She flicked through her notepad one last time. Satisfied with the information it contained, she hid it away and responded to Phoebe, agreeing to meet her at the hotel at four o'clock.

❖

"Where did you disappear to this afternoon?" Phoebe rushed through the door only seconds after Stella, laden with shopping bags.

Stella began a rehearsed lie about meeting up with an old colleague for coffee, before Phoebe interrupted. "Shh, I don't really care." She threw her bags on the tiny sofa. "I've been shopping."

Stella raised her eyebrows at the quantity of bags. "So I see."

"But I can't concentrate on that right now," continued Phoebe, desire in her eyes.

"Want me to give you something to focus your full attention on?"

Stella stood firm as Phoebe came to her, cupping her face before kissing her longingly.

A deep, sexy sigh escaped Stella as her tongue parted Phoebe's lips, forcing her to grip on tightly.

Phoebe slipped a hand beneath Stella's top, roughly pushing her bra aside before urgently fondling Stella's breasts.

"I thought we were going to lie down for a while?" Stella enjoyed Phoebe's hands all over her, undressing her now.

"We will. Soon." Phoebe struggled with the buttons of Stella's shorts. "Jesus, get these off, will you?"

"Are you always so demanding?" Stella stepped out of her shorts.

"Maybe you shouldn't wear underwear tomorrow. I think I like the idea of you naked under your clothes, just for me." Phoebe tugged at Stella's knickers and quickly dipped a finger between her legs.

"That," Stella said, indicating the moisture on Phoebe's finger, "is the reason I have to wear underwear."

"Have you been wet all day?"

"Haven't you?"

"I have, actually. I've thought of nothing but fucking you since this morning." Phoebe stopped as she threw her own bra across the room. "I'm sorry. I meant making love to you."

"It's okay." Stella squeezed Phoebe. "I like that you want to fuck me, and I like that you use the word. Just make sure you make love to me sometimes, too."

"I promise. But for now I want to make you weak at the knees."

"I'm already weak at the knees."

They kissed and groped each other until they were both highly aroused. Phoebe gently asked, "Tell me what you want?"

"I want you." Stella suckled Phoebe's nipples.

"Then tell me how."

"Really?" Stella was hesitant.

"I mean it. Tell me what you want before I take you any way I like."

"Can you save taking me any way you like for later? I kind of like the sound of that."

"Of course. Now tell me what you want."

"Okay." Stella went to the bed and lay on her back. "Straddle me."

Phoebe grinned and rested her knees either side of Stella's hips. She played with Stella's nipples, squeezing and massaging them.

"That's enough. Keep your hands to yourself."

Phoebe cocked her head. "Are you delusional as to the position I'm in as opposed to the rather vulnerable position you're in?"

"Don't test me, Phoebe. Now move up."

Stella felt the thin film of moisture from Phoebe's desire cover her stomach as Phoebe edged upward. Her ability to make Phoebe so wet astounded her.

"Higher," said Stella.

Phoebe moved upward.

"Higher."

Phoebe moved over her chest.

"Come on, Phoebe. Don't make me keep asking."

Phoebe manoeuvred into position, grinning and bracing herself against the wall as Stella's tongue entered her.

CHAPTER TWENTY-FOUR

Having been on this tour far too many times to recall, it was no surprise to Stella that the next few days passed by in a blissful blur. Stella was falling in love. Their night in the Munich beer hall was unremarkable. The only thing Stella remembered was that she and Phoebe had made love before they went, and then again upon their return. Almost everyone on board had become aware that they were sharing a room, but no one really commented or seemed to care—so much for Janet's rules. It would become apparent when the hat went around for tips if any clients had been bothered by the fact that Stella was off limits. Such was the hectic nature of this particular tour, Stella wasn't even sure she should ask for tips. Not for herself anyway. Russo, on the other hand, deserved a medal.

A hot summer's day saw nearly all the group participate in rafting, cycling, swimming, or fishing as they relaxed in Hopfgarten, a quaint Austrian village in the Tyrol. But beyond her official duties, Stella preferred the sanctuary of her hotel room. So, it seems, did Phoebe, testing Stella and her time management skills. Stella utilised every spare minute to her advantage, notching up valuable hours of study time, including taking a crash course in spying and sleuth work via the Internet, paying special attention to the art of following someone. In direct contrast, she found gathering information from Phoebe a difficult task. It was like drawing blood from a stone.

"So, you're awfully calm, given what your plans are in Lucerne tomorrow." Stella mixed a drink for them both.

The icy glare from Phoebe was a clear warning.

"Come on." Stella threw on a T-shirt—this wasn't a conversation to be had naked. "Cut me some slack here. I'm going out of my mind with worry."

"And I thought I was doing such a good job of distracting you."

"The distraction is wonderful, don't get me wrong, but I'm on the verge of making you my prisoner for the next two days simply to keep you safe."

"Well." Phoebe grinned. "Under any other circumstance that would be welcome."

"Let me help. Give me something useful to do."

"The most useful thing you can do is stay out of it so I don't have to worry about you."

"I won't be leaving your side in Lucerne," said Stella.

"You will because you have a tour to look after. Look, honey, leave it to me, okay? I don't want you to get hurt." Phoebe patted the bed next to her, summoning Stella, who refused to budge.

Where the tears came from, Stella didn't know, but they came on strong, and they worked a treat. "I can't stand the thought of something happening to you," she blubbered. "Every second of our time in Lucerne, I'll be beside myself with dread."

Phoebe's harshness softened. She pulled Stella onto the bed, engulfing her in a strong embrace. Stella's body shook under the weight of her fear. She couldn't stop crying.

"Look," Phoebe said. "I can tell you nothing is happening tomorrow. The entire meeting will be done and dusted by lunchtime the following day, okay? So please, stop worrying." Phoebe squeezed tightly. "I promise to call you immediately after it's all over. All going well, you can buy me lunch."

Bingo! Stella at least had a time frame. She needed to push for a location now. Her mind raced through some of Lucerne's most exclusive residential areas. With a few possibilities, she wondered about their proximity to any public places. Surely Phoebe wouldn't be stupid enough to meet too close to where Sebastian lived.

"Will your friend be there? The nanny?"

"Stella! Just let it go."

"*What?* I'm only asking."

Phoebe's frustration was beginning to boil over. "Look, there's nothing to it. I'll meet them somewhere. It will be out in the open, all rather innocent. It won't be a deviation from their normal routine. I'll spend some time with Sebastian, and I'll leave. Simple."

"Simple?" Stella sat up, suspiciously eyeing Phoebe. "What about the bodyguards?"

"What bodyguards? Who said anything about bodyguards?"

Shit! Stella wanted to kick herself. She wasn't cut out for a career in intelligence; that was becoming clear. She quickly recovered. "The ones you said beat you up after you hung about the school." It was a long shot. Phoebe never mentioned they were bodyguards. Stella held her breath.

"Oh, no. It was the school that reported me. He was only a hired thug. Oscar has many of those floating around."

"So, Sebastian only has the nanny to look after him?"

"As far as I know, most of the time it's just his nanny. She has a black belt in karate or something like that. She's no pushover."

Stella wasn't sold. "I find it hard to believe, with all his money, the boy doesn't have a bodyguard."

"He does. She's his nanny." Phoebe laughed. "He's not in line for the throne, you know? Yes, Oscar is a powerful man. Yes, he's well protected, but anyone who's anyone out there knows that to harm Sebastian would be a call to arms. Oscar Dean isn't to be messed with like that. Sebastian has all the protection he needs, I'm sure."

Stella's eyes widened. "See? You just said it yourself. Oscar Dean isn't to be messed with. Phoebe, you have to call this off."

"Calm down. I've no intention of kidnapping him or extorting money. I'm no threat. I only want to meet the boy. That's all."

Stella was far from convinced. She left Phoebe in the bath and made an excuse to leave the room, her satchel slung casually over her shoulder, concealing her precious notepad. She settled in a beautiful beer garden, ordered a refreshing cranberry juice, and jotted down the information Phoebe had disclosed.

Next on the list was an attempt at successfully following someone. She'd downloaded the key steps involved and was keen to put them to the test. The problem she faced was that she wasn't a stranger to Phoebe. The Internet gave endless examples on how to tag someone you didn't know, but this was a unique scenario. Phoebe knew her and probably knew how to detect being followed. For today, however, Stella would practice on a stranger.

Hopfgarten was small, and she might have been overly cautious, but all three targets appeared to remain oblivious to Stella's tailing. She was tested on occasion; one target frequently stopping while Stella continued on, finding a hiding place and then picking the target up later. She pretended to be on a call once or twice and rushed past her target, again conveniently picking them up shortly afterward. It was a good result, and the experience yielded valuable lessons, all aiding her master plan. Yes, additional concentration was required, but she returned to the hotel satisfied with her progress.

CHAPTER TWENTY-FIVE

Stella struggled to keep her eyes open as the coach sped along the autobahn toward Lucerne. Last night she had intended to snuggle up to Phoebe and rest, desperate for a full night's sleep before rising early to study her notes. Phoebe, it seemed, had other plans.

Their lovemaking had been intense, experimental, and had lasted for hours. Phoebe had made it count, exploring Stella's body entirely. It fleetingly crossed Stella's mind that Phoebe could have lied, that today was the day, but there was nothing she could do about that now. *Please let it be tomorrow.*

On the outskirts of the picturesque city of Lucerne, Stella handed out her city map, spoke about Lucerne itself, and arranged to meet the group at a coach park late that afternoon. A trip up Mt. Pilatus was planned for the evening, arriving at the summit via cog rail, dining in the famous restaurant with stunning views, before descending via cable cars as the sun slowly set. With the amazing weather they were experiencing, it would be a memorable sight.

The best way Stella knew to describe Lucerne, was crisp and fresh. It would often seem like all the beautiful people lived in this city—even Stella could feel a little intimidated in Switzerland.

It would be late by the time they reached their accommodation, and the hotel bar was the gathering place that evening. All in all, this left Stella a mere two hours to prepare. While her group were exploring, or most likely shopping, she hurried to her first stop, a cheap department store three blocks away from the bustling souvenir and watch stores that hugged the Reuss River. With time at a premium,

Stella went directly to the boys' clothing section and selected an entire outfit.

The fitting room assistant gazed at her with a confused expression, but Stella ignored her and secured herself behind the locked door and stripped. First she tested the shorts—dark brown with light blue writing down the side. They fit. Next, she slipped on a white T-shirt and was amazed at how androgynous she looked. She slid on a white cap and hardly recognised herself. As per the instructions on the Internet, a disguise was required for the difficult task of tailing someone known to you. The tricky part was to appear different from your usual self, without standing out in a crowd. Stella was pleased with her progress, and after carefully selecting additional items, made her purchase and delivered the goods to the hotel.

She tipped the contents of the shopping bag on to the bed and quickly ripped off the tags, scrunching the clothes in an attempt to tarnish that crisp, new look. She stripped again and stood before the mirror to tightly wrap wide bandaging around her chest, flattening her modest breasts. Stella attempted this three times until she could secure it swiftly in place in less than fifteen seconds. The boy's underpants, with the trendy thick waistband, were surprisingly comfortable, and the shorts went with them nicely, low-slung and trendy. The cheap runners looked too new, so she opened the window and scraped them along the roughly rendered sill. Next she threw the white cap on the ground and stomped all over it—no kid had a clean white hat. Stella then extricated the insides of cheap bud-shaped earphones, leaving only the shell. They were an effective prop, but she needed to be able to hear.

Finally, she stood appraising herself in the full-length mirror. *Would Phoebe recognise me?* She hoped not. This was her only chance.

With her supplies stuffed in a cheap skater-boy backpack, she squeezed it into the bottom drawer of the bedside table before calling Phoebe.

"Hey, you. Where have you been?" A hint of annoyance crept into Phoebe's voice.

Stella remained firm. "You do realise I'm working at the moment, don't you? I had a few things to attend to for the girls in the office."

"Oh, okay. I missed you this afternoon, that's all." Stella experienced a pang of guilt at Phoebe's kind words. "Melanie and I found a great shopping arcade and we've gorged ourselves on fondue."

Phoebe sounded so calm, and Stella realised there had probably been enough time that afternoon to meet up with Sebastian. She was relieved to know nothing had happened, but it was unnerving to hear that Phoebe had spent a relaxing afternoon with Melanie. For her own part, she had rushed around making last-minute preparations in her attempt to provide Phoebe with a second pair of ears and eyes, albeit without Phoebe's knowledge.

But Phoebe was a planner. She was methodical and detail driven and certainly wouldn't have waited until today, the last minute, to finalise this operation. The stress Stella was experiencing was hers alone. Phoebe was calm and most likely on schedule.

The cog rail journey to the summit of Mt. Pilatus, the steepest in the world, produced the obligatory wonderment at ascending a mountainside with a maximum gradient of forty-eight percent. But it was the anticipation of the impending activities that excited most, and only a handful let fear overcome them. Those with an adventurous spirit could toboggan over a kilometre down the mountain or experience the thrill of the giant tubing slide, over sixty metres long. The photo opportunities atop Mt. Pilatus were endless, and Stella was required to pose for many group shots.

She was relieved to finally remove the fake smile from her face and sit opposite Phoebe and sip coffee. She felt safe up here. In contrast, looking down on beautiful Lucerne, she felt nothing but dread. She attempted to relax, but was a million miles away, her mind constantly flashing with images of Oscar, Simon Threadbody, the nanny, Sebastian, and beefcake bodyguards with dark sunglasses and thick necks matching their thick heads.

"Where are you, Stella?" Phoebe asked, worry in her eyes.

"Pardon?"

"Just now. You certainly weren't here with me. Where did you go?"

It crossed Stella's mind to tell the truth, tell Phoebe how worried she was, how eagerly she wanted to help. But she wasn't willing to upset Phoebe now. She convinced herself lying was for the greater good. "I was thinking about last night." Stella managed a lazy wink. "I think I'm exhausted."

"Really? You actually look worried."

"Can you blame me?" Stella wanted to wring Phoebe's neck, beg her not to go, but it was imperative she remain calm. "I'm focusing on taking you to lunch tomorrow so we can celebrate your successful morning and the fact that you managed to stay alive." Although Phoebe had voiced concern about the lengths Oscar would go to protect his grandson, Stella had pushed the disturbing thoughts to the far reaches of her mind. Safety in numbers and providing a witness, should it all go pear shaped, was Stella's focus. She wanted to be available to call the authorities or provide backup if required. What she hoped, beyond anything, was to be a silent observer with Phoebe never having to know she was there. She pushed her luck one last time. "So, what's the latest I can expect your call?"

Phoebe frowned.

"Look, I'm going to be worried sick. I *am* worried sick. You've planned this, I know you have, so I'm guessing you have a definitive start and finish time." Stella raised her eyebrows defiantly. "So, when can I expect a call to breathe a sigh of relief and stop worrying?"

Phoebe's features softened. "Midday. I promise to call you no later than midday."

"And will you be close by?"

The look Phoebe gave Stella was more than enough to indicate the conversation was over.

❖

The group struggled to settle through dinner. Pumped full of adrenaline and astounded by the views from the mountaintop restaurant, they chatted loudly and as usual, it was a rowdy descent via the cable cars with a spectacular sunset providing the backdrop.

Russo was a maniac on the ride to the hotel, and even though it was nearly ten thirty by the time the last person was handed their room key, the group were keen to drink late, and unfortunately, Stella was obliged to at least make an appearance.

Predictably, Phoebe declined. She was snug in bed by the time Stella was heading out.

"Don't be too long, eh?" Phoebe yawned.

"I'll try not to wake you."

"Don't worry about that. I'm used to the curve of your body now." A shy little grin twisted the corners of her mouth. "I look forward to bedtime when I can pull you close." Phoebe was lying on her side and indicated the space in front of her. "You belong here," she said. "In my arms."

In that moment, something in Stella broke. Snapped completely. The fraying thread she clutched so tightly, the thin cotton-like tendon that linked her to reality, albeit a fragile link, gave way. She had fallen headfirst in love with Phoebe Lancaster. This was suddenly very serious. Up until that moment, Stella had been moved more by Phoebe's actions, rather than her words. Although always improving, Phoebe often struggled to articulate how she was feeling. Stella experienced a warm sensation build in her stomach and it filled her with happiness. This time, Stella was lost for words.

"Hey, aren't you forgetting something?" Phoebe filled the silence.

Stella checked for her wallet, phone, and room key. "No. What?"

"You don't know?"

"Phoebe, what?"

Phoebe pointed to her cheek. "Kiss?"

Tomorrow loomed. For a brief moment, Stella had let it slip her mind. Now, staring down at Phoebe, Stella wanted to cry, beg, and magically transport them beyond tomorrow morning, to safety. Instead, she swallowed hard, crossing the room to gently kiss Phoebe.

"Don't be long, lover."

Stella rushed for the door. She had to escape. She waited for many moments in the hall, gaining composure, before crossing the courtyard to the bar and ordering a double vodka.

The group were understandably in good spirits. Adrenaline and alcohol was a sure-fire combination for a fun evening. Thinking back, it felt surreal and difficult to believe one tour could contain so many undesirable incidents. What wasn't difficult to believe was the terror she felt in Corfu. Now, less than a fortnight later, she was preparing to don a disguise and follow her lover through Lucerne in an attempt to keep her safe from God-only-knows who. This unknown factor was Stella's greatest worry. Her preparation had been the best she could hope for under the circumstances, but was it enough?

At midnight, the crowd began to thin. Stella looked on in amusement as all the single girls chasing Russo slowly departed one by one. He was busy playing cards with a group of boys, uncharacteristically focused on winning poker rather than scoring a girl for the night.

CHAPTER TWENTY-SIX

At six in the morning, logic told Stella that it was highly unlikely Phoebe would be meeting her son so ridiculously early, but there was no way she could sleep again. Her heart raced as nervousness gripped her.

It was too late now for any more studying, planning, or scheming. All that remained to do was worry.

Determined not to be caught off guard, Stella rose at seven and silently showered. She was unwilling to let Phoebe out of her sight and sat in the uncomfortable wicker chair opposite the bed and watched her sleep.

Her unoccupied mind clicked through bad scenario after bad scenario. Her phone provided some distraction. She played cards, deleted old and unwanted contacts, played hangman until the three-letter words became unbearable, texted her mum—even though she knew she probably wouldn't reply until later—and although she despised Sudoku, she managed a game or two of that. Finally, when Stella was close to climbing the walls, Phoebe woke.

"What are you doing?" Phoebe wiped sleep from the corner of her eyes.

"What? Nothing. Why?"

"Are you just sitting there watching me?"

"What's wrong with that? I like you. I'm allowed to look at you."

"You *like* me?"

"Uh-huh. You're okay."

"Really? Just okay?" Phoebe propped herself on one elbow, her pyjama top revealing much of her cleavage.

"Well." Stella moved to the edge of the bed. "I suppose you're better than just okay." She poked her finger toward Phoebe's top, pulling it down further and leaning forward to take a peak.

Phoebe brushed her away. "I think you have to *really* like someone before you can have free, unobstructed access down their top."

"Okay. I really like you."

"How much?"

"Loads. More than you'll ever know. Want me to show you?" Stella winked.

"Nice try. But I need to get up. Stuff to do today." Stella frowned "Now, come on." Phoebe kissed Stella deeply. "I promise to make it up to you tonight."

"Tonight? Don't for one second think we won't be back here immediately after lunch."

"You're awfully demanding. I assume you're waiting to eat breakfast with me? Last supper perhaps?"

The bottom felt like it fell out of Stella's stomach. She ushered Phoebe into the bathroom and paced back and forth, attempting to refocus on the task at hand. As Phoebe hummed under the running water, Stella mentally recapped her plan.

At breakfast, neither of them ate substantially. Stella drank two coffees and poured a third before reminding herself that being distracted with an unrelenting desire to pee, was ill-advised. Worried now that she had already drunk too much, she buttered cold toast and forced it down in the hope it might act as a sponge.

"Well." Stella rose from her chair. "I have some errands to run for Janet." She rolled her eyes as part of the routine. "So, you'll ring me, yes? At about midday?"

Phoebe appeared lost for words at the abrupt departure, but only momentarily. The brief wave of surprise was soon replaced with her usual composed demeanour. "By midday. I promise."

The dining room had started to fill up. Stella surveyed at least half her crew. "I can't kiss you here, sorry."

Phoebe nodded. "I understand."

The knot in Stella's stomach tightened. "You stay safe, okay." It wasn't a request. It was an order.

"By midday, honey. I promise."

Stella had nothing else to say, but everything to lose. She forced a smile and returned to the room.

The instant Phoebe was out of sight, adrenaline surged through her, and she focused one hundred percent on the task at hand. She had no idea exactly how long Phoebe would take to make a move but wasted no time in gathering her pre-packed satchel and rushing from the hotel. It wasn't even eight thirty, but Stella wasn't taking any chances.

Stella knew the street well, crossed the road and slipped through her favourite arcade before weaving her way back through the adjoining alleyway, effectively sneaking through the rear of the shops on the arcade front.

"Hey, Stella. What are you doing back here? What's wrong with the front door these days?"

Excellent! It was Maxwell, café owner and long-time friend. Maxwell's had provided a much needed escape on many occasions when she first began touring. She had sought solace there long before she learned to substitute alcohol for soft drink, long before the client-free evening was scheduled in Corfu, and long before she realised taking time out in a hotel bar was deemed an open invitation for absolutely everyone to invade your personal space and quiet time. It was Maxwell who'd first said to her, "Stop babysitting those people, Stella. They are grown adults." He'd also added, "And stop drinking so much. You drink like a grown man, yet you must have the liver of a child."

Yes, Maxwell was exactly who Stella had hoped to see. "Ah, Maxwell, you handsome man. I have a big favour to ask, and I'm in a big hurry."

Stella had the lie already planned; she was playing a trick on Russo and needed to use the bathroom. She would change into her disguise and take up a vantage point in the front of the café. She told Maxwell she had to wait until the signal came from her crew before rushing out the door. Hook, line, and sinker, Maxwell swallowed it and became excited to be part of the setup. "I'll bring you coffee, Stella, make you look less obvious."

Within seconds, Stella emerged from the bathroom looking like a young boy, her chest expertly flattened by the bandage, her earphones in place, and her shorts slung comfortably low.

Maxwell ushered her to a window table and, inhaling deeply, Stella attempted to control her exhilaration and anxiousness all at once. She glanced at her watch and sighed. Since leaving breakfast, it had taken less than ten minutes to be in place. Her eyes remained on the hotel entrance as she stuffed her mobile phone into her left hand shorts pocket. She removed a small canister of pepper spray from the backpack and secreted that securely in her waist band, fearful it may look suspicious elsewhere.

As per advice obtained on the Internet, Stella had changed her mobile ring tone. It was advisable to have your phone on silent, but she preferred not to in case Phoebe needed her. There was no guarantee, in the heat of the moment, that she would feel the thing vibrate silently in her pocket. Her hands needed to be free, so holding it was out of the question. Phoebe had heard Stella's phone ring numerous times, and recent studies indicated that people identified ring tones of friends and family, sparking recognition in their mind and an association to the person whose phone was ringing. The last thing Stella needed was her phone to go off near Phoebe and the recognition of the ring tone draw attention to her.

Stella was completely over-thinking the situation. She shifted the backpack on the chair next to her about ten times in preparation for a dash out the door. She could do nothing now but watch and wait, praying that Phoebe hadn't slipped past her already.

Stella waited.

And waited. She constantly glanced at her watch. Eight forty-five came and went, and Stella watched her untouched cup of coffee go cold. Eight fifty-five, and Maxwell slid a ham and cheese croissant in front of her, laughing that perhaps the joke was on her. Ten past nine, no movement, although Stella could have done with a visit to the bathroom, except now it was out of the question. Nine thirty and Stella's phone startled her, her leg knocking the table, spilling the cold coffee. She groped like a mad woman before pulling the phone from her pocket. She was disappointed it wasn't Phoebe but answered, her eyes refocusing on the hotel entrance. "Hey, Russo. What's up?"

"Well, don't sound so happy to hear from me."

"I'm thrilled, trust me."

"Yeah, whatever. Look, have you had breakfast? Fancy a slap up treat at Maxwell's? My shout."

Maxwell's? Shit! Think! Then, as if miraculously in secret agent mode, Stella replied, "No thanks, buddy, not today, and you don't want to either. I just walked past Max's, and a whole bunch of our lot are packed in there. I'd give it a miss if I were you."

Russo sighed. "Little bastards. Why can't they be satisfied with the hotel? Oh well, I might stay in bed for another hour or so then, hit the cafés for lunch. Ring me if you're at a loose end. Although by then, you and Miss Lancaster might be gazing into each other's eyes over some very sticky fondue." Russo laughed at himself.

"Bugger off, Russo."

"Love you too, babe."

The line went dead.

Stella settled back and resumed her wait.

Jesus, I'm not cut out for this. She seriously began to wonder if Phoebe had snuck out another way. The thought of being nowhere near Phoebe when she met up with Sebastian caused a nauseating ache in her already knotted stomach.

Her torment was short-lived. Stella launched into action only minutes later when, dressed in tailored navy shorts, runners, and a singlet top, Phoebe strode purposefully from the hotel entrance.

"I gotta go, Max." Stella hurried from the café, ignoring Max's excitement as he rushed from the kitchen to see her off.

She fell into step, keeping approximately ten metres behind Phoebe. In contrast to what it was supposed to do, her disguise left her feeling vulnerable and exposed. At this juncture, the battle was winning the mind games in her head and maintaining composure. She inhaled slowly and focused. Stella altered her gait in an attempt to walk like a young boy, that is, she hunched over and scuffed her feet, imagining for a moment she had a pair of socks stuffed down her knickers. Without appearing too obvious, she checked her phone, ensuring it wasn't on silent and was accessible in her left pocket. She found it disconcerting to have both earphone buds in, so she removed one and ensured the cord was secure and plugged into absolutely nothing down her T-shirt. Finally, Stella adjusted the backpack so it clung snugly to her small frame and relaxed into her boy stride.

She remained on the lookout for anyone with an air of familiarity. It was true that perhaps Oscar didn't even know Phoebe was in the country, but it was also a possibility that Simon Threadbody knew exactly where she was. She needed to be in the zone, prepared and alert.

The time was nudging nine forty-five, but the pace hadn't quickened. Based on this, if Stella knew Phoebe well enough, the scheduled time to meet Sebastian was most likely ten thirty. Phoebe would arrive early and survey the area. Phoebe's methodical planning gave Stella a morsel of comfort.

Bathed in gorgeous sunshine, they appeared to be walking in the direction of one of Lucerne's most affluent inner city suburbs. The tree-lined avenues were home to huge townhouses, all protected by solid wrought iron fences or thick, well pruned hedges, far too high to see over. Stella had studied the map umpteen times, so this was not unexpected. Unfortunately, there were few reasons for tourists to visit this way, so it became more challenging to blend in with a crowd.

Without warning, Phoebe stopped, pulling to the side to answer her phone. *Shit!* Stella had been too preoccupied scanning the area and visualizing the map to be prepared for this. With only the slightest falter in her stride, and against all her instincts, she continued on, head down. Don't stop, she repeated over and over in her head. Stella cursed her lack of focus; she should have been expecting the unexpected. Reading on the Internet that you should continue past your subject and pick them up later was one thing, but actually passing within a metre of Phoebe was another. Stella's racing heart pounded in her chest, amplified by the tight bandaging that she was sure, all of a sudden, constricted her breathing.

From beneath the brim of her hat, she saw Phoebe lean against a thick stone wall, speaking into her handset. Panic gripped Stella; Phoebe was staring back up the street, directly at her. Was her disguise good enough? Would being found out jeopardise their relationship and Phoebe's attempts to see her son? She fought against every cell in her body not to stop. It all looked and sounded so easy in theory. She pushed onward, her ears filling with the sound of fear. Stella gritted her teeth, and despite herself, lowered her head even further.

Just as she was about to pass, Phoebe turned toward the wall, her back to Stella, oblivious to everything. Stella glanced around hurriedly sucking in deep breaths to regain what little composure she had. Her next step was to locate an appropriate place to pull over and wait for Phoebe in order to resume her tail. Twenty metres away, on the opposite side of the road, she spotted a bus stop. Every instruction she'd read on the Internet told her not to look back and it took all her will power not to check that Phoebe hadn't shot off in another direction. Stella crossed the street and strode toward the sheltered bus stop.

Every move she made was fraught with the possibility that she was over exaggerating and drawing attention to herself. She slouched like she imagined a young teenager would and pretended to read the timetable. She was indescribably relieved to watch Phoebe finish her conversation and resume her journey.

The entire area was littered with carefully manicured parks occupying street corners. Some parks were private, only accessible to those lucky enough to live in the houses on the immediate perimeter, but many were open to the general public. Stella hoped to God if the meeting was in a park, it was a public one.

After leaving a suitable distance, she crossed back over the road again to resume her tail. They walked for only another two blocks before Phoebe turned left into a well-equipped children's playground. This reserve was nestled on a long narrow strip with streets at each end and old, expensive apartment buildings on either side. Trees and wooden play equipment were strewn the length of the park atop lush green grass.

If she knew Phoebe as well as she thought she did, she guessed she would be stopping soon at a vantage point allowing her to scan both entrances and the full length of the park. Stella began wandering toward a large tree to take cover. She passed a serious battle taking place between what looked like a herd of plastic dinosaurs and a fleet of Matchbox cars. She nodded awkwardly at a group of mothers, before finally reaching her destination.

There had been no script to follow on the Internet in relation to the actions of a teenage boy loitering in a park, so on the off chance that Phoebe, or anyone else for that matter, happened to be looking in her direction, she wanted to appear authentic. Drama was hardly her favourite subject at school, but she casually threw her backpack on the ground and slumped against the tree trunk fiddling with her phone.

Most kids these days barely looked up they were so used to staring at the tiny screen. She wouldn't win an award for her acting, but then in her experience, most teenage boys looked awkward anyway. Phoebe settled on a bench about thirty meters away, checking her watch.

Stella's position wasn't ideal, but it would have to do. Due to the trees, in which she sought some cover, her vision of both entrances was partially obscured. A better vantage point would have her too near the clearing and perhaps too obvious.

If Stella had thought she was nervous before, it compared little to how she felt now. Now, she was terrified. She could feel the bandage around her chest moistening with sweat, and it took remarkable concentration to stop her legs from jiggling. She wondered how long she could slouch like a bored teenager before raising suspicions. At ten twenty-five, after noticing Phoebe stare in her direction for a long time, Stella shifted her hat a little lower. She knew she wasn't supposed to, that kind of manoeuvre attracted attention instead of deflecting it, but her nerves were frail. She clenched her jaw. Phoebe looked away, but then, following the new direction of Phoebe's stare, Stella realised she could have removed all her clothes, stood on her head, and still not attracted Phoebe's attention.

From the far end of the park, Stella watched a woman arrive hand in hand with a young child. Sebastian was a fine looking boy.

The greeting appeared awkward. Hesitantly, Phoebe embraced the nanny with a brief hug and a peck on the cheek. Next, the introduction to her son—Stella had no idea if he was of average height for his age, but Phoebe knelt on one knee, extending her hand to the shy, unsure young boy. Stella hadn't realised she was holding her breath until her lungs demanded air. Of course, watching all this unfold was like watching a slide show. Stella couldn't watch everything at once. She looked periodically toward Phoebe and her son, between scanning both park entrances and keeping check on the nanny. Phoebe must have suggested she push Sebastian on the swing because like a shot, they raced to the long line of swings and she began pushing him, high and fast.

Besides the anxious knot in her stomach, Stella was touched by the reunion. Although Sebastian would have no recollection of the last time they were together, Phoebe had given birth to that little boy, and Stella was so pleased for her to finally be reunited, albeit for an agonisingly brief encounter. Also in the back of her mind was the tiny wave of relief that confirmed Phoebe had been telling the truth. Seeing for herself a proud mother play with the child she had never really met, alleviated many of Stella's harboured seeds of doubt.

Stella pushed all sentiment aside and regained her focus. Besides a handful of teenagers and families strolling through the park or settling on a picnic rug, there wasn't a great deal of action, but she remained vigilant. As much as she loved the fact that Phoebe was at last meeting her son, the tension was almost palpable. The sooner they were out of this park, Lucerne, and even Switzerland, the better.

From the moment Sebastian arrived, time slowed down, and Stella found herself checking her watch every few minutes. Phoebe and Sebastian moved from the swings to the slide, from the slide to the roundabout, and then began a game of checkers on the life-size board. Stella felt creepy, watching over the top of her phone.

The park really was beautiful. Nearing lunchtime, it began to fill up with twenty-somethings playing Frisbee, groups of middle-aged couples enjoying bocce, and countless mothers with prams and toddlers.

At eleven twenty, Stella could almost taste the end relief, it was so close. Phoebe had promised to call her by midday, so this little party would be coming to an end soon. She had suspected Phoebe's time with her son would be about an hour, any longer and his absence may have been suspicious. It had all gone so smoothly, her preparation was well worth the effort. In less than ten minutes, all this stress could be put behind them.

Yes, falling deeply in love with Phoebe Lancaster was going to be amazing. She's mine, Stella thought as she watched Phoebe scruff the hair of her little boy. She hoped Phoebe could work something out with Oscar in relation to custody of Sebastian, but whether it was just the two of them or a threesome, it made Stella astoundingly happy.

Then it all went wrong. Horribly wrong.

CHAPTER TWENTY-SEVEN

The nanny's phone rang and her head snapped around. Stella followed her gaze. Her eyes locked on a man dressed in jeans and a smart jacket entering the same gate she and Phoebe had passed through on the north side. The man was too far away to pinpoint exact features, but it didn't matter; she knew who he was.

Stella had a split second to make a decision. Should she cause a commotion, head toward him and hope Phoebe saw the kerfuffle in time enough to leg it? Although she knew Phoebe was on high alert, this was the son she hadn't seen growing up. Would she be too engrossed in Sebastian to escape in time? Beyond this, there was also the real risk of Stella being caught if she distracted him too closely. If he discovered she was disguised, the outcome was unpredictable. Her fate would be in his filthy hands.

Her time was up. Stella swung her pack over her shoulders and crossed the middle of the park. Exposed and no longer amongst the shelter of the trees, she hurried toward Phoebe.

"Mum. Mum! I want to go now!"

Stella advanced at a rapid pace and Phoebe's face indicated that she recognised Stella's voice, if not her appearance. Either way, it had the desired effect. Phoebe's eyes left Stella and focused on something behind her.

Stella chanced a quick glance in the same direction and clocked sight of the man striding toward them, pressing his fingers on an ear piece and speaking into what Stella guessed was a concealed microphone.

"We need to go now!" Stella's tone was serious, but her voice trembled with fear. She tightly secured Phoebe's hand. There was no time to make this little drama presentation any more authentic. Phoebe grabbed her bag from the park bench, bid the nanny and Sebastian a quick good-bye, and marched off, dragging Stella along behind her.

"Fuck, Stella. Do you know who that is?"

"Yes. I know. And I'm guessing he knows who we are, too."

"It would be too much to expect him to just be satisfied with scaring us off."

Stella glanced behind her. The man kept his stride, marching past Sebastian and ignoring the young boy's attempts to greet him. In fact, the man brushed the child aside without even flinching. "He's still coming, Phoebe!"

They weaved through the barriers designed to stop motorcycles from entering the park and burst onto the street, Stella heading one way, Phoebe the other.

"This way," Phoebe snapped.

Stella recovered and accelerated to catch up. She saw the man, less than twenty metres from the gate. "Should we split up?" she asked, following Phoebe across the road.

"No. We have to stick together."

As they rounded the street corner, Phoebe's long stride found her a metre or two in front of Stella who was struggling to keep up. Stella checked again and the man turned the corner after them, breaking into a steady run. Stella wondered how they would maintain their pace for an extended period of time, let alone increase it.

"We can't outrun him," panted Stella.

In response, Phoebe darted up a narrow alleyway. Stella knew what she had in mind, but they just couldn't seem to put enough distance between them and him. There was no time to disappear and hide.

"Follow my lead." Phoebe pulled bins over to obstruct the path in the narrow alley and Stella followed suit.

They gained precious seconds when he tripped over the contents, but was it enough? All Stella and Phoebe could do was run for their lives.

Stella's legs were burning from lactic acid build-up, especially her thighs, and she wondered how far you could push your heart to pump valuable oxygen around your body before it gave up. She refused to consider the consequences facing them if they were caught.

Stella checked behind. Yet again, the distance was closing. Their hunter pressed on, relentlessly leaping over every obstacle before him.

In one last-ditch effort, Phoebe pulled Stella left down a narrow path, and then right behind a block of flats.

Stella recognised they had made a critical miscalculation.

CHAPTER TWENTY-EIGHT

Simon Threadbody pulled up, gasping as he rounded the corner. Stella and Phoebe had their backs against a brick wall. Nowhere to run and nowhere to hide. His prey was trapped. He whistled aloud and hunched over to draw some much needed oxygen.

Stella wanted to wipe the smug grin off his face, but she could barely breathe, let alone muster enough energy for a bodily assault. Regardless, Simon was almost twice her size.

He made a show of his flashy equipment when he pressed something in his jacket pocket and said. "Track my GPS signal and get Oscar to me right away." His gruff voice was nothing like the sophisticated persona he conveyed, but then, neither was his posh tone. He paused to listen to a voice on the other end. "Just tell him Phoebe Lancaster is *dying* to see him."

If the gruelling sprint through the affluent streets of Lucerne hadn't knocked the wind from Stella, she found herself desperate for every precious breath now. Her pathetic effort to eat breakfast plagued her, and although she attempted to keep the food down, she threw up the entire contents of her stomach and stumbled along the wall, lightheaded and dizzy.

Simon laughed.

Phoebe pulled Stella close and glared at him. "You shut your mouth."

He shrugged and paraded back and forth in front of them, his chest puffing out triumphantly with every breath regained. "Hey, I'm as surprised as you that she lasted that long. She's improved since last time."

"What?" Phoebe stood protectively between Stella and Simon. "What do you mean?"

"Well, last time I chased that little minx, she gave up well before today's big effort." He winked at Phoebe. "She must be trying to impress her latest squeeze."

Stella stepped from behind Phoebe. "So, it *was* you?"

This time Simon laughed long and hard. "Yes, you stupid little dyke. Jesus, I tried to warn you about this one." He pointed to Phoebe. "But, oh no, little Miss Smartass here knows best. You don't take a hint, do you? You fucking thick or something?"

"Simon!" Phoebe barked. "Don't you dare speak to her like that."

He advanced toward Stella, frowning menacingly. "You get about with a murderer, seriously dangerous things begin to happen around you and to you, and you flat out refuse to heed *one* warning," he said. "That, in my book, makes you a very silly little girl indeed."

Adrenaline was again beginning to surge through Stella. She could take all the insults anyone spat at her, but she would not tolerate Simon Threadbody, a piece of scum, accusing Phoebe of murder. "We all know who killed Rebecca, Simon."

"You know nothing, stupid girl," he spat.

"So, you were sent to hunt me?" Phoebe spoke calmly. It seemed Simon didn't scare her at all.

"Come now, Phoebe. Do you really think if I'd been sent to hunt you, you'd be standing there alive?" He chuckled to himself. "I could have killed you a million times over by now."

"Then what?" Phoebe asked. "Are you just playing a little game? Toying with your prey?"

"Don't be so bloody melodramatic. You've watched too many movies. Oscar asked me to have you followed, see what you were up to." He shook his head. "What were you thinking? Coming to Europe wasn't a smart thing to do, my girl."

"I should have known Oscar was behind this. As if you'd have the authority to hunt me," said Phoebe.

Simon's head snapped toward her. "I have all the damn authority I need. Tailing you myself was *my* idea." He sighed. "Although it didn't begin well. That poor girl on the Metro was a slight miscalculation." He shrugged and smiled as Phoebe and Stella exchanged glances when they realised he was talking about Pippy. "Besides that though, the little traumas you encountered along the way were just a bit of fun. No harm intended."

"You beat the daylights out of her." Phoebe pointed to Stella. "That was just a bit of fun, was it?"

He shrugged. "Well, *I* enjoyed myself."

Stella was beginning to crack under the insanity and pressure of the situation. She thought she was going to be raped in Corfu. Was this bastard really going to rape her? Her sweaty palms, her racing heart, and the sense that she could wet her pants at any moment were a testament to her fear. Although a tiny voice inside her head warned her not to antagonise Simon, a stronger and louder voice in her heart was taking a different route, for a very different reason. "You could have killed me, you asshole. But you'd be used to that feeling wouldn't you? Wouldn't exactly be the first time you found yourself with blood on your hands."

Simon glanced from Stella to Phoebe and back again. "She told you *I* did it, right?"

"I *know* you did it!"

"No." Simon became serious. "You *want* to believe I did it. You *need* to believe I did it, because if I didn't"—he flippantly pointed toward Phoebe—"she did. And you can't possibly be in love with a murderer, can you?" Simon was a showman with a captive audience. "Well, I suggest you learn to watch your back, young lady. One day you just might find yourself with a kitchen knife firmly lodged in it."

"Are you still spinning that line, Simon?" Phoebe's tone was venomous, and Stella was proud of her composure.

Simon ignored Phoebe, addressing Stella again. "You've got a fiery lover on your hands there. I warn you not to provoke suspicion in your relationship. My darling Rebecca's death was a consequence of her mistrust."

Stella noticed Phoebe flinch at Simon's term of endearment, but she pressed on regardless. "Phoebe mistrusted Rebecca, so she killed her? Hardly makes sense."

"I thought you'd be a better liar, Simon. You aren't really what I expected." Stella had gained confidence from Phoebe's strength. "First you tell the police an intruder killed Rebecca, and now you're adamant it was Phoebe."

Simon shrugged. His indifference grated Stella, and she hated him even more.

"Seems everyone did it but you. How convenient. But then, you were cooking the books, weren't you?"

Simon laughed. "Have you been telling little tales, Phoebe? Tut, tut, tut." The smug grin appeared again. "If I gave a fuck, I'd invite you to check the books for yourself. You'll find nothing to substantiate your hollow claim." He was becoming impatient and eyed Phoebe. "I think this little charade of yours has gone on long enough. Perhaps you should consider yourself lucky to be a free woman and be grateful you appear to have committed the perfect murder."

Stella couldn't let it go. "Do you really expect me to believe she just walked up and stabbed Rebecca?"

"Oh shut up, you insidious idiot. The truth won't make you feel better about fucking a murderer." Simon lowered his voice. "You lick the pussy of a cold-blooded killer. Deal with it."

"Enough!" Phoebe had turned deathly pale. She took Stella's hand. "I have something to tell you."

Stella's heart sank. She wasn't expecting this. A movie, played in fast forward, recounting the last few weeks, streamed across her eyes. She didn't want to hear this. "It's okay. I believe you." Stella thought if she said it aloud it would be true. "You already explained it to me, didn't you? You told me the truth, right?"

"Please, just listen to me."

Stella nodded, dread filled her.

"I heard them arguing in the kitchen. I'd been watching a movie, but I'd stopped it to take a call. When the call was over I went to the toilet, and that's when I heard them arguing."

"Do you really think she's going to believe you?" interrupted Simon.

Phoebe pushed on. "Suddenly, I found myself standing between Simon and Rebecca. We were all screaming at each other. Simon brought up the crap about Oscar wanting Rebecca to marry him. He said I was just a useless dyke who needed a good fucking by a real man. I couldn't control my anger and I told him he'd have to pay for sex for the rest of his life, just like he'd done for years. It was stupid and childish to goad him. I infuriated him. I disgusted him and he picked up a knife."

Stella looked toward Simon.

He laughed. "Oh, I'm as intrigued as you are to hear this little tale of shite."

Stella returned her attention to Phoebe who continued. "Rebecca began screaming at him to put it down. I was screaming at her to get out, and screaming at him for threatening her and especially with a knife. Simon was screaming at us both. Then, it happened so quickly I can barely recall it. Simon came at me, red with rage, the knife raised. He looked me in the eye, and I knew he'd gone completely mad."

Simon lunged for Phoebe, grabbing her by the throat. "You be careful what you say next, you little bitch."

"Get off her!" Stella launched herself on his back and he released his grip. She doubted her actions caused him to let go, more that Oscar was probably only minutes away.

"What are you afraid of, Simon?" said Phoebe. "The truth or something? There's no one here to dispute either of our stories. Just let me finish." She turned to Stella again. "The moment Simon came at me, I made the biggest mistake of my life. A fatal mistake that I must suffer from until the day I die." Phoebe swallowed hard. "I moved. One step. One lousy step to the right, and the knife that was meant for me stabbed Rebecca in the heart."

Simon slapped Phoebe hard around the head. "Shut your fucking mouth."

Phoebe used the wall to maintain her balance.

"Leave her alone!" Stella wiggled her way between them ignoring Simon. She felt aghast but relieved at the same time. Then she felt ill. Phoebe looked like she wanted to die. "It was a reflex action. Anyone would have done the same thing. Oh, baby, you poor thing."

Phoebe shook her head. "It was the wrong reflex action, Stella. My first priority should have been Rebecca, not myself. I had one defining moment in my life. I failed. She died because of me." Phoebe fell to her knees, crying.

"Oh, come now, Phoebe. You always were so bloody theatrical. The little slut had it coming one way or the other," Simon spat on Phoebe's hair.

"Fuck you, Simon. Rebecca is dead. How is that melodramatic?"

"Then perhaps you shouldn't have stepped aside," he said.

Stella glared at him. "You spineless asshole!"

He bent low and spoke in Phoebe's ear. "You're nothing but the filthy dyke who could have killed Rebecca Dean." His foul breath was forced up her nose with the vehemence of his words.

"Except you did it," said Stella.

Simon straightened. "Yeah, well, shit happens, doesn't it? You heard her say it. She as good as killed her, so who cares?"

Shakily, Phoebe stood. "I care, you filthy fucking liar."

"And so do I." The voice was deep and came from around the corner.

Suddenly, as if the cloud of madness and lies surrounding them vanished, Oscar Dean and four thickset men entered the small, secluded alleyway.

"You disappoint me, Simon," Oscar said, placing his hands squarely in his tailored trouser pockets.

Oscar gave the slightest of nods and the men advanced toward Simon, efficiently manhandling him against the wall, swift jab punches ensuring his compliance.

"No, wait, Oscar. I'm just playing with these stupid girls." He pointed to Phoebe. "She killed Rebecca, I swear."

"Don't you mean *that little slut*?" Oscar tilted his head as if waiting for an answer. "That was what you referred to my daughter as, wasn't it?"

Oscar turned to Phoebe. "Well, this is a little messy, now, isn't it?"

"Only you would find this scenario messy, Oscar. The rest of the world would be horrified." Phoebe stood firm.

Oscar looked to his men. "Get him out of my sight."

Stella realised she had been standing motionless since Oscar arrived. Her legs felt as heavy as lead, especially after running from Simon. "He's been tormenting us for nearly a month now."

Oscar looked toward her, poised to answer, but Phoebe interrupted with a more pressing issue. "You heard him say it, Oscar. I didn't murder Rebecca."

"No, but you could have saved her." He shook his head.

"And don't you think I'll live with that guilt, that torture, for the rest of my life?"

Oscar thought for a moment then nodded. "Yes, I think perhaps you will. You should have told me it was Simon. The outcome might have been different."

Stella finally found the courage to move close to Phoebe. It was all the support she dared show in the circumstances.

"I gave Sebastian to you because I was frightened I was going to jail, I was frightened of you, and I felt guilt so immense I couldn't even think straight. You wouldn't have believed it was Simon, and I'd have been worse off than I already was."

"You gave me my grandson because it was the right thing to do."

"And now the right thing for you to do is let me see him."

Oscar laughed.

"I loved Rebecca with all my heart, and the only thing I have left of us, and her, is Sebastian. Please, Oscar, can we come to some compromise on this? For God's sake, he's my son!"

"I have no obligation to do anything for you."

"I know that," said Phoebe, sad resignation littered her words. "But he deserves to know the truth eventually. He deserves to have his mother in his life, and he deserves to know who his other mother was, who Rebecca was."

"He's a happy and contented little boy. He doesn't need disruption in his life."

"Of course not. I understand that. But having me in his life doesn't have to be a disruption." Phoebe was begging. "Please, he spends his days with a nanny, someone paid to love him—"

"Money is not the issue here. I can pay ten more nannies to love him if need be."

"But my point is you don't have to. I love him because he's my son. I would protect him with my life—"

"Just like you protected Rebecca?"

Phoebe burst into tears, and Stella lightly touched her hand before pulling away, not wanting to spook Oscar with an inappropriate display of affection that might sway him against even considering the prospect of Phoebe being in Sebastian's life.

Through sobs, Phoebe managed to say, "I failed once. Please give me a chance to make it up to you and Sebastian."

Oscar paced back and forth.

Phoebe continued. "I know you disagree with my lifestyle—"

"I thought Rebecca was with you just to spite me." Oscar stared Phoebe squarely in the eyes.

"She used to say how you took her to every hockey game, never missed a play or musical, how you attended her presentation evenings and how you supported every decision she made, stupid or otherwise." Oscar smiled briefly. "But the one decision she struggled with, the one thing she really needed support with was her sexuality, and you just turned your back on her."

Oscar's gaze fell to the ground.

"She never stopped being your little girl. In her eyes, you stopped being her dad."

"I've heard enough." Oscar turned to leave. "I'm disappointed you went behind my back to see Sebastian. I trust it won't happen again."

"Please, Oscar. Please just—"

He held his hand aloft and faced her for the last time. "Next time you want to see him, call me first. I won't tolerate this sneaking around. We'll be back in Australia for the summer. I expect I'll hear from you then."

Phoebe's eyes lit up. "What? Really?"

"You heard me. I won't repeat the offer."

Phoebe rushed toward him but pulled up short of actual contact. "Thank you so much. I promise you won't regret it."

Stella had one last question for him. "What will you do with Simon?"

Oscar looked impatient, but he stopped long enough to answer the question. "I'll call the authorities and I presume he'll be extradited and tried in Australia."

Phoebe looked shocked. "You won't deal with it yourself?"

Oscar laughed. "It's not the nineties anymore, my dear. Those days are long gone." He turned the corner and left without looking at them again.

CHAPTER TWENTY-NINE

Stella couldn't believe what just happened, and neither could Phoebe by the gobsmacked expression on her face. Tenderly, she touched Phoebe's cheek. "Are you okay?"

Phoebe simply nodded as tears flowed freely.

Stella slumped against the wall and Phoebe followed. "However I expected today to turn out, I certainly wouldn't have predicted this in a million years."

Phoebe closed her eyes for a long moment. Stella presumed thoughts of Rebecca consumed her at this time. For a long while, neither of them spoke.

"I should kick your ass. You put yourself in extraordinary danger today, Stella."

Stella knew it had all been worth it. After hearing Simon's confession and Oscar's offer, she was overwhelmed by relief.

"Thank you for believing in me," said Phoebe, her tears showing no sign of abating. "And although I wish you hadn't become involved, I'm glad you were here."

"I gave up even considering you killed Rebecca a long time ago," said Stella.

"At least there's no glimmer of doubt in your mind now."

"Honestly, there was never any doubt."

A smile crept across Phoebe's face. "I'm so very relieved that the person I care about the most now knows the whole truth."

"I won't lie," said Stella. "Today has been the most remarkable and terrifying day I have ever experienced. But I hope this is the beginning of something truly special between us." She moved in to gently kiss Phoebe. "Something special between the three of us, when Sebastian is in your life." For the first time since laying eyes on the mysterious Phoebe Lancaster, Stella allowed herself to envisage a long and fulfilling future together.

"That would make us a family."

Stella nodded. "Well deduced."

"Are you ready for that?" Phoebe appeared only the slightest bit concerned about the answer.

"I don't think I've ever been more ready."

They kissed again, this time with more urgency.

"Why, Little Miss Tour Manager," said Phoebe. "Are you falling for the girl with the shady past?"

Stella laughed, knowing it was far too late for that. Wincing as her legs cramped, she pushed away from the wall, pulling Phoebe with her. "Come on, old girl. Take me home and fix me a hot bath. The way I feel now, I'll never be able to run again."

Phoebe straightened and stretched her back. "I'm surprised your little legs moved so fast, to be honest." She grinned.

"Really? Well, how about you take me back to the hotel and take full advantage of my need to be horizontal?"

"Don't you have a coach load of clients who need organising this evening?"

Stella took out her phone and called Russo. She explained she felt unwell and was returning to the hotel to sleep it off. He seemed happy to take charge. Finally, they trudged to the main road, looked up to the street sign and called a taxi.

Phoebe took Stella in her arms. "Looks like you're stuck with me now."

"Looks like it." She buried her head in Phoebe's shoulder. "You know? Somehow I think I'll cope just fine."

"You were incredibly brave back there."

"*Me*? The way you handled Simon was amazing. And Oscar. All the stuff I've researched about Oscar, I really thought he would have been far more formidable."

"Researched?" She looked Stella up and down. "And what exactly are you wearing?"

"You're not a fan of my new look?"

"No. And less of a fan of being seen holding hands with someone pretending to be a teenage boy," said Phoebe.

"Oh, I don't know. Maybe this is where I've been going wrong."

"Who says you've been going wrong? But let's not change the subject. You followed me?"

Stella shrugged. "What was I supposed to do?"

"And you researched Oscar?"

Stella laughed and pulled her notepad from her backpack. "I researched everyone."

Phoebe flicked through the book. "Jesus, Stella, this is comprehensive. When did you decide to follow me?"

"Krems."

Phoebe rolled her eyes and smiled, seemingly outsmarted by an amateur.

Krems seemed so long ago. Stella's memory of Krems was filled with passion in the back of a limousine.

"I remember you offered me an extra pair of ears and eyes. You probably saved my life today, Stella." Phoebe suddenly saddened. "And I've put your life in danger the entire tour. I'm so sorry, baby."

"It wasn't your fault. Simon was playing a little game. How were we to know?"

"A little game that saw you black-and-blue from his cowardly beating. He deserves to rot in jail for the rest of his life."

"I won't argue with that. But you deserve to forgive yourself for what happened to Rebecca."

Phoebe shook her head.

"Listen to me." Stella eyed her squarely. "You made a mistake. You aren't a bad person and you weren't holding the knife. Simon made choices that day, and while I know you'll never forget what happened, and you'll always blame yourself, you have to begin the process of forgiveness. You've punished yourself long enough."

Stella watched Phoebe take herself back to the past. "I don't know how it all went so wrong. I don't know how it escalated into something physically violent so quickly. It was a stupid argument about stupid money and I wound him up, I know I did. He was ready to go off and I pushed him, I backed him into a corner and he went mental. I pushed him too far, and he and I will pay for that for the rest of our lives."

❖

The four walls of the hotel provided the refuge they both needed after such an emotional and dramatic day. For the time being, neither wanted to be interrupted by the rest of the world. When Oscar handed Simon over to the police, they knew they'd be required for statements, but until then, they basked in the fact that Sebastian would no longer be a stranger, and that Phoebe's name would be cleared once and for all.

Stella sensed someone at the door, watching, so she emerged from under the deep bath water to find Phoebe staring at her.

"I'm finally free, Stella, and I have a son."

Stella was reluctant to be the voice of reason, but she had to say something. "You don't think Oscar will renege do you?"

"Something tells me he won't. Grief can do strange things to you. I don't know if he's the conniving bastard I always thought him to be." She shrugged. "I wish he and Rebecca had given each other a chance."

The day's events had finally caught up with Phoebe, and the sheer expression of relief was evident in her radiant smile.

"Come join me." Stella had finally made it into the bath. Her muscles both rejoiced and complained about the heat, but in no time at all, they relaxed and tingled with the joy of weightlessness.

Without protest, Phoebe removed the hotel robe and slipped into the water, facing Stella. "I'm so tired. I feel like I could sleep for a year." She closed her eyes.

Stella took her trembling hands. "It's finally over, baby."

"My son is a nice little boy," said Phoebe.

"Just like his mum." Stella leaned forward and kissed Phoebe. "I'm so proud of you."

They soaked in the bath, relaxing in silence until Stella said, "Have you got enough energy to take me to bed and show me how you intend to keep me happy?" She slid her hand down between Phoebe's thighs.

Phoebe reacted to her touch, tenderly massaging Stella's breasts. "I think if I pace myself—go nice and slow—I should be able to keep my energy levels up."

Stella moaned as the pressure on her aching nipples hardwired itself to her centre, sending the early stages of her orgasm directly to her clitoris. "I'm exhausted. I think I'll be a cheap shout tonight." Stella knew it wasn't exhaustion that made her come so easily.

"That's funny," Phoebe said softly. "I've never noticed you to be anything *but* a cheap shout."

Stella pinched Phoebe's inner thigh in protest.

"Ouch! You can't come if I won't let you."

"And why would you want to do that to me?" Stella writhed as Phoebe's hand circled lower.

"Because you're sexy when you beg."

"Then I won't utter a word. That'll fix you."

"It's not your words that get to me. You beg me with your eyes, darling." Phoebe sucked Stella's neck. "And I never want to stop seeing that desire."

Stella couldn't take it any longer. She hauled them both from the bath. "I want you inside me."

"That's the best offer I've had all day."

She winked at Phoebe.

A whirlwind tour of Europe in less than a month wasn't long enough for many things—building a house, reading Tolstoy, writing a novel, or becoming a nun, but it *was* long enough for Stella to fall in love.

About the Author

Michelle is Tasmanian born and now resides in the UK, just north of London. She relishes outdoor and travel adventures with her wife, writes by the seat of her pants, and often lives life by the same philosophy.

She believes that life is about opportunities: You choose to take them or you don't. Someone far more famous than her once said, "If you always do what you've always done, you will always get what you've always got." Motivated by this, Michelle likes to explore opportunities that come her way.

The urge to write seemingly stalked Michelle until she finally succumbed in her mid-thirties. Surprise was her initial reaction, but now the author title inspires her on a daily basis.

Getting Lost is her debut novel. Go on, seize the opportunity and get lost! You never know what you might find.

Books Available from Bold Strokes Books

Twice Lucky by Mardi Alexander. For firefighter Mackenzie James and Dr. Sarah Macarthur, there's suddenly a whole lot more in life to understand, to consider, to risk…someone will need to fight for her life. (978-1-62639-325-7)

Shadow Hunt by L.L. Raand. With young to raise and her Pack under attack, Sylvan, Alpha of the wolf Weres, takes on her greatest challenge when she determines to uncover the faceless enemies known as the Shadow Lords. A Midnight Hunters novel. (978-1-62639-326-4)

Heart of the Game by Rachel Spangler. A baseball writer falls for a single mom, but can she ever love anything as much as she loves the game? (978-1-62639-327-1)

Getting Lost by Michelle Grubb. Twenty-eight days, thirteen European countries, a tour manager fighting attraction, and an accused murderer: Stella and Phoebe's journey of a lifetime begins here. (978-1-62639-328-8)

Prayer of the Handmaiden by Merry Shannon. Celibate priestess Kadrian must defend the kingdom of Ithyria from a dangerous enemy and ultimately choose between her duty to the Goddess and the love of her childhood sweetheart, Erinda. (978-1-62639-329-5)

The Witch of Stalingrad by Justine Saracen. A Soviet "night witch" pilot and American journalist meet on the Eastern Front in WW II and struggle through carnage, conflicting politics, and the deadly Russian winter. (978-1-62639-330-1)

Pedal to the Metal by Jesse J. Thoma. When unreformed thief Dubs Williams is released from prison to help Max Winters bust a car theft ring, Max learns that to catch a thief, get in bed with one. (978-1-62639-239-7)

Dragon Horse War by D. Jackson Leigh. A priestess of peace and a fiery warrior must defeat a vicious uprising that entwines their destinies and ultimately their hearts. (978-1-62639-240-3)

For the Love of Cake by Erin Dutton. When everything is on the line, and one taste can break a heart, will pastry chefs Maya and Shannon take a chance on reality? (978-1-62639-241-0)

Betting on Love by Alyssa Linn Palmer. A quiet country-girl-at-heart and a live-life-to-the-fullest biker take a risk at offering each other their hearts. (978-1-62639-242-7)

The Deadening by Yvonne Heidt. The lines between good and evil, right and wrong, have always been blurry for Shade. When Raven's actions force her to choose, which side will she come out on? (978-1-62639-243-4)

Ordinary Mayhem by Victoria A. Brownworth. Faye Blakemore has been taking photographs since she was ten, but those same photographs threaten to destroy everything she knows and everything she loves. (978-1-62639-315-8)

One Last Thing by Kim Baldwin & Xenia Alexiou. Blood is thicker than pride. The final book in the Elite Operative Series brings together foes, family, and friends to start a new order. (978-1-62639-230-4)

Songs Unfinished by Holly Stratimore. Two aspiring rock stars learn that falling in love while pursuing their dreams can be harmonious— if they can only keep their pasts from throwing them out of tune. (978-1-62639-231-1)

Beyond the Ridge by L.T. Marie. Will a contractor and a horse rancher overcome their family differences and find common ground to build a life together? (978-1-62639-232-8)

Swordfish by Andrea Bramhall. Four women battle the demons from their pasts. Will they learn to let go, or will happiness be forever beyond their grasp? (978-1-62639-233-5)

The Fiend Queen by Barbara Ann Wright. Princess Katya and her consort Starbride must turn evil against evil in order to banish Fiendish power from their kingdom, and only love will pull them back from the brink. (978-1-62639-234-2)

Up the Ante by PJ Trebelhorn. When Jordan Stryker and Ashley Noble meet again fifteen years after a short-lived affair, are either of them prepared to gamble on a chance at love? (978-1-62639-237-3)

Speakeasy by MJ Williamz. When mob leader Helen Byrne sets her sights on the girlfriend of Al Capone's right-hand man, passion and tempers flare on the streets of Chicago. (978-1-62639-238-0)

Venus in Love by Tina Michele. Morgan Blake can't afford any distractions and Ainsley Dencourt can't afford to lose control—but the beauty of life and art usually lies in the unpredictable strokes of the artist's brush. (978-1-62639-220-5)

Rules of Revenge by AJ Quinn. When a lethal operative on a collision course with her past agrees to help a CIA analyst on a critical assignment, the encounter proves explosive in ways neither woman anticipated. (978-1-62639-221-2)

The Romance Vote by Ali Vali. Chili Alexander is a sought-after campaign consultant who isn't prepared when her boss's daughter, Samantha Pellegrin, comes to work at the firm and shakes up Chili's life from the first day. (978-1-62639-222-9)

Advance: Exodus Book One by Gun Brooke. Admiral Dael Caydoc's mission to find a new homeworld for the Oconodian people is hazardous, but working with the infuriating Commander Aniwyn "Spinner" Seclan endangers her heart and soul. (978-1-62639-224-3)

UnCatholic Conduct by Stevie Mikayne. Jil Kidd goes undercover to investigate fraud at St. Marguerite's Catholic School, but life gets complicated when her student is killed—and she begins to fall for her prime target. (978-1-62639-304-2)

Season's Meetings by Amy Dunne. Catherine Birch reluctantly ventures on the festive road trip from hell with beautiful stranger Holly Daniels only to discover the road to true love has its own obstacles to maneuver. (978-1-62639-227-4)

Myth and Magic: Queer Fairy Tales edited by Radclyffe and Stacia Seaman. Myth, magic, and monsters—the stuff of childhood dreams (or nightmares) and adult fantasies. (978-1-62639-225-0)

Nine Nights on the Windy Tree by Martha Miller. Recovering drug addict, Bertha Brannon, is an attorney who is trying to stay clean when a murder sends her back to the bad end of town. (978-1-62639-179-6)

Driving Lessons by Annameekee Hesik. Dive into Abbey Brooks's sophomore year as she attempts to figure out the amazing, but sometimes complicated, life of a you-know-who girl at Gila High School. (978-1-62639-228-1)

Asher's Shot by Elizabeth Wheeler. Asher Price's candid photographs capture the truth, but when his success requires exposing an enemy, Asher discovers his only shot at happiness involves revealing secrets of his own. (978-1-62639-229-8)

Courtship by Carsen Taite. Love and justice—a lethal mix or a perfect match? (978-1-62639-210-6)

Against Doctor's Orders by Radclyffe. Corporate financier Presley Worth wants to shut down Argyle Community Hospital, but Dr. Harper Rivers will fight her every step of the way, if she can also fight their growing attraction. (978-1-62639-211-3)

A Spark of Heavenly Fire by Kathleen Knowles. Kerry and Beth are building their life together, but unexpected circumstances could destroy their happiness. (978-1-62639-212-0)

Never Too Late by Julie Blair. When Dr. Jamie Hammond is forced to hire a new office manager, she's shocked to come face to face with Carla Grant and memories from her past. (978-1-62639-213-7)

Widow by Martha Miller. Judge Bertha Brannon must solve the murder of her lover, a policewoman she thought she'd grow old with. As more bodies pile up, the murderer starts coming for her. (978-1-62639-214-4)

Twisted Echoes by Sheri Lewis Wohl. What's a woman to do when she realizes the voices in her head are real? (978-1-62639-215-1)

Criminal Gold by Ann Aptaker. Through a dangerous night in New York in 1949, Cantor Gold, dapper dyke-about-town, smuggler of fine art, is forced by a crime lord to be his instrument of vengeance. (978-1-62639-216-8)

The Melody of Light by M.L. Rice. After surviving abuse and loss, will Riley Gordon be able to navigate her first year of college and accept true love and family? (978-1-62639-219-9)

Because of You by Julie Cannon. What would you do for the woman you were forced to leave behind? (978-1-62639-199-4)

The Job by Jove Belle. Sera always dreamed that she would one day reunite with Tor. She just didn't think it would involve terrorists, firearms, and hostages. (978-1-62639-200-7)

Making Time by C.J. Harte. Two women going in different directions meet after fifteen years and struggle to reconnect in spite of the past that separated them. (978-1-62639-201-4)

Once The Clouds Have Gone by KE Payne. Overwhelmed by the dark clouds of her past, Tag Grainger is lost until the intriguing and spirited Freddie Metcalfe unexpectedly forces her to reevaluate her life. (978-1-62639-202-1)

The Acquittal by Anne Laughlin. Chicago private investigator Josie Harper searches for the real killer of a woman whose lover has been acquitted of the crime. (978-1-62639-203-8)

An American Queer: The Amazon Trail by Lee Lynch. Lee Lynch's heartening and heart-rending history of gay life from the turbulence of the late 1900s to the triumphs of the early 2000s are recorded in this selection of her columns. (978-1-62639-204-5)

Stick McLaughlin: The Prohibition Years by CF Frizzell. Corruption in 1918 cost Stick her lover, her freedom, and her identity, but a very special flapper and the family bond of her own gang could help win them back—even if it means outwitting the Boston Mob. (978-1-62639-205-2)

Edge of Awareness by C.A. Popovich. When Maria, a woman in the middle of her third divorce, meets Dana, an out lesbian, awareness of her feelings brings up reservations about the teachings of her church. (978-1-62639-188-8)

Taken by Storm by Kim Baldwin. Lives depend on two women when a train derails high in the remote Alps, but an unforgiving mountain, avalanches, crevasses, and other perils stand between them and safety. (978-1-62639-189-5)

The Common Thread by Jaime Maddox. Dr. Nicole Coussart's life is falling apart, but fortunately, DEA Attorney Rae Rhodes is there to pick up the pieces and help Nic put them back together. (978-1-62639-190-1)